Merman's Kiss

Dee J. Stone

First Edition.

ISBN-13: 978-1505319835
ISBN-10: 1505319838

Merman's Kiss

Chapter One

My head throbs like someone smashed it against a pile of rocks.

I try to move my limbs, but they feel like they're buried in cement. When I pry my eyes open, I'm blinded by something bright and strong. The sun? My eyes snap shut and tears seep out.

The throbbing travels from the back of my head to my forehead. I moan as images come. Memories. It all rushes back to me. The killer waves this morning, almost as high as towers. The itchy sensation pricking every nerve of my body as I imagined riding them. My stupid self ignoring the warning bells telling me it was too dangerous. Paddling into the ocean and popping onto my board. Getting swallowed by the massive wave. Thrashing my arms and legs as my mouth desperately sought oxygen, only to get salt water instead. My limbs growing weaker until I blacked out.

Something touches my fingers. No, touching isn't the right word. Rubbing, maybe? It feels nice. Soothing. Slowly, I open my eyes. A face stares down at me. The sun shines behind his head, creating a halo.

An angel? Am I in heaven?

He has dark blue eyes and long, golden hair brushing his shoulders. Definitely an angel. I *am* in heaven.

"Cassie!" a voice calls.

The angel disappears and I hear a splash. I try to raise my head, but the throbbing turns into hammering, and I groan. When I turn my head to the side, I realize I'm on some sort of boulder in the middle of the ocean.

"Cassie!" the voice calls again. It sounds like my best friend, Leah. I hear an engine. She must be on a boat or Jet Ski.

I open my mouth to call to her, but nothing comes out. The action alone takes up so much energy that my eyes droop.

Through the fog in my head, I hear the engine approach. A hand shakes my shoulder. "Cassie? Are you okay?"

I open one eye. "Leah?"

She's sitting on a Jet Ski, dressed in her wetsuit. Her green eyes are wide in alarm. "Thank God you're alive."

When I try to sit up, my head spins. "Easy," she says, climbing out of the Jet Ski and settling near me on the boulder. She wraps an arm around my shoulder and helps me into a sitting position. "We need to get you to the hospital."

"I'm fine," I mutter. "What happened?"

"You wiped out. I saw you go down and I grabbed the Jet Ski to go after you. I'm taking you to the hospital. You have a nasty bump on your head."

I finger the spot. Ouch. "How did I end up on the boulder?"

Her eyebrows crease. She scratches her dark brown hair. "Did you swim here and pass out?" She takes me in her arms, hugging me close. "You have no idea how freaked out I was when I saw you lying here. I'm so glad you're okay." She pulls out of the hug. "I was searching forever. I really thought…" Her voice cracks. "I really thought you died. Don't you ever do anything like that again!"

I stare down at the small waves hitting the boulder. "There was a guy. An angel. An angel saved me."

"An angel?" She surveys the area. "I didn't see anyone."

"Maybe I went to heaven."

She doesn't say anything. I know what she's thinking—that I hit my head and am talking nonsense. Am I?

"And when you called my name, he disappeared. I'm telling you the truth, Leah. I'm not crazy."

"O-kay. What did Angel Guy look like?"

Those eyes. So deep, so blue, like the ocean. And golden hair that I've never seen before, not even in the movies. "He was beautiful."

Her eyebrows crease again. I know she doesn't believe me, but I couldn't have been hallucinating. The hands rubbing my fingers were real. His face was real. *He* was real.

Or was he? I shake my head because none of this makes sense. Maybe I am hallucinating.

Leah gets on the Jet Ski and helps me climb on behind her. I'm still a little groggy and dizzy, but my headache is disappearing by the minute. She steers us toward the shore.

I look back at the boulder. He had to be real.

We make it to the beach and climb off the Jet Ski. Leah wraps her arm over my shoulder. "Feeling okay?"

"Fine." I keep looking back toward the ocean, hoping for—I don't know. For Angel Guy to pop out of thin air and reveal himself?

"I still think you should see a doctor. We hear so many stories of people hitting their heads and thinking they're fine, when they sustain major head injuries and—"

"Leah, quit worrying. You're worse than my mom." Mom has never really liked me spending most of my free time hitting the waves. I guess as her only daughter, she wants someone more...like her. A daughter who would go shopping with her and give her fashion advice and stay up into the early hours of the morning talking about guys.

3

Leah stops in front of Misty's Juice Bar, the place she's currently working at, and faces me. "You're just so reckless, Cass. I know I'm not a great surfer, but even I know you shouldn't have been in the ocean with those waves."

I press my lips together.

She touches my arm. "I know you're still hurting from the breakup with Kyle—"

"We are *not* talking about that." I nod toward the shop. "Your boss is giving you the death glare. I'll see you later, okay?"

Rubbing my head, I notice the pain is almost completely gone. I squint toward the ocean. It's wishful thinking, hoping my board will somehow emerge. Chances are it's in pieces at the bottom of the ocean.

My eyes move to the sky, which is growing a little gray and cloudy. We'll probably have a storm later today or tonight.

When I enter my beach house, a familiar scent tickles my nose.

"Mom?" I hurry into the kitchen and find her sitting at the table, munching on a chocolate bar and flipping through a magazine. I take in her familiar chin-length, dyed red hair and light pink nail polish.

"Cassie!" She stands and pulls me into her arms. I bury my face into the side of her neck, feeling the stiffness of her business suit against my arms. She's been gone for over two weeks. As much as I enjoyed the freedom, I missed her terribly.

She steps out of the hug and studies me like she hasn't seen me in years. "You look great, honey. Except, what happened to your head?" She reaches to touch the bump, but I move back.

"Oh, nothing. I tripped on the stairs. So um, how was your trip?"

"Busy, but good."

I peer into the living room, where her suitcases are lined against the wall. "Need help unpacking?"

She bites her lower lip, regret clouding her eyes.

My heart sinks. "You're leaving again?"

She sighs and drops down on the chair, running her hands through her hair. "I fly out again tonight. Sorry, Cass."

I walk to the cupboard and rummage around until I find my gummy worms. Mom works in sales. She travels all over the country selling a new line of women's cosmetics. It's been her dream job ever since she started college. Then I came along when she was in her last semester and ruined her plans. She got her degree, but had to kiss the dream goodbye. Dad was chivalrous and married her, but he left us when I was ten. Not very chivalrous. Now that I'm eighteen and will start college in the fall, Mom can finally live her dream.

I stick a worm between my teeth and slice it in half. She was a complete mess when my dad left us, and now she's finally putting her life back together. I can't take that away from her, no matter how much I miss her.

She gets to her feet and takes me in her arms again. "I'm sorry, sweetie. I didn't think I'd have to travel this much." She draws back and looks into my eyes. "You know you're always welcome at Uncle Jim and Aunt Lisa's and the gang if you get too lonely. And Leah's parents would love to have you over any time."

I don't say anything, just continue to devour my worms. I stayed with Leah the first few times my mom was away. We had a blast. But after a while, I wanted my mom. That's how it's been for the last few years of my life—just Mom and me. But I suppose I need to get used to this, to the future. College, a real job, my own apartment.

She touches one of my blonde braids that's curled over my shoulder. "And there's always your dad."

I push away from her.

"Okay, okay. I'm sorry." She reaches for me again and plays with the bottom of my braid. "He's trying, Cass. At least give him a chance."

"Mom—"

"That's all I'm going to say. Just to give him a chance."

I clench my teeth.

Mom squeezes my shoulder. "We have the next six hours to spend together. Let's make the most of it. What do you say?"

I force a smile onto my lips. "Okay."

Chapter Two

"I still have no clue where I'm going this fall." Leah bends down and picks a pebble off the beach.

I shield my eyes as I stare out toward the ocean. The waves are flat this morning. Leah and I hoped to squeeze in some surfing, but the ocean has a mind of its own. Most of the other surfers have gone back home. "You need to decide soon," I say. "It's mid-June."

Her fingers close over the pebble. "I won't let Frankie pressure me into following him to New Jersey. I won't. *New Jersey?* That's so far away."

We pick up walking again. I miss doing this—strolling along the beach, enjoying the beauty of nature and the company of my best friend. The only times I'm at the beach is when I surf and when I'm teaching my surfing class.

"He shouldn't pressure you to leave Florida," I say. "If he loves you, he should try to make a long distance relationship work."

She tosses the pebble into the ocean. "Why do men suck?"

I kick my toes into the wet sand. "Because they are made of suck."

My dad pops into my head, followed closely by my ex, Kyle. I shake my shoulders, hoping to cast the memories into the ocean.

After a few seconds of silence, Leah says, "You okay with living alone?"

I shrug. "It's growing on me."

"She loves you, you know."

Yeah, I know. She had me when she wasn't ready. Now she has a chance to start over. Maybe any mom would do the same.

"Hey, Cass?"

"Hmm?"

"What's that down there?"

I shield my eyes again as I squint in the distance. I can't make it out, but someone—or something—is lying by the tide.

"You think it's some drunk?"

I squint again, but the sun makes it hard to see him clearly. "I'm not sure."

We head over to him, it, whatever, and I stop short when I can see him clearly. And I say *him*, because—

"Holy shit. He's naked." Leah clamps her hands over her mouth. "He's *naked*."

I jump back like his lack of clothes might inflict me with a contagious disease. The guy looks around our age, maybe a little older. His skin is very light, like he hasn't spent enough time on the beach. His arm is draped over his face, so I can't see if I know him. But based on his body type—nope.

I know he's alive, because his chest rises and falls.

"Oh my God, those muscles. And that hair." Leah's eyes are ravaging his body.

"Maybe we should call the—oh my God." I fall down on my knees and push his arm off his face.

"Cassie, what are you...?" She grabs my arm. "Don't *touch* him!"

That beautiful face. The golden hair. My mouth hangs open. "It's him."

"Him? Him what?"

"Angel Guy." I look up at her. "This is the guy who saved me." I stare down at his face. I didn't hallucinate. I didn't imagine him. My heart flutters in my chest. He's real.

Leah releases my arm and falls down next to me. "*This* is the guy who saved you?"

"Unless you're hallucinating with me, yes, this is the guy."

She throws her hands on her mouth again.

"He fell from heaven," I mutter. Then I hear what just escaped my mouth. How ridiculous do I sound right now?

"Well, Angel Guy is looking mighty human, if you ask me." She raises an eyebrow toward his...yeah.

My cheeks boil. "We need to get him out of here." I run my hands down my wetsuit. If only I brought my towel with me.

"Um. Maybe we should call 911?" Leah says.

"Are you crazy?"

"Cass, I don't know who he is, but he's not an angel who fell from heaven. He's probably stoned."

"He saved me."

"Maybe he had a death wish yesterday, too." She gets to her feet and tugs on my arm. "We need to call for help and let them deal with—"

"Can you run back and get my towel?"

Her eyebrows shoot up. "Are you serious? You can't be thinking about—"

"He saved me, Leah. If not for him, I'd be dead."

She folds her arms over her chest. "He left you to rot on that boulder."

"No, he sat with me until you showed up."

Her arms fall away from her chest. "What?"

I nod. "As soon as you called my name, he ran."

Her eyes scan him again. "He's naked, Cass."

"Please get my towel. Please, before anyone else shows up."

She presses her lips together. I beg with my eyes. Her forehead creases as she frowns. Then she throws her hands toward the sky and marches off.

"Thanks!" I call after her.

She waves her hand.

I paste my eyes on my savior, studying every part of his face. I lean forward and brush some of that golden hair off his forehead. It's silky, too silky for wet hair. He doesn't stir. His broad chest continues to rise and fall.

"Who are you?" I whisper. "Why did you save me?"

Voices and giggles sound in the distance. My head springs up. A group of high school kids are headed this way. I scan the area for Leah and find her trekking back, my cream-colored towel slung over her arm.

If the kids see him on the sand naked like this, they might call 911. If they take him away, I don't know what I'd do.

An idea enters my head. I can't believe I'm even contemplating this. I throw myself over him, like we're lovers on the sand.

He smells like salt water. And something else, something exotic. I never smelled anything like it before. I analyze his face. His jaw is completely smooth, no sign of stubble. He looks human, but there's an unearthly, almost god-looking quality to it.

"What the hell?"

My gaze shoots up to Leah, who's standing before me with a startled expression on her face.

I scamper off him and grab my towel, throwing it over his man parts. "I didn't want anyone to see him," I mumble.

"Okay, smarty pants. What do we do now?"

I wrap the towel around his hips and tie a knot on the side. "We carry him to my house."

"We *what*?"

"I don't suppose you secretly have teleportation powers?"

She snorts.

"Help me lift him."

"I don't know how you always get me to do this sort of stuff," she mutters under her breath as she joins me on the sand. We each lift an arm over our shoulders and heave him to his feet. "Holy hell," she says. "What has this guy been *eating*?"

My body is collapsing under his weight. "We can do it."

She grinds her teeth. "You so owe me."

We start dragging his body toward my house, but it's not as easy as I thought. Even though we're both toned and have decent muscles, we're no match for this guy's weight. We fall down on the sand and catch our breaths. My body is drenched in sweat. When I glance at Angel Guy, he's still out cold.

"We'll never make it," Leah pants.

I can't just leave him here. I won't. "He saved me," I say. "I need to save him."

"How noble," she mutters. Then her face brightens. "Wait, I've got an idea."

She springs to her feet and runs after a group of college-aged guys. She talks to them, motioning toward me and Angel Guy. After a minute or two, the guys follow her toward us.

"This is the friend I'm talking about," Leah says. "We had a party here last night, and he got wasted."

One of the guys, tall with dark hair, whistles. "Totally wasted."

"Yeah, totally," Leah says. "Think you can help us out?"

The guys exchange glances.

"I'll pay you," I blurt.

Leah raises her hands in a what-the-hell gesture.

The dark-haired guy says, "No worries. We'll help you get him home. Free of charge." He flashes a dimpled grin at Leah. She smiles back, her face growing a little red.

"Thanks so much," I say. "Really. I appreciate it."

The three guys step closer to Angel Guy. Two of them raise his arms over their shoulders while the third one lifts his legs. I lead them toward my house.

I feel everyone on the beach eyeballing us as we trudge through the sand. I ignore them and continue on. We make it to my house in ten minutes. I unlock the door and show them into the living room, motioning for the guys to drop him on the couch. They do. Sweat shines on their foreheads. I guess he was a burden on them, too.

I thank them again and they head for the door. But before the tall, dark-haired guy leaves, he looks back at Leah and flashes her another smile.

"Ooh," I tease once the door shuts behind him.

Leah shrugs. "Whatever." Her eyes land on the guy sprawled on my couch. "So what are you going to do with him?"

He's lying there, one leg hanging off the couch, the other bent toward his chest. His face is buried in a cushion. "I have no idea."

Leah glances at her watch. "Crap!" She runs to the door. "My shift started."

"You're going to leave me with him?"

She throws her hands on her hips. "Whose idea was it to bring a passed-out naked guy into her house?"

I give her a look.

"I'll come by as soon as my shift ends, okay? In the meantime…" Her eyes rake over him. "Try to wake him up? Maybe you should call someone over in case he turns out to be a creep. Maybe the police?"

I shake my head. "I'll be fine."

"Just be careful."

Once the door closes, a chill runs down my spine. I'm alone with him. Just yesterday I wasn't sure if he was real. Now he's in my living room.

I hug myself. I *am* crazy. He could be a murderer, for all I know. But he did save me from death.

I get down on my knees and study him. He looks peaceful. Kind of how Sleeping Beauty would look if she were a guy. I laugh to myself. Sleeping Beauty? I must be losing it.

My hand moves on its own and brushes some golden strands off his right eye. Maybe he *is* the male version of Sleeping Beauty and needs a kiss from Princess Charming. I snort.

"Hey," I whisper. "It's just me and you now. You saved me yesterday, and I owe you my life." I push some more strands aside. "Why won't you wake up?"

I fall back on my knees and play with one of my braids. Then I reach for his hand and slide my fingers through his. His hand is cold and very soft, something I wouldn't expect on a guy. It almost feels feminine, even though it looks very masculine. His skin is extremely white, nearly translucent. I squeeze, hoping to get a reaction from him. But he continues to lie there, his chest rising and falling in a steady rhythm.

An idea pops into my head. I make my way to the kitchen and fill a glass with ice-cold water. When I return to the living room, there still isn't any change. I bite my lip before splashing the water onto his face.

Nothing. He's still lying there, the water dripping down his face, his chest, and all over the couch. "Great," I mutter.

But I'm not giving up. I refill the glass and splash his face another time. I jump back when his arms and legs flail around. He springs up and looks around frantically. Then his eyes land on me.

I stumble back. His eyes—they're even more mesmerizing than I remember. Dark blue like the deep ocean, but also bright. It looks like light is coming out of them. My heart races so fast I think I might faint.

He blinks at me as if he's never seen a person before. Then his gaze moves down the length of his body, and his eyes widen. He scuttles back like leeches are attached to every part of him. If not for the wall, I'm sure he would have toppled right over the back of the couch.

I take a hesitant step forward, but freeze when his gaze flits to mine. He looks terrified, like a little kid who lost his way home. My chest rises and falls rapidly as ragged breaths escape my mouth. Maybe he hit his head swimming or surfing and lost his memory?

He just stares at me, blinking like he can't believe where he is.

I take another step closer and try to muster a sweet, friendly smile. "Hi. I'm Cassie Price. I found you passed out on the beach and brought you to my house."

His face looks blank. Maybe he doesn't understand what I'm saying? If he's an angel or whatever, maybe he doesn't communicate like we do.

"Do you...do you understand me?"

He opens his mouth a bit, then quickly shuts it. Opens it and shuts it. He wraps his fingers around his neck and croaks. Then he coughs.

I take a step back.

He opens his mouth again and sputters something I don't understand. I move closer. "I'm sorry?"

His eyebrows knit together. "D-Damarian."

"What?"

He stares down at the towel around his hips, then slowly touches it. Oh God, is he going to take it off?

"My…name," he says softly, bringing a hand to his muscled chest. "Damarian."

I feel my jaw hang open as I try to process his words. Damarian. That's his name—Damarian.

He's rubbing his hand up and down his right leg, feeling his calf muscle. Then he raises his leg in the air and bends it. Raises it and bends it again. The expression on his face is pure wonder. Like he's never seen a leg before.

"Do you recognize me?" I ask. "From yesterday? You rescued me when I wiped out surfing." Something that hasn't occurred to me suddenly fills my mind. Maybe he nearly drowned saving me yesterday and that's how he ended up unconscious on the beach.

His intense eyes land on me. They bore into me, inspecting every feature on my face. He shifts on the couch until both his legs hang over the edge. He stares down at them, then at the floor, looking perplexed.

"Are you okay?" I ask. "Do you need help getting up?"

He places both his hands on the couch's armrest and slowly heaves himself to his feet. He lets go of the armrest and sways a bit before crashing down on the couch.

I rush over. "Are you okay?"

His eyes widen at his legs. "Not quite as simple as I imagined."

Now that some of the weirdness is gone—sort of—I hear his voice. It's like nothing I've ever heard before. It sounds almost musical. But still masculine.

He curls his toes. He raises his hand and widens his fingers apart, bending close to examine the space between them.

What exactly is he doing?

"Um…Damarian?"

His head snaps up for a second before he focuses on his fingers. "How peculiar, the way they part." He fits the fingers from his other hand between them and slides them up and down.

Am I in the same room as a nutcase?

Damarian rests his palms on the couch and lifts his body. He slowly raises his right leg and presses down on the floor. He does the same with his left. He starts to walk on shaky legs as if balancing on twigs.

When he sways, I reach out to help him, but he recovers. What exactly is he? Who is he? He's acting like he's never walked before.

After taking a few steps forward, he turns to me and grins, his face bright. "Magnificent."

I shift from one foot to the other and tug on my left braid. My gaze drops to the towel that has loosened around his waist. I hope it doesn't fall off.

All of the sudden, he grabs both sides of his neck and bends over like he's trying to catch his breath. His chest rises and falls as though he ran a marathon.

"Damari—"

He lets out a wail and collapses to the floor, curling into a fetal position and scratching at the sides of his neck.

I bend down to touch his shoulder, when he lets out a howl and I lurch back. It doesn't sound human, but like a whale crying out in pain.

It's so loud that I'm forced to cover my ears.

"What's wrong?" I yell over the dreadful sound. "Why are you doing that?"

He's murmuring something I can't hear. I scoot closer to try and make it out.

"W-w-ater."

"Water?"

He releases another wail, scratching his neck harder. Examining it closely, I realize it's all red. A rash?

"I…need…water."

He's wheezing now. That mixed in with the sound causes me to leap to my feet with my heart pounding. Water. He said he needs water.

I grab the glass off the coffee table and rush into the kitchen. I don't wait for the water to get cold—I just fill the glass and hurry back to him. I kneel down and hold it out. "Here."

His face is no longer as translucent as it was earlier, but peach-colored. He opens his eyes, and I notice they're a lighter shade of blue. When he sees the glass in my hand, he shakes his head. "Me…in water."

"What?"

He squeezes his eyes shut and croaks, "My body…in water."

I gape at him. "You need to be in water?"

He nods weakly.

"I have a pool," I say, jumping to my feet. "Can you stand?"

He nods again, weaker. I throw his arm over my shoulder and help him to his feet. He's so heavy, my shoulder's about to snap. More determined than I've ever been in my life, I muster up all my strength and we stumble toward my indoor pool. I practically have to drag him down the stairs. He's still howling and wheezing, and it seems to be worsening with each step we take.

"We're almost there," I assure him.

He doesn't respond as his head lolls onto my shoulder and his hair brushes against my nose. I inhale his ocean scent, and for a second I feel like I'm surfing. But his screeching makes me quicken my pace. His neck is extremely irritated.

We enter the pool room and I lead him toward the ladder. His eyes crack open and his body perks when he's sees the water. I'm about to help him down the ladder, but he dives inside. A second later, his head breaks the surface. He thrashes around. The sounds don't disappear and he keeps sinking like his body is too weak. Or maybe he can't swim? What if he drowns? Why did he insist I bring him here?

My hands tremble. He's dying and I don't know how to help him.

He moves his mouth, but I can't hear him. I lean over the edge of the pool.

"S-salt."

"What?"

"Salt...need...salt."

Salt? What the hell? But his eyes look terrified and pleading, and I nod and rush to the kitchen. Salt. Salt. I rummage through the shelves until I find it. When I bring it to him, he motions for me to spill it into the pool.

He can't be serious. He falls to the bottom of the pool. I open the salt and pour it in.

Damarian swims to the area that's concentrated with salt. Then he breaks the surface and cries, "Salt. More salt. More salt."

More? This is all the salt we have in the house. The only way to get more is to run to the store. I don't understand why he's even asking me to do this.

He splashes around and yells, "Seawater."

Seawater? I hold out my hands in a helpless gesture.

He sinks to the bottom of the pool and breaks the surface again. "Seawater. Please." It sounds like it takes every last bit of his energy to utter those words.

"I don't have seawater," I shout over all the thrashing. "I'm sorry."

I bite my lip and spin around, pressing my palms to my temples.

Then an idea hits me. I rush back to the edge of the pool. "I have synthetic sea salt in my basement." Mom bought me a huge tank with marine fish and a bucket of sea salt a few years ago. My fish didn't last more than a week and the bucket's been gathering dust ever since.

Still flailing, although with less energy, Damarian nods urgently. "Yes! Sea salt."

"But why would you need that?"

"Please!"

I dash toward the basement and stumble down the steps. Where did Mom stash the bucket of sea salt? I open one of the storage rooms and see it sitting there with other useless things piled on top. I throw them off and grab hold of the handle. Holy crap, it's heavy.

I pause when I don't hear anything from upstairs. I strain my ears. No shouts. That's not a good sign. Groaning, I use all my might and drag the bucket to the stairs. Sweat gathers on my forehead as I heave the thing up, one step at a time. I don't know how I do it, but I manage to get it to the top step. Using all the strength I have left, I drag it to the pool room.

Damarian is lying on the bottom of the pool.

I push the bucket to the edge and lean over. "Damarian!" He doesn't move. "Damarian!"

I stare down at the bucket, then at him. He can't possibly mean…? He's just *lying* there. I peel off the lid and tilt the bucket over. The salt rushes out, like it needs him just as much as he needs it.

Damarian rises to the surface and thrashes around, throwing water everywhere. My wetsuit and flip-flops get drenched. I back up to one of the lounge chairs. After about thirty seconds, he stops. So do the noises and wheezing.

The room grows silent. Now I hear how heavy my breaths are. My forehead is covered in sweat.

"Thank you," he says.

I sigh in relief. I have no idea what just happened, but I'm glad he sounds normal again. "No problem. Are you okay?" I move toward the pool and look down. His arms are treading the water. Something shiny peeks out from underneath him. I squint. Dark blue, like sapphire. It looks like a...

I stagger back, trip over my feet, and land hard on my side.

Mermaid.

Chapter Three

No, merman. Merperson.

I shut my eyes and mutter, "It can't be."

Taking a deep breath, I get to my knees and crawl to the edge of the pool. He stares at me. The shine is back in his intense, blue eyes, but there's also a hint of fear. His skin has regained its translucent color. I don't want to venture to the lower half of his body. I don't want to see something that shouldn't be there.

He leaps in the air and jumps into the water. His sapphire tail creates an arc that gleams in the sunlight creeping in through the windows. I stumble back, my heart thumping in my chest. This doesn't make sense. It can't be. Except, everything *does* make sense. He saved me when I almost drowned because he *was there*. He saw me wipe out, maybe even fished me out from deep in the ocean. He ended up naked on the beach, because he has a *tail* instead of legs.

He pops up in front of me. I yell and scurry back.

"I am sorry, Cassie Price," he says. "I did not intend to startle you."

I just gape at him.

"Please, do not be alarmed. It is I who should be alarmed."

Taking another deep breath, I shuffle a little closer to him. He looks friendly enough, but I'm not that naïve to trust him.

"Who…you're a mermaid," I breathe. "I mean, a merman."

He stares at his tail before returning his gaze to me. Unease clouds his face. "Yes."

"Mermaids don't exist."

"Not to humans, no."

The unease on his face has grown to fear. Anxiety, terror. "I won't tell anyone," I say.

"You will not?"

I shake my head.

A sigh escapes his lips. "Thank you."

I shift my position and sit cross-legged on the floor, studying him just as he studies me. "You saved me when I wiped out yesterday morning and left me on the boulder."

I hear his tail swooshing in the water. I'm tempted to bend over and look at it. From the small glimpse I got earlier, it's beautiful. But I doubt he'd like that. It'd be like him studying my legs.

He nods.

He wasn't an angel, but a mermaid. Mer*man*. "Why?"

He doesn't say anything. It looks as though he doesn't know the answer himself. Then he says, "Children of the sea are not to engage the humans."

That's pretty obvious. But he broke the law. For me. Why? And why am I making such a big deal out of it?

"You were beautiful," he murmurs. I look at him, butterflies gathering in my stomach. "On the water. Sailing. I watched the water swallow you. I was certain you would die." He lowers his head before raising it back to me. "I could not allow that to happen."

More butterflies gather in my stomach and goose bumps crawl over my skin. "And this morning?" I ask. "Why were you unconscious on the beach?" I can't bear the thought that this happened because he rescued me. Maybe he swam out of his way to save me. Maybe merpeople can't swim too close to shore.

"The storm," he says. "I should not have been swimming."

The storm was pretty massive last night. "And you got hurt?"

He stares off in the distance. "I do not remember. I was swimming away…"

"From what?"

He doesn't answer. Unease clouds his face again. Clearly he doesn't want to talk about it.

"So…what happened before?" I ask. "With the rash on your neck and the wailing. You needed to be in water? Salt water."

"This is my first time as a human. I do not know."

My eyes analyze his face and upper body. He's very broad and heavily muscled. Then my gaze moves to his neck. The rash is no longer there, but something else is. I can't quite make it out.

I uncross my legs and crawl closer to him, reaching out my hand. "Can I?"

He looks unsure, but nods.

I lower my hand toward his face and take hold of his chin, tilting it to the side. Two small things protrude from both sides of his neck. I study them for a few seconds until I realize what they are. Gills. "They were all red before," I say.

Damarian is staring up at me. My breath catches in my throat. This is the closest I've been to him since he's woken up. It's the first time I see his eyes clearly. They're so blue I could drown in them.

I should be terrified. He's a different species, one I know nothing about. He could be dangerous. But I'm not scared. There's something about him that makes me feel like I can trust him. Like I can get closer.

He slowly brings his hand to my face and runs his fingers across my cheek. His hand is cold and sticky. I put mine over his and pull it away from my face. I hold it on my palm. His hand looks human-like, but it's webbed. Thin pieces of skin between each finger. That's why he was studying his human hand so strangely earlier.

He moves his hand to one of my braids and softly tugs on it. "You bind your hair."

I laugh a little. "It's easier to surf that way."

His eyebrows knit. "Surf. Is that what you were doing yesterday?"

"Yeah."

"Is it quite dangerous?"

"Sometimes."

His brows knit even more. "Then why do you engage in such an activity?"

Now I giggle. "Hey, you gotta live a little, right?"

His lips tug into a small smile. "Father would not agree."

It's weird to hear him talk about others—other merpeople. To think there are more out there. "Are there a lot of you?" I ask.

He opens his mouth, then shuts it. I wait for him to answer, but I realize he doesn't plan to. For a second, I feel upset, hurt for some reason. But it dawns on me that he doesn't feel safe telling me. His kind has to remain hidden. We are supposed to believe they don't exist.

"I'm sorry for prying," I say.

He nods.

My eyes trek to his tail swaying in the pool. It continues to shine in the sunlight, like crystals. He follows my gaze, and my cheeks heat up. "Sorry for staring," I mutter.

"It is all right. I am fascinated by human legs."

"Can I...?" My eyes search his. He nods.

I jump into the pool. He's still at the shallow side, so the tail touches the floor. I'm about to take a deep breath and dive under to take a peek at it, but Damarian lifts it for me. It has sapphire scales with a matching fin. I reach out to touch it, then pull my hand away. It's sticky and slimy.

"May I?" he asks, gesturing to my legs.

I heave myself onto the edge of the pool and hold out my leg. He studied his own legs earlier, but he can get a better look at human legs by examining mine. He lifts a hesitant hand to my bare right leg and wraps his fingers around my calf. My wetsuit reaches my knees. His touch is soft, gentle. He moves it lower and lower, over the bump of my ankle until he reaches my toes. He glances at me before gently pinching them, one by one. Then he bends them. He brings his other hand to the same foot and parts two of my toes. Every place he touches burns and tingles.

His eyes widen in wonder. "Peculiar to have fingers on your legs."

"I guess it's to help us walk."

He takes hold of my hand and touches my fingers with his webbed hand. He parts my index finger and middle finger, feeling the space between them. "Very peculiar."

My whole body heats up and my breathing grows uneven. I can't believe I'm getting turned on by a fish.

Damarian drops my hand. "What is that noise?"

"Noise?"

"Ringing."

I strain my ears, but don't hear anything. It's hard to hear outside noises from in the pool room. Maybe merpeople have special hearing? "It's probably the phone."

"Phone?"

"Yeah. We use it for communication."

He gives me a blank look.

"It's like this handheld device that…you know, never mind." I doubt informing a creature from the ocean about our methods of communication will accomplish anything. Unless he's dying to learn about us, which doesn't seem likely from what I've learned about him so far.

"It is incessant," he says.

"It is?" I rise to my feet. "It's probably important. Do you mind if I check it out?"

He shakes his head.

I head for the door and turn the knob, but glance back at the merman. He's swimming in the pool, occasionally leaping in the air and diving into the water like a dolphin.

I hear the phone shrilling when I'm halfway up the stairs. It's not my cell phone but the home phone, which means two things: this call is really important, or this call is anything but important.

I dash into the living room and reach for the phone. "Hello?"

"Cassie, where are you?"

I fall back against the couch when I hear Uncle Jim's frantic voice. I check my watch. Crap, my surfing class. I got so caught up with the merman that it slipped my mind.

"Sorry, Uncle Jim, I just—"

"I got a call this morning from a parent informing me that her son's surfing teacher failed to show up."

I run my hand down my face. "Dammit."

"Are you okay? What's going on?"

Well, if you *really* want to know, I rescued a naked guy from the beach this morning and he turned out to be a merman. Now he's swimming around in my pool filled with salt water because he can't survive on land.

"I'm okay," I tell him. "I just got caught up with some…stuff."

"What did we discuss last month, Cass?"

I sigh. "That if I was really serious about this job, I'd make an effort to show up every day and not blow it off like I did at my last job."

Now he sighs. "You know how much these surfing lessons mean to me."

"I know."

Uncle Jim injured himself surfing last month, and I begged him to let me substitute for the class. I was working at a shop near the beach, alongside the dreaded Ex and I needed something, *anything,* to take me away from there. Uncle Jim was great for giving me a chance, and I realized I loved teaching kids to surf. But he can be a real hardass sometimes. To him, missing a class is like missing a meeting with the president.

"I'll cancel the class for today," he says. "Will you come in tomorrow?"

Merman in the pool. I have no idea what'll happen by tomorrow. "I'll let you know tonight, okay?"

He agrees and hangs up. When I return to the pool room, Damarian is still swimming around. I watch him for a few seconds. This doesn't look real. I feel like I'm in a fairy tale.

I sit down, dangling my legs over the edge of the pool. What do I do with him?

He pops up a short while later, sprinkling water all over me. "Hello." He grins.

I'm glad he's having fun in my pool. "Did I thank you for saving me?" I ask.

"Have I thanked *you* for saving *me?*"

I smile and my cheeks grow warm. I stare down at my toes sweeping the surface of the water.

He places his cold hand under my chin and lifts my head until our eyes meet. "You are kind for helping me," he says softly. "My king has taught us not to trust humans. You destroy our home by throwing waste into the sea. You injure whales and other creatures by trapping them in your nets. If one of us were to be discovered, we will all be hunted." His hand moves to my cheek. "I watched you struggling in the sea," he continues. "Such a helpless creature. I could not believe what my king has told me. You did not seem menacing or dangerous. I could not have allowed you to die." He tucks some hair behind my ear. "Any other human would have exposed me."

I don't say anything, because I don't want to admit how right he is. Had Leah and I been five minutes too late, other people could have stumbled upon Damarian. Assuming they wouldn't call the cops, they would have dumped him into a pool with salt water, just as he asked me, and they would have seen his shiny tail. The next step would have been a call to the news stations.

"I am very grateful to you," he says.

"Thanks for saving me," I whisper. "Another merperson might have let me drown."

He nods.

The room grows quiet.

After a bit, Damarian says, "I will need to return to the sea."

My heart drops. I don't know why. It's obvious he wants to return to the ocean. It's not like he came on land on purpose so he could learn about humans or have an adventure. Washing up on shore was an accident. He doesn't want to stay here.

"Okay," I say, trying to mask my disappointment.

We're both quiet. My toes dip into the water and his webbed hands finger the tiled floor.

"How do you turn back into a human?" I ask.

"I am not certain."

"You don't remember changing?"

28

His eyebrows crease. "Last I recall is swimming in the storm."

"You'll need to change back to a human if you want to get back to the beach and into the ocean."

"I understand."

But how exactly does that happen? There could be a million possibilities. "Did you do anything before you changed?" I ask. "Eat anything? Did someone do something to you?"

He shakes his head.

I sit here, stumped, watching his tail sway in the water. Is it possible that all he needs is to be out of seawater for a while? After all, he washed up on shore and remained like that for a few hours. He might have changed after being out of salt water for some time. It's kind of like throwing a fish back into the ocean once you catch it. It flaps around, desperately searching for water. Once you throw it back in, it swims away, as good as new.

I scan Damarian for a few seconds. I don't know this guy, but I don't want him to just go. Is that weird? Maybe I'm looking for a distraction to make me forget about my mom and dad and Kyle. But he wants to go home—he *needs* to. He belongs in the ocean, just like I belong on land. I'll do anything to help him.

"Maybe you need to be out of seawater for a while and then you change," I tell him.

He nods slowly as he digests my words. "That is a fair assumption. Perhaps we shall attempt it." His face fills with anxiety and fear.

I reach for his hand. "It'll be okay. If it doesn't work, we'll try something else. I'll help you in any way I can." I swallow a lump forming in my throat. "You'll be home soon."

"Thank you. You are most kind, Cassie Price."

"You can call me Cassie."

He stares into my eyes. "Cassie."

I don't blink. It's like some force is pasting our gazes on one another. I feel something spark between us.

I pull away and stand. "We should test it out now to see if it works. But if it does, we'll have to wait until late night or early morning to go to the ocean, before the fishermen come out. No one can see you."

"I understand."

He glances around the pool. So do I. I have no idea how to do this. The easiest way would be to drain the pool, leaving Damarian without salt water and hopefully prompting his change back to a human. But that's too risky. What if it doesn't work? I might not be able to refill the pool in time.

Damarian puts his hands on the edge of the pool and tries to heave himself up.

"Oh, yeah! Good idea." If he manages to hurl himself out of the pool, he will no longer be in salt water. And if he doesn't change into a human, he can always jump back inside.

But hauling his body over the edge proves to be harder than we thought. His tail is too long and heavy, and his arms tremble as though they can't support the lower half of his body. He huffs and puffs like he's losing all of his energy.

Unlike humans, he can't throw one leg over the side of the pool for leverage. His hands slip and he crashes down into the water.

I rush to the edge. He splashes around a bit before gathering himself. "Are you hurt?" I ask.

"I am all right, thank you," he says, his chest rising and falling quickly. He looks down at his tail. "I do not believe I am able to climb out."

"Give me your hands. Let's work together." The only other option I see is to drain the pool, and I really don't want to do that unless we have no choice.

Merman's Kiss

Damarian raises his hands toward me. I'm not sure I can pull him over— he must weigh much more than the average human guy. But if we work together, we might be able to do it.

I take his hands, gulp in a deep breath, and pull with all my might.

It's like pulling on a tree.

But I'm not giving up that easily. I pull harder while he tries to throw his tail over the edge of the pool. I feel my face grow hot as I pull harder and harder. Damarian presses his lips together and groans.

My arms grow weak. He groans louder. I don't know if we can do it.

Just as I'm about to give up and lower him back into the pool, Damarian swings his tail with so much force that I'm thrown back and hit my head against one of the lounge chairs.

My head throbs. But as I rub the spot, I grin. Because Damarian is out.

Chapter Four

We've been waiting for a few minutes.

Damarian half-lies on his back, putting all his weight on his elbows. His tail lies next to me like a dead fish. It looks a little different out of water. Still beautiful, but less mesmerizing and shiny. I have an urge to run my hand down it again, to feel it for one final time. But I curl my fingers into a fist. Damarian tugs the towel tighter around his waist.

He seems pretty dry. I don't know how long we need to wait, or if this is even going to work. Pushing my knees to my chest, I ask, "How old are you?"

"Soon I shall reach my two hundred and fortieth moon."

I raise an eyebrow. I guess merpeople consider one year as twelve moons? That would make him almost twenty. "Are you considered an adult in the merworld?" I ask.

"Yes."

I run my hands up and down the back of my legs. "I just became an adult a few months ago. I guess that's a few moons in your world."

He nods. "Is it difficult?"

I press my toe into one of the cracks of the tiles. "I don't know. Yeah, I guess." It's exciting to start a new part of my life, to move forward and discover who I am. But it's also scary.

"Humans do not differ that much from children of the sea," he says.

I look at him. He's right. From my short time with Damarian, I learned that he and I have the same emotions. We have a will to be good people and do the right thing. We have compassion for a race we don't know or understand.

"Maybe you can tell that to your king," I joke.

He doesn't return the smile, just stares at the spot in front of him. I'm guessing he plans on taking this secret to the grave. I'm pretty sure his family and friends would give it to him for swimming in a nasty storm, washing up on the beach, turning into a human, and actually speaking to one. My heart muscles constrict at the thought that I'll never see him again.

I scan his body, specifically his tail, waiting for the transformation. His eyes are on his tail, too. We continue to wait.

And wait.

And wait.

Nothing happens. Maybe this won't work after all. Maybe his transformation to a human was a one-time thing or a mistake. Maybe he *can't* turn back.

My eyes trek to Damarian. He looks terrified.

I rest my hand on his arm. "Are you okay? Is it coming?"

"I feel…odd." His chest rises and falls like he's having a small panic attack.

"It'll be okay," I say softly, moving my hand to his webbed one and giving it a light squeeze. "Just remember to breathe."

He nods. I'm not sure if it's sweat gathering on his forehead or the water from the pool.

Suddenly, Damarian groans. He collapses to the floor, his tail bouncing. I scramble to my knees and watch, holding out my hands to grab him or help him or *something*. His head knocks onto the floor and he produces another groan.

I'm about to reach for him, but his tail changes. The sapphire scales slowly turn white and his fin fades away. I gasp as toes replace it. Damarian cries out in pain as the rest of his tail disappears into legs.

With my hands on my mouth, I stare at them. Just like this morning, they're that translucent color, matching the rest of his body. He lies there, his eyes shut tight, his mouth slightly opened. The towel is wrapped around his hips.

I crawl closer. "Damarian?" I rest my hand on his shoulder and shake it. "You okay?"

His eyes flutter and he moans.

"You hit your head pretty hard. But you're human again." I try to sound happy and encouraging, but I'm really freaking out. Witnessing a merman shift into a human was the most mind-blowing thing I've ever seen.

He opens his eyes, then closes them. "I am exhausted."

"Do you want to take a nap? We have some time before nightfall."

"All right." His voice drifts away.

"I mean, on a bed."

They're still closed and his breathing gets heavy. Did he fall asleep?

I watch him for a bit. He looks peaceful and beautiful.

My eyes start to droop. Sleeping must be contagious. From carrying him home this morning and into the pool and freaking out that a *merman* is in my house, my body is in major need of a nap, too. Curling down next to him, I close my eyes.

***

My eyes open. It's pitch black. Someone groans next to me. I smell the familiar scent of the ocean and everything comes back. Naked guy, merman, Damarian.

I see a form and immediately know it's him. "Hey," I say.

"Hello."

I press the small light on my watch. It's only eight PM. We have a long way to go before we can get him back in the ocean. "You've been out of the water a while."

"Yes."

I cross my arms over my chest and shiver. I'm still a little wet. "I guess as soon as the salt water's gone, you change into a human." My voice echoes throughout the empty pool room.

"Yes, I suppose."

But we don't know the rules one hundred percent. We don't know how long he can go on without needing salt water or if anything else can trigger his need to change back into a merman. If that need arises, I'll have to put him in the pool.

Damarian seems a bit shaken. I reach out and rest my hand on his knee. At least, I think it's his knee. It's still hard to see anything. "Are you okay?"

He pauses for a few seconds. "Yes."

"I'm so sorry. It looked like it was very painful."

"It is all right."

"Do you want to dress into warm clothes?"

"Yes, thank you."

I turn on the lights. Damarian is all dry, except for the towel and his hair, which is semi-wet. It's so golden and silky. It practically begs to be worked through.

After returning to him, I hold out my hand. I'm not sure how well he can walk. He was very shaky in the living room, and I half dragged him into the pool. He doesn't have a lot of experience.

He brings his hand to mine. It's so soft and no longer webbed. I help him to his feet and he wobbles a bit. I smile. "It's not as hard as it looks." I take both his hands in mine and lead him toward the door. His steps are labored and shaky, but he's doing it. "Just a little more practice and you can pull off a human guy." I laugh.

His lips tug into a smile. "I prefer the tail."

"I don't blame you."

We make our way to the living room. That's when I hear relentless knocking.

I freeze. "The door."

"Pardon me?"

Crap.

I grab his hands and pull him into Mom's bedroom. I push him down on the bed. "Stay here, okay?"

"What is the matter?"

I can't just leave him here. What if he needs salt water? The knocking continues. I'll just get rid of the person and hurry back.

"I promise it'll only take a minute."

Taking a deep breath, I make for the door and open it a crack. Leah stands before me with an annoyed yet worried expression on her face. "Finally! I thought you were kidnapped."

My body sags in relief. "Good, it's only you."

"Who else would it be?"

She pushes past me inside, but I grab her arm. "No, don't come in!"

She turns around and raises an eyebrow. "What's going on? Where's Angel Guy?" Her eyes sweep me up and down. "And why are you still in your wetsuit?"

I bite my lip and avert my gaze to my toes. Leah's my best friend and we tell each other everything. But I promised Damarian I wouldn't tell anyone about him being a merman. I can't betray him. But then again, I can't betray Leah, either.

Her eyes scrutinize me. "Don't tell me he actually grew angel wings."

I search her eyes, knowing I can trust her. But I don't have to tell her anything now. Damarian will be back in the ocean tonight, and then I'll tell her everything. "Hey," I say, fingering my braid. "Um…"

"What?"

"There's *a lot* I need to tell you. But I can't right now."

"O…kay?"

I shift from one foot to the other. "Just trust me, okay?"

She wrinkles her nose and crosses her arms over her chest. "Hmm, I don't think I can do that."

"Leah, please."

She giggles. "I'm kidding! Of course I trust you. So I guess I'll leave?"

"Yeah, I'm sorry."

She waves her hand. "It's okay."

She walks out the door.

"Hey, Leah?"

"Yeah?"

"Does your dad have any old shirts and pants I can borrow?"

Both eyebrows shoot up. "What the hell?"

"Trust me?"

"Okay. I'll see what I can find."

"Thanks." I throw my arms around her and hug her tight.

When she pulls back, she says, "Oh, this story better be good."

Trust me, it is. I close the door after her and dash back into Mom's room. Damarian is not lying on the floor wailing in pain. Good. He's sitting on the bed, looking through one of Mom's fashion magazines.

I step toward him. "I'm going to get you clothes soon. But in the meantime, do you want to eat anything? I'm pretty sure swimming all night and changing into a human, and then changing into a merman and then back into a human has left you starving."

He looks down at his stomach. "I suppose."

I lead him to the kitchen. He's still unsteady on his legs, but he's doing much better that I don't have to stop every second to help him. I sit him down at the table and open the refrigerator to find some food. What exactly do merpeople eat?

I look back at him. "Do you only eat fish?"

He's running his hands up and down the tablecloth. "What is this?"

"A tablecloth. It protects the wood of the table and is used as a decoration."

He lifts it and examines the table. "We use stone as tables."

That's interesting. What I'd give to grow a tail and swim down there with him. To discover how the merpeople live. "You don't have any evil octopus witches who can turn humans into mermaids, do you?" I ask.

He looks at me, startled.

I giggle. "Just kidding. So what would you like to eat?" I open the pantry and scan its contents. I doubt pasta or rice would go well with the fishguy. "What do you eat in the ocean?"

"We eat fish," he says. "Crabs, seaweed. There are those who have an appetite for octopuses and squids." He says the last bit with a confused expression, probably because of that comment I made before. "Other creatures we find in the ocean as well. But ordinarily, we eat fish."

That makes sense. The ocean must be like a buffet to them. "Is it dangerous to hunt?" I ask.

"Father..." His voice trails off and he clamps his mouth shut, shaking his head. I guess I'm prying.

I return my attention to the pantry and notice a can of sardines.

Perfect. When I wave it out before him, and say, "Sardines," he grins. "I only realize now how famished I am."

I hand him the can and sit down across from him. He looks down at it, furrowing his eyebrows.

"You pull that." I point. "And it should open."

He nods and drags the can open. His eyes widen like I handed him a gourmet meal. He grabs a few and dumps them into his mouth.

I try not to laugh, but it's cute how he devours them. I probably look just like that when I munch on my gummy worms.

He swallows. "Forgive me for my rudeness. Would you like some?"

"No, thanks. I'm not really a fan of fish."

He stares at me, his mouth slightly ajar. "What do you eat?"

"There are a lot of things we eat, other than fish. Meat from animals, fruits and vegetables, grains, milk and cheese. Candy."

"Candy?"

I push off my chair and open the cabinet that stashes my worms. I hold one out to him.

He eyes it carefully. "That is what humans use to capture our fish."

I study it. That's true. But the fish belong to humans just as much as it belongs to merpeople. I'm not going to start an argument, though.

"Taste it," I urge.

He's hesitant, but reaches for it and bites down. His eyes widen in wonder when he realizes how gooey it is. "This is quite tasty. I very much enjoy it."

"Your kind doesn't really hate humans, do you?" I ask.

He swallows the last of the worm, then chews on more sardines. "No. But we are told to fear them to ensure our safety."

The more they fear us, the more they'll stay hidden. His king is right to do that. If humans were to discover that merpeople actually exist, their lives would be ruined forever.

He scoops the last bit of sardines with his finger. "Do you have more of this?"

"Sure." I head over to the pantry and toss him another can. It slaps him in the chest. "Sorry! You were supposed to catch that."

"Catch?"

"Yeah." I pick it up from the floor, hand it to him, and rejoin him at the table. "Throw it at me."

He glances at the can before throwing it. I don't expect him to throw hard, but he does. I nearly miss it.

His eyes shine with intrigue.

"Now you try." I chuck it at him and he catches. "Good job!"

He smiles the widest I've ever seen.

"Did your mom ever tell you not to play with your food?" I joke.

His gaze moves to mine. "I do not understand. We slaughter the fish before we eat them."

I lean forward. "How do you do that?"

He shifts in his seat, studying me. I sit perfectly still as his eyes roam every inch of my face. I guess he feels he can trust me, because he says, "Father along with my younger brother and I hunt for food. As soon as we see an edible fish, we attempt to seize it. There is a location on the fish we must bite in order to kill it. Then we place all the fish in a large oyster shell and bring it home to the rest of the family."

"Wow. That's pretty cool."

He raises his eyebrows. "The sea's temperature is cool. The deep sea is extremely cold and dark. We do not venture too deep unless needed. The king sends a party to explore into the deep sea. It is the only area we have not fully explored."

I just stare at him, getting swallowed into his fantastic, magical world.

"Are you all right?" he asks after a few moments.

I blink and feel my cheeks boil. "Yeah, fine."

Someone's knocking on the door. Leah. I jump to my feet, tell Damarian I'll be back in a few minutes, and make my way to the door. My best friend stands there with two shirts and a pair of jeans.

"Thanks," I say, taking the clothing and giving her another hug.

She peers into the house. "All this is seriously piquing my curiosity." Now she's on her tippy toes, craning her neck and looking deeper into the house.

"Tomorrow," I promise. "I'll tell you everything tomorrow. Every last detail."

She falls back on her feet. "You're lucky I'm an awesome best friend."

"I know." I gather her in my arms and hug her again, this time tighter. "Thanks again for the clothes."

"No problem."

When I'm back in the kitchen and hand the clothes to Damarian, he eyes them like I might eye a corset. "I cannot imagine this being comfortable." He holds the jeans upside down over his chest.

I laugh, turn it around, and hand it back to him. "Believe me, you don't want to be running around with nothing more than a towel. Although, I'm pretty sure some girls on the beach would love that."

He presses the jeans on his legs. "This substance…it is rough."

"Well, that's jeans." At least Leah didn't bring tight-fitted ones. I can imagine Damarian's reaction to that. "Just go into that room and get dressed. Wear the shirt this way, with the words and pictures on your chest. I'm going to change in my room."

He nods and disappears into the other room. I make sure the front door is locked before going up to my room. I fall on my bed and breathe heavily. This is the first time I'm truly alone since rescuing

Damarian, and it's finally sinking in. A merman. *Merman.* They exist. They really exist. I might be one of the only people in the entire world to know about them.

I catch my reflection in the mirror. Frizzy, hay-colored hair in two braids. Brown eyes too big for my face. I groan and get to my feet. Next to such a beautiful creature, I really look like a toad.

I rummage around in my closet and settle on a plain white T-shirt and jeans. When I return to the kitchen, I find Damarian already there. His shirt's on the right way, so he gets points for that. But the jeans…not so much.

"The zipper goes in the front," I say, hiding a laugh.

He scowls. "I do not appreciate human coverings, but this feels all right."

"Okay. Suit yourself."

He scratches his thighs, his attention on my jeans. "You wear them as well."

"Yep." I head to the fridge, grab a Coke, and toss him a can. "Stay hydrated, just in case. Do you feel like you might need salt water?"

"I feel well."

"Good. Here." I reach over and open the can for him.

He looks mesmerized as the bubbly liquid makes it way down his throat.

I lean back against the counter and study him. Dressed in normal clothes, he looks like he belongs here. Well, more like in a fashion magazine. Human clothes definitely do him justice.

He's studying me, too. "How long before I may return to the sea?"

I glance at my watch. It's only nine PM and people might still be at the beach. I hope Damarian can hold out for a few more hours. If not, he'll have to return to the pool. "Not for a little while."

He nods. I can see how badly he wants to go home. Not that he looks like he's being kept hostage, but he looks lost and confused, bewildered, and most of all, homesick.

"Come," I say. "Let's watch some TV to pass the time."

"TV?"

I grin. "I think you'll love it."

***

It's three in the morning. Damarian passed out while watching a crime show. He didn't understand how TVs work, and no matter how much I tried, I couldn't explain it. So after a while, his eyes drooped and he was out cold.

Sleep hasn't crossed my mind. Not when I have a merman lying next to me.

I don't want to wake him. He looks so young and carefree. I study each feature, burning the image of him into my memory. This is something I'll take to the grave, after telling Leah, of course. I'm not sure she'll believe me, but I don't care about that now. I brush some hair off his forehead. I'll miss him.

I shake his shoulder. He stirs, opening his eyes. They cloud with confusion for a second, but then clear. "Hello, Cassie."

"It's show time."

"Show time?"

"It's just an expression. It means you're ready to go home."

His face washes with relief. He follows me toward the hallway and out the front door. I take his hand and lead him toward the beach. He's a pro at walking now.

"I feel a bit ill," he tells me when we're almost there.

My heart races. "We better get you to the ocean."

We sprint to the beach. I look around to make sure no one's here. We walk further inside, to an area where people don't normally hang out. An area with a lot of rocks. I help him climb up. "You can dive from here," I say, then bite down on my bottom lip. We're assuming he'll shift into a merman once he hits the ocean. But what if he doesn't? He won't be able to swim as a human. I'll have to jump in after him and bring him to shore.

Damarian pulls at his shirt. I reach for the hem and help him drag it over his head. My eyes dip to his jeans. Those need to come off, too. I raise my hands, but drop them to my sides, heat creeping onto my face. Damarian slips his hands into the waistband and pulls them down, stepping out of them. He's *naked.* He doesn't seem embarrassed. Maybe he doesn't understand how embarrassing it should be for him to be naked in front of me.

He faces the ocean. Clearing my throat and keeping my eyes above his stomach, I step next to him. The waves are a bit strong tonight. I scan around again and sigh in relief when I don't see anyone. Then I grab Damarian and pull him into a hug. He wavers and almost loses his balance. "Sorry," I say and laugh. "You're probably not used to hugs."

"Hugs?"

"Yeah. It's what friends do to one another when they say goodbye."

"I understand." His hands slowly come around me. My heart pounds in my head and goose bumps crawl over my arms. This feels really good. More than good. I don't want to let go.

But I need to. I step out of his hold and look at him. "You'll be okay?"

He scratches his neck. "Yes."

My vision grows blurry. I run my sleeve across my nose. "Goodbye, Damarian."

He stares into my eyes. "Goodbye, Cassie. You are the kindest human I have ever met."

That makes me smile. "You're the most amazing merman I ever

met."

He smiles crookedly. "And I shall be the only merman you ever meet."

I laugh. "Yeah."

He faces the ocean, then turns back to me. A hint of fear and anxiety clouds his features. He raises his hand and caresses my cheek with the back of his fingers. My entire body heats up and my cheek burns from his touch. I can hardly breathe.

He slowly bends forward and the next thing I feel is his soft, warm lips brush across mine. My eyes flutter closed. A second later, he pulls back. My eyes fly open. Damarian backs away, his gaze locked on me.

Turning around, he dives into the ocean.

I drop down on the rocks and stare into the water, my heart beating rapidly, my cheek still scorching, my lips tingling. I don't see anything, only the waves crashing violently. I count a few seconds, hoping he's changing into a merman. I rest my palms on the rocks and lift off my knees, ready to jump in if I need to.

His tail pops out of the ocean. The moon shines on it, making it look like crystals. It brightens the ocean. Then it disappears under the water. My heart drops. That's it. It's over.

I'm about to turn away, but something splashes in the water. Damarian's golden head emerges. My breath catches in my throat. His eyes bore into mine for what feels like hours until he jerks away and dives back into the ocean.

I wait a few minutes. But I don't see anything other than the waves. He's gone.

Chapter Five

Leah slides another smoothie across the counter. "I wonder if a person can die from too much fruit and sugar."

Frowning, I grab the cup and bite hard on the straw. I'm not even sure what the flavor is this time—I told Leah to surprise me. I don't taste anything because every part of me is numb. I might as well be drinking water.

Leah leans in close, her dark brown, wavy hair falling over her shoulder. "What happened last night?"

I suck hard on the liquid. I can't believe the mood I woke up in this morning. It almost feels like I was in a serious relationship and had my heart broken. I don't get it. He was just a merman, a fish from the ocean. Who kissed me. I can still feel his warm lips on mine.

I rub my forehead. The memories need to vanish from my mind because they aren't supposed to be there to begin with. A broken heart from a creature I only met for a day? Something is seriously wrong with me.

Leah mops the counter with a rag. "Remember, you promised," she half-sings.

I know, and I plan on telling her. Just right now...I feel like I jumped into the ocean with Damarian, except I drowned while he swam away. And I hate that I feel this way. After Kyle broke up with me four months ago and ripped my heart out of my chest, threw it on the floor and stomped on it, and then shoved it back inside, I promised myself I wouldn't let myself fall madly in love with anyone. Not unless I was absolutely one thousand percent sure he's the right guy for me. Now I can't get a merman out of my head.

Leah's eyes fill with concern. "Cassie, I'm really worried about you. What's going on?"

I drop money on the counter and slide off the stool. "Meet at the beach after work?"

"Sure."

I turn to leave, but she calls my name. I face her. She lifts the counter and pulls me into a tight hug. "What's that for," I mumble.

"Because I know you're hurting for whatever reason."

That brings tears to my eyes. I stay in her arms for a little bit before picking up my surfboard and heading out to the shore. My students should start arriving soon. I sit down on the wet sand and face the ocean. I stare at the waves, feeling them hit my toes.

Someone blocks the sun. Shielding my eyes, I raise my head. Uncle Jim stands before me. I hug my knees to my chest and rest my cheek on one. "If you're going to scold me, don't bother. I'm in a crappy enough mood as it is."

He slowly lowers himself next to me. His leg's no longer in a cast, but he still has trouble walking. I help him settle down. "I'm not going to scold you, sweetie," he says.

Sweetie. Uncle Jim's not a mushy guy. Something's up. I look at him. "What's going on?"

"Have you spoken to your mother?" he asks.

She called this morning, but I wasn't in the mood to talk to her. "Is she staying in Philly for the whole month or something?"

I mean that as a joke, but the expression on his face doesn't make this funny.

I scramble to my feet and glare at him. "Are you serious?"

"Cassie—"

I grab my surfboard and run into the ocean. I don't get it. I'm her kid. I know I'm eighteen and legally an adult, but I'm still a kid. I need my mother. Yes, I'm admitting it—I need my mom. I always have. Growing up without a dad and Mom working crazy, late hours to pay the rent, I never felt like she was really there. It was like she was floating through life, waiting for a big break. Now she landed a decent job with a good company and we can live comfortably without having to worry about money. And she chooses to *run*. I'm leaving for college in the fall, all the way in Texas. This is really the only time we have together.

I paddle deeper into the ocean, but I don't wait for a wave. I don't jump on my board. I just sit on it with my legs dangling off the sides. For some stupid, idiotic reason, my time with Damarian felt magical, special. Like maybe something good finally happened to me. Now that he's gone, real life has knocked me over the head and left a lump the size of a beach ball.

I'm an adult now. I'm supposed to embrace life with open arms and accept everything thrown my way. But I'm not ready. Not at all.

The waves crash into me. Salt water enters my mouth. I spit it out.

Squinting toward the beach, I find that most of my students have arrived. I swim back to shore.

***

"Cassie!"

I turn around and see Leah running toward me. She drops down next to me on the wet sand, but not close enough for the tide to hit her. She's coming straight from work and hasn't changed into a

48

swimsuit.

"What's up?" she asks.

I dig my toes into the sand. "Are you ready?"

"Hell yeah."

I start my story. I tell her how I managed to rouse "Angel Guy" from his unconscious state, how he was like a baby learning to walk for the first time. How he developed a rash on his neck and begged for salt water.

"I didn't know what to do," I say, staring down at my toes buried in the sand. "I was freaking out. Then I remembered the sea salt in my basement. You know, when my mom bought me that fish tank for marine fish?"

She nods. Her eyebrows have been raised since I started the story and have remained that way.

"He wasn't an angel," I say.

"No, duh."

"He was something so much better."

Now her eyebrows furrow. "Better than an angel?"

"You'll never believe me."

"Try me."

I draw an image in the sand with my finger. "He turned into...this."

Leah bends forward to study it. "A fish? He turned into a fish?"

I shake my head and point to the tail, circling over the fin.

Her face shows nothing but confusion. She stares at the picture. Then her green eyes snap to mine. "Mermaid?"

I swallow. "Mer*man*."

Her jaw drops and she looks at me like I've really lost it.

"Don't say I hit my head when I wiped out."

Her mouth moves, but no sound comes out. She stares down at my drawing for a few seconds before focusing her attention back on me.

"I'm not crazy, Leah. He was swimming in the ocean that night during the storm and he somehow washed ashore. That's why he was naked. He changed into a human after being out of salt water for too long."

Still, her mouth doesn't move.

"You even noticed it yourself, how he doesn't look human. His translucent skin and golden hair. That's not natural."

"Mermaid?" she croaks.

"Mer*man*," I correct.

She shuffles over until she's right in front of me. The waves crash over her knees, but she doesn't seem to notice. She's looking at me with an incredulous expression.

"He's back in the ocean now," I say. "Back with his own kind." Where he belongs.

"Mermaid?" she croaks again.

I laugh as I rub away the image of the mermaid tail. "Mer*man*, Leah."

"Rescued you from drowning."

"Washed ashore, completely naked. Woke up in my house. Would have died if I didn't give him salt water."

"Mermaids don't exist," she says. "This is insane."

I hold out my hands. "You can't deny the evidence. Someone saved me when I wiped out, and it couldn't have been a person. No one was near me and I was probably sinking to the bottom of the ocean."

She hugs her knees and stares out at the waves. "There really are mermaids living out there?"

I nod. "And they're intelligent and emotional, just like us." Not to mention kind and caring.

She covers her face and laughs. "This is crazy."

"I know."

She uncovers her face. "Looks like you starred in your very own movie—The Little Merman."

"You can't tell anyone about this, Leah. Promise me you won't."

"I swear I won't. What's his name? Does he have a hot name? He has to have a hot name."

"I don't know if I should tell you…"

"Aw, Cassie. Please, please, please?"

I sigh. I can't ever say no to her when she begs like that. "Okay. Damarian."

"Damarian?"

I nod.

"Yep. Definitely hot."

I laugh.

We sit in silence for a few seconds, watching others swim in the ocean. Leah turns to me. "Will he be back?"

I shake my head.

"How can you be so sure?"

"They need to hide from us. Washing up on the shore could have been a major disaster. He'll never risk that again."

She nods slowly. "And you're okay with that?"

I give her a nonchalant face. "Why shouldn't I be?"

"You have a connection to him. He's your hero, your knight in shining armor—well, your fish in shining scales. And you're his hero, too."

I dig my fingers into the sand and doodle. Then I shrug. "There's nothing I can do about it." Tears threaten to prick my eyes, but I push them away. "I guess I feel…I don't know. Empty."

"Why?"

I draw my knees to my chest and rest my cheek on them. "Ever since I woke up on that boulder, I felt something. I don't know what, but I knew something saved me. Now I know who it was. I was *with* him the whole day. He even kissed me. Sort of. Then he just swam away. I'll never see him again."

Leah's mouth falls. "He *kissed* you?"

"It was more like a brush."

"That must mean something."

I shrug. "Maybe that's how they say goodbye. I don't know. I don't want to think about it. I need to push it out of my head or else I'll drive myself crazy."

She moves closer and lays her hand over mine. She doesn't say anything else—she doesn't have to. It's enough to just have my best friend near me and let me pour my heart out. Having Leah by my side makes me feel less alone.

Someone clears his throat from behind us. Both Leah and I raise our heads. I blink a few times, not believing who is standing before me. Jet-black hair, tall, tanned chest.

"Hey," he says, swallowing so hard that his Adam's apple bobs.

"Kyle," Leah says. Then she shoots me a just-say-the-word-and-he's-gone look.

He's dressed in a wetsuit, carrying a surfboard. A lump forms in my throat as I catch sight of the one he's holding. Light blue with waves on it. My present to him a few months before he broke my heart. I should snatch it out of his hands, but I pry my gaze away.

"Hey," he says again.

I'm tempted to say, "What do you want, Kyle?" but I bite my tongue and doodle on the sand.

"How are you, Cass?" he asks.

We haven't seen or spoken to each other in a month. Somehow we've managed to avoid bumping into each other on the beach. I'm sure that's all his doing, since he works at a shop near the beach and probably knows my comings and goings.

Kyle, being ever Mr. Sweet, can't help himself but ask how his ex is doing. To make sure she hasn't had an emotional breakdown or whatever. I'd rather eat this wet sand than answer his question.

I stare straight ahead at the ocean.

"Hey, Kyle!" someone yells. It's a pretty redhead, all wet and holding a surfboard. She must have just come out of the water.

"Well, see ya around, I guess." He takes off in the direction of the redhead.

"What a jerk," Leah mutters. "Has the nerve to ask how you're doing."

"Don't be too hard on him," I say, my throat parched as if I did eat sand.

"See, that's the problem with you, Cassie. The guy tore your heart out of your chest and left it to rot. You forgive too easily."

"I don't forgive him." It's just hard to hate him when he did nothing wrong. He stopped loving me and ended things. He did it the right way.

Leah goes off on me, but I try not to listen. She's been saying the same thing ever since he broke up with me—that I need to have a backbone. Trusting guys has always been an issue for me since Dad left my mom for some woman he met online. Now he's married to her and lives a few miles away with their two kids and however-many pets.

When I met Kyle at the start of my senior year of high school, I thought he would be that one person, other than Leah, whom I could trust. We had an insane amount of things in common and just understood each other. I really thought he was the right guy for me.

"You want someone to love you so bad that you'd let him walk all over you."

"Leah—"

"I've introduced you to so many great guys. Guys who deserve to have someone like you."

"I know. I'm screwed up, okay? We don't need to go over that again."

She takes me in her arms and squeezes me tight. "You're not screwed up. There's someone out there for you, and he'll love you just for you."

I bring my arms around her. I want to believe her, but I don't think it'll ever happen.

Chapter Six

I bring up a Google page and type in "Mermaids." The first few links that pop up are Wikipedia, images of mermaids, the 1990 movie, and other sites with the same keyword. I check out most of the links on the first two pages, but none of them have any accounts of an actual mermaid.

I puff out some air and fall back in my chair. If I saw a merman, there *has* to be someone else in the world who did, too.

Poising my fingers over the keys, I type "I saw a mermaid." That brings up a lot of hits. Most seem to be YouTube videos. I click on the first one. It shows a young woman claiming she saw an actual mermaid when she was vacationing in California. She talks about how she swam too far into the ocean with her younger brother and how they saw something odd in the water.

Then the video shows a girl wearing a fake tail swimming in a pool.

I roll my eyes and stop the video. Awesome, a fake.

A whole bunch of similar videos show up. Telling myself to give this another chance, I watch one, then another. When I've watched five, I rest my elbows on my desk and bury my forehead in my palms. Maybe I really am the only one in the entire world to have stumbled upon a creature from the sea.

I'm about to close the webpage when a video catches my attention. I don't know what it is about it—maybe the expression on the man's face, the intensity and determination in his eyes. I click on it.

He looks middle-aged and starts off the video swearing that this isn't a joke. As much as I want to believe this video may be what I'm looking for, skepticism clouds my mind. Still, I sit back and watch.

He says he usually wakes up before the other fishermen because he likes to be alone and because he believes he'll get a better catch at a much earlier hour. Last year (which is really two years ago, since he made the video last year), he was fishing on his boat like he usually did, when all of the sudden he saw something odd in the water. He didn't pay much attention to it at first, since there are a lot of things in the ocean, but after a minute or two, he saw a shiny green fishtail. He put aside his fishing pole and bent over to take a closer look. He assumed it was a species of fish he hadn't seen before. But then he saw dark hair and an arm. He thought it was a body and immediately sailed back to shore and got help. They searched the ocean for days, but couldn't find anyone. That's when the guy put the pieces together and realized it wasn't a human, but a mermaid.

I scroll down the page and read the comments. Most are hateful and call him a liar and an attention seeker. Not that I blame them. The story does sound crazy, and I know I wouldn't believe him, either. I click on his profile to check out some of his other videos, but he doesn't have any.

Could he have been telling the truth? He didn't say where he lives, so I don't know if it's the same ocean I saw Damarian in. I mean, do merpeople live only in the Atlantic Ocean? Are they all over the place like humans? This guy could live all the way on the west coast or something.

Just as I'm about to check some more videos, hoping for other real stories, my cell phone rings. I scan the screen and my heart drops a little. Mom. I haven't spoken to her since she left two nights ago. I'm not sure I even want to talk to her. I don't need to hear how awesome she's doing now that she's a free woman.

But I can never ignore her. I mumble, "Hello."

"Hi, sweetie!"

She sounds way too energetic, like she's pretending she's really excited to talk to me.

"What's up?" I say.

"How are you doing?"

"Fine."

She must notice the sarcastic tone, because she says, "Uncle Jim spoke to you."

"Mhm."

"I'm so sorry, Cass. I really thought I'd be gone for only a week. But Martha put me in charge of a new project she's introducing—"

"Got it." I close the YouTube page and sit back. "So I guess I'll see you whenever?"

"Cassie."

I sigh. "Sorry." I don't mean to lash out at her—I know how much she sacrificed for me when I was growing up. I know how much she missed out. I guess…it's not that I'm lonely. Okay, maybe a little. Lots of people my age would die to have a place all to themselves. But it's not all that it's cracked up to be.

"Listen, sweetie," Mom says. "I want you to call your father."

I shoot forward in the chair. "Not again."

"You're eighteen now. It's time to let go of childhood grudges and give your father a second chance. Do you want to regret this for the rest of your life? The ball's in your court, Cassie. Good night, honey, and I'll speak to you tomorrow."

I wish her a good night and hang up. Getting to my feet, I fall down on my bed and hug a pillow. She's right. I am holding onto a childhood grudge. How long am I going to punish my dad for something he did years ago? I unlock my phone and scroll through my contacts. He's listed as "Mark."

My thumb hovers over his name, but I can't click on it. I just can't. I press my phone against my chest. I'm not ready to forgive him and let him back into my life. I don't know if I'll ever be.

I don't know if I'll ever be able to welcome any man into my life.

Chapter Seven

One week later

My eyes snap open when I hear knocking on the door. I groan and roll over on my bed. I have no idea what time it is, but I know it's way too early for someone to be pounding on my door. Today's my day off and I plan on sleeping in until lunchtime, then hanging out at the beach.

But the knocking doesn't stop. I smash my pillow over my head.

Knock. Pound. Knock.

"Go away!" I yell into the pillow.

Pound. Pound. Pound.

I throw the pillow off and drag myself up and toward the door. If it's a kid pulling a prank or someone trying to sell me something...

"What do you want?" I shout through the door.

"C-Cassie?"

I freeze.

That voice. I would recognize it anywhere. I bend forward to look through the peephole. Golden hair. It can't be...

My shaky, sweaty fingers close over the knob. It won't open. *Of course it won't open if it's locked.* I unlock it and pull the door open, knocking it into my left side and producing a small yelp. He stands before me, dressed in what looks like women's pink shorts.

He follows my gaze and laughs sheepishly. "It was all I could find."

I blink at him. Then at the shorts, which are really, really short and tight…and his chest, his naked chest. I force my eyes back to his face. Damarian. What the hell is he doing here?

His eyes move back and forth between mine. "I have startled you."

"N-no." I clear my throat. "I mean, no of course not." The door widens a little and I stumble to the left. I didn't realize I was putting my weight on it.

He holds out a hand. "I am sorry for arriving here unannounced. I…" He drops his hand to his side and searches the area around him. I peek out. Random passersby are starting to stare at the half naked guy wearing only tight women's shorts.

I slam my hand to my forehead, snapping myself back into it. "Sorry. Come in." I widen the door and step back as he squeezes past me. I get a whiff of that ocean scent. His hair glistens with water, but the rest of him is pretty dry.

After closing the door, I slowly raise my eyes. His bore into mine. Then they move a little lower, to my lips. They tingle as I remember the feeling of his light kiss. His gaze drops even lower. I glance down and realize I'm wearing a loose white shirt and light blue underwear. My cheeks sizzle.

Making a run for my room, I call out, "Make yourself comfortable while I change and find something for you to wear."

When I get to my room, I cover my face and laugh. Out of embarrassment, excitement, confusion—I don't know. I find myself on my knees and laughing so hard my sides ache.

Once I calm down, I search my closet for something to wear. I lean against the clothing, almost losing my balance and crashing into the closet. He's here. He's *here*. Why is he here?

I settle on jeans and a purple shirt. Opening my bottom drawer, I pull out Leah's father's jeans—the ones I gave Damarian last week. I didn't have the willpower to return them to her. Like I didn't want to let go of him, which is stupid, I know. I find his shirt and inhale its scent. Even though I washed both the shirt and jeans, they still smell like him. Like salt water.

Damarian is sitting on the living room couch. I hold out the clothes. Recognition enters his eyes and they light up. "You have not returned them to your friend?"

My mouth opens, but no words come out. I don't know what to say—that I spent every night of the last week wishing and hoping he'd return?

"You can throw out the shorts," I tell him. "Unless you'd rather keep them."

He smiles crookedly. "That would not be a wise choice."

My own cheeks lift. "No, it wouldn't."

He nods and disappears into the room next door with the clothes. I fall on the couch and let out a breath. I feel like someone's squeezing my body when Damarian's in the same room as me.

My fingers wring in my lap. My knees shake.

He emerges a few minutes later, wearing the clothes the right way this time and looking incredibly hot. I do a quick sweep of him before resting my eyes on his face. "Um…hi," I say.

"Hello."

He sits down near me. I chew on one of my braids. Sitting so close to him…it's causing every hair on my body to stand up.

"Wh…" I clear my throat again. "I mean…why…where…?"

He shifts on the couch. "I…" He pushes some hair off his right eye. "When I returned home…" His eyes flick to the blank TV screen before returning to my face. "I could not forget you, Cassie."

My heart dances wildly, sending hot blood throughout my body. I clench my fingers to my palms as the room gets uncomfortably hot.

"I had to return to land," he continues.

I stare into his eyes and he into mine. He raises a hand and brings it to my cheek, stroking it with the back of his fingers.

"I couldn't stop thinking about you, either," I whisper.

He lowers his hand and we sit side by side. The room grows silent. I wring my hands again. Damarian sits straight, his gaze on the blank TV.

"Did anyone see you?" I ask.

He shakes his head. "I believe not. I left home late last night and swam to land. I remained there until I shifted into my human form. Then I discovered that garment..." He motions his head toward the shorts that he threw on the recliner. "When the sun rose, I traveled to your home."

The risk, the danger. All for me. Every part of me is bursting to ask why—why me? What's so special about me? I know I'm the first and only human he's had contact with, but he's a *merman*. The ladies in the ocean must be goddesses compared to me.

I make circles on the carpet with my toes. "How long are you staying?"

Our eyes meet. "I am not certain."

I continue making circles. "I guess you have nowhere to stay..."

He doesn't say anything, just looks helplessly around my house. A few seconds pass before he gets up and says, "I apologize. I do not know what I was thinking...arriving here, thinking I could remain with you." He takes a step toward the door, but I grab his arm.

"I'm sorry if I made you feel unwelcome. Please, sit down."

He nods and sits.

"I'm just...overwhelmed, I guess. You're more than welcome to stay. I...I'd love for you to stay."

His face washes with relief and he smiles.

I stand. "We need to go shopping. Find you clothes. And we'll need to stock up on that sea salt just in case."

He nods. He looks terrified and anxious, but also excited. I grab my purse and reach for his hand. The way it slides into mine—it's like a perfect fit. I feel the spark all the way in my toes.

I lead him out the door and toward my car, well Mom's car. He stops short, his hand gliding out of mine. He stares at it.

"What is this?" he asks.

"A car."

He raises an eyebrow. "Car?"

"Yep. That's how we humans get from one place to another. These legs don't have super speed like that tail of yours."

That makes him smile. I open the passenger door for him and he slides in. Then I get into the driver's seat. I'm about to buckle my seatbelt when I realize Damarian needs to be buckled in, too. I glance at him. "Um..."

"Yes?"

"The law requires...you know, I'll strap you in." I bend forward and reach for his seatbelt. The thing's tangled. As I try to untangle it, I feel his eyes on me. I turn my head. His face is so close to mine that I feel his warm breath tickling my cheek. Our eyes are locked on one another. The air gets knocked out of me.

We just stare into each other's eyes for what feels like forever, until a group of kids across the street shriek as they chase each other down the block. I tear my gaze from him and focus on untangling the belt. When it's free, I stretch it across his chest, my heart hammering, my fingers shaking. I slide back to my seat, buckle myself, and wrap my fingers around the steering wheel to steady them.

The only thing I hear is our breathing—his soft, mine heavy.

I clear my throat. "So we're going to the mall. That's where you can buy shirts, pants, shoes…" He's been walking around barefoot all this time.

"Yes," he says.

I start the car and drive toward the mall. Damarian's face is pressed against the window, soaking in our world. I peek at him from time to time, watching the way he silently marvels at everything.

"How do you stay hidden?" I ask.

He stares at the spot in front of him, frowning.

"Sorry. I shouldn't have asked that."

It hurts that he can't trust me, but of course he can't. I don't blame him. Just…I'm still not so sure why he came back.

"We're here." I kill the engine and reach over to release Damarian's seatbelt, making sure not to touch him or get sucked into his eyes. "Just pull the latch and the door should open."

He does as I say and climbs out of the car. I feel this wall between us. Not that we were ever really open with one another. I want to know everything about him, learn about his life, about *him*. Did he come back for me or because he's curious about humans?

"Um…this way," I say, leading him toward a clothing store. A few people glance at his bare feet and quickly avert their gazes, probably thinking he's crazy. I stay close to him so he won't get lost in the large store.

His jaw drops a bit as he surveys the main floor and the escalators. "This is where humans acquire garments?"

"That, among other things." I take his arm and bring him toward the escalators. "Men's clothing is on the second floor."

"What is this?"

"Escalators. They're used to transport people from one floor to another."

His eyes widen as he watches a woman and toddler get on it.

"It's a lot of fun. You'll see." I take his hand and step closer to the escalator. His grip on me tightens, as though he's about to walk to his death. I give him a reassuring squeeze and raise my leg, urging him to do the same. We step on it.

Damarian looks behind him for a second before returning his focus on me. His eyes fill with intrigue. Then he nearly loses his balance. I tighten my hold on his hand and tell him to grab onto the rail.

"This is most peculiar," he says.

We reach the second floor and get off the escalator. Damarian stops short when he sees the many items on display. "How does one know what to acquire?" he asks.

"Now that's a good question."

I hate shopping, but doing it for Damarian...it doesn't make me hate it so much. Maybe because he's so dependent on me right now, and I want to make his stay here as comfortable and perfect as possible. My only problem is that a dog has better fashion sense than me.

"Well, you can't go wrong with jeans," I say, showing him a pile on one of the racks.

His lips form a straight line. "I am not one to appreciate such rough garments."

That makes me giggle. "Okay. You can try khakis or cargo pants. I mean, there are more kinds of pants, but that's all I know..." I lead him to another rack and hold out a pair of khakis.

He takes it and runs a hand down the length of it. "This is softer." He lifts his eyes to me. "Do most human males wear the rough fabric?"

It's cute how he doesn't want to stand out. "Most guys your age would probably wear the jeans, but a lot of guys wear khakis, too."

He continues feeling the pants. "This would feel more comfortable."

"Okay. Um…your size…" This is another area where I'm clueless. "I guess you can try on a few sizes and see which fits best."

"All right." He slides his thumbs into the jeans he's wearing.

"No!" I nearly shout, placing my hands over his. "Not here. There are fitting rooms."

He looks lost.

"Rooms to try the clothes on. It's not really modest to undress in a room full of people." I gesture to the other shoppers. Some are peeking at us, which causes my cheeks to warm up.

"I understand." He looks around. "Where are these fitting rooms?"

"Let's look for some more clothes so you can try them on at once. You want to look for shirts?"

"Yes."

We spend the next few minutes checking out T-shirts. Damarian picks out a few and we head for the fitting rooms.

"I'll wait out here," I tell him. "Only men are allowed in there."

He nods unsurely.

"There's a mirror inside, so you can check out how you look. I'll be out here if you want to show me."

He nods again and disappears into the room.

I fold my arms over my chest and lean against the wall. Goose bumps pop up all over my arms, and they're not due to the air conditioning in this place.

Five minutes pass and no Damarian. I hope he's okay.

Ten minutes pass. I crane my neck to look inside, but I can't see much.

When fifteen minutes have passed, I start to pace around. I hope he's okay and not unconscious on the floor. I have no idea how long he's been out of salt water.

I crack a few knuckles.

He finally emerges, dressed in the khakis and a light gray shirt. I falter back as I take him in. He looks good. Really good. Like he stepped off a runway.

I blink and smile. "What do you think?" I circle around him to make sure it fits well. As far as I know, he looks amazing.

"They feel comfortable."

"Cool. Did you try on the other shirts?"

"Yes. They all feel comfortable."

"Okay, good. Do you want to buy some more or are you good?"

"I am well, thanks."

I stare at him. "I mean…are you satisfied with your clothes?"

"Yes. Thank you for all your help."

I feel my cheeks heat up. "No problem." I turn away and chew on my pigtail. "Shoes?"

He looks down and stretches his leg out. "Is it a requirement?"

I scrunch my nose. "Yeah. I know it feels good without shoes, but you'll get hurt if you don't wear any."

"All right."

We make our way to the shoes section. After a few minutes, he chooses flip-flops.

"Do you want anything else?" I ask.

"I do not believe so."

I think for a few seconds. What would a human guy need? "Underwear," I say. "Of course you need underwear. And pajamas."

He looks baffled.

"Well, you need underwear to wear under your..." I shut my mouth and lead him toward the section that sells male underwear. I study the items for sale. Boxers, briefs, boxer briefs. I scratch my head. "Hmm, I guess we should go with boxers, since you can't stand tight things."

"All right."

"Now for pajamas." We make our way to the right section. After examining the pajamas, Damarian settles on dark grey pants. "You probably will feel more comfortable sleeping shirtless, but we should buy some tank tops just in case." I swallow as my eyes flash to his chest. I yank them away. "Okay, we're all set."

We wait in line at the cash register. Damarian stands quietly, watching all the activity around him, observing the way people shop, how they interact with one another. After a few minutes, he says, "Why are we waiting?"

"We need to pay."

His eyebrows furrow. "Pay."

"Yep. You can't get anything for free here. If you want it, you've got to pay for it."

His eyebrows furrow even more. "Pay. But I have not—"

"Next in line, please!"

He follows me to the cashier, where I place his clothing on the counter. I feel him grow uneasy and hear him shuffling from one foot to another. It's interesting how his human instincts are kicking in.

The woman scans the items and says the price. My heart drops a bit. That's a lot of money. Biting down on my lip, I pull out my credit card. I hope Mom won't kill me.

"Cassie," Damarian says.

I look at him.

"Those are my garments. I should provide the pay."

"It's okay. Don't worry about it."

"But I insist. I will provide for the pay somehow."

"It's okay."

"Cassie, I do insist."

The woman's eyes go from me to Damarian, back and forth. I clear my throat and say, "Credit, please."

When everything's done, I thank the woman and grab the bag. I march quickly to the door and see Damarian trying to keep up. When we're close to the doors, he gently places a hand on my arm. "Cassie…"

"You're new here. You don't have any money. This is my gift to you, okay?"

His eyes search mine, and I can see he doesn't like it. But he knows he has no choice. I open the door and hold it out for him.

"We have no such method in the sea," he says.

"What kind of method do you have?"

"We trade. If my friend has an item I require, I offer an item of equal value."

"Barter," I say. "We did that years ago." At least, I think we did. I don't really remember much of history class.

"Is there any way I can relinquish you of the burden of my pay?" he asks.

I unlock the car and place the bag in the back seat. "We're friends, Damarian. Friends give each other gifts. Think of this as a Welcome Back to the Human World gift."

We climb into the car. "I must offer you something in exchange," he says.

I reach for his buckle and strap him in. "I'd really love it if you'd drop it."

He leans back and huffs, crossing his arms over his chest.

I burst out laughing.

He stares at me.

"Sorry. You're just acting very human right now."

He looks down at his folded arms. "Is that so?"

"Yep." I start the car. "Next stop is to the pet shop for some sea salt."

Chapter Eight

The second we enter the pet shop, Damarian comes to a short stop. His gaze immediately goes to the fish tanks lined up across the wall.

I curse to myself before following him. I know what he's going to say. I shouldn't have brought him inside. I didn't think this through.

He flashes me accusing eyes. "They are captured." He points to five goldfish swimming around in a medium-sized tank.

"No, they're not."

"They are imprisoned."

"They're here on display so people can buy them as pets. We treat them well, Damarian. Humans give their pets a lot of love and attention."

He clenches his jaw.

I fold my arms. "Hey, it's not like they can actually understand what's going on or feel anything."

He gapes at me. "To what are you referring?"

"Their brains are not advanced like ours and they don't feel emotion."

"You are mistaken." He touches the side of the glass and narrows his eyes.

I glance around the shop. The owner is attending to a small family and the other customers are looking around. "Damarian, what are you doing?" I hiss. I hope he doesn't plan on breaking the glass and letting all these fish free.

He closes his eyes. I rest a hand on his arm. "Damarian?"

He opens his eyes and rubs his forehead. "I cannot communicate with them in this human form."

My mouth falls open. "Communicate? You...you speak to fish?"

"Can I help you?" The owner steps toward us.

"Yes—"

"Please release the fish," Damarian says in an authoritative voice.

The owner looks taken aback. "Excuse me?"

"I'm sorry," I say, holding out my hands. "He's just..." I clear my throat. "Do you have any synthetic seat salt? For marine fish?"

He glances at Damarian for a second before turning his full attention to me. "Yes, I do." He leads me farther into the store. I look back to make sure Damarian doesn't plan on doing anything stupid, but he's just staring intently at the fish in the tank. Right before I turn into the next aisle, I see him go over to another tank, one with tropical fish.

The owner shows me the sea salt. It's the same one I have at home. I ask for two buckets. I'm not sure how long Damarian plans on staying, but I'm not taking any chances. From what just happened with the fish, I won't be surprised if he goes back home today, taking all the "captured" fish with him.

I feel a pang in my heart as those thoughts swirl around my head.

Damarian is watching the marine fish when the owner and I walk up to the counter. He doesn't look upset now. He looks...sad. Like he's longing for something. It dawns on me that seeing marine fish probably reminds him of home, of the life he left.

Merman's Kiss

I pay for the sea salt and ask Damarian to help me carry them to the car. I know he doesn't want to leave, but he nods and takes both containers, a serious expression on his face. I watch the way he carries them with no effort. Man, the guy is strong.

When we're in the car, silence fills the air.

Damarian says, "I apologize for my behavior."

I squeeze the steering wheel. "It's okay. I get why you were upset."

"I do not understand the ways of humans. It was quite difficult, seeing my brethren captured in such a manner. But now I understand that they are not captured. And you are correct in assessing that fish do not hold the same emotional capacity as the children of the sea, nor are they highly intelligent."

"But you can communicate with them," I say.

"Yes."

I look at him. "What do they say?"

"They care for their young, just as we do. They scavenge for food to survive. They do not appreciate being hunted."

"It's no different than when you hunt for food."

"I agree."

I start the car and drive toward home. The ride is completely quiet. I focus on the road and Damarian stares out the window. I don't know what to think. I don't know if he's pissed at me, pissed at humans. Maybe he's had enough of our life and wants to go home.

It bothers me that I care so much, that I've grown so attached to him.

I park the car and we climb out. Damarian carries the sea salt and clothing into the house. "Maybe you should go into the pool, just in case," I tell him.

"Yes, perhaps."

"Okay. Let's put the clothing away first."

I lead Damarian to the guest room, which is down the hall from my room. I take his clothes and place them in the closet and the drawers. He stands at the door, and I feel his eyes burning into my back.

I turn around.

"The bed," he says.

"Yeah?"

"It is larger than the one in the other room."

I take one of his shirts out of the drawer and refold it. "That's the couch. But yeah, this is a king-sized bed."

His eyebrows shoot up. "King. I was not aware that humans have a king."

I place the shirt in the drawer. "Well, not all countries do. America doesn't. We have a leader, but he's not called a king. Other countries like England and Sweden have kings and queens."

He eyes the bed. "I do not understand why you have a king's bed."

I lie down on it and stretch my arms. "It's just called a king-sized bed because it's big. When my parents first got married, I guess they thought they'd have many guests. This is my favorite bed in the entire house. As a kid, I used to sneak in here in the middle of the night and crawl in. My mom got so mad."

He steps closer and slowly lowers himself onto the bed. He sinks in a bit and stares at it. Then he bounces. "How it differs from my bed."

I sit up and fold my legs. "What are the beds like in the sea? What do you sleep in?"

"Large oyster shells with seaweed."

A mental image of merman Damarian lying in an oyster shell flashes across my eyes.

He stands up. "May I swim now?"

I stand up, too. "Sure."

We make our way to the pool room. This will be the second time witnessing his transformation into a merman. The second time I'll see a mythical creature right before my eyes. Damarian stares down at the water.

"What's wrong?" I ask.

His head snaps to mine, like he was in a trance. "I am all right."

I see the anxiety on his face. I reach for his arm. "It'll be okay."

He shuts his eyes for a second. "The transformation…it is quite painful."

That makes my heart cry for him. My hand slides from his arm to his hand, until my fingers are locked with his. "I'm sorry." And I feel so guilty. He's risking so much to do this, and I still don't know why. If it's because of me, I feel horrible for everything he has to go through.

Taking a deep breath, he raises his arms to dive in.

"Wait."

He looks at me.

"You should probably take off your clothes. I'll close my eyes." I place my palms over my face.

I hear him slowly remove his pants and then his shirt. After a few seconds, he grunts and I hear a splash. I uncover my face and crawl to the edge of the pool. Damarian is flailing around, but not because he can't breathe. It looks as though his internal organs are on fire and he's thrashing around in agony. Water hits the walls of the pool room, the chairs, and me.

After about thirty seconds, he calms down. I wipe the water off my face and peer down. His beautiful sapphire tail greets me, gleaming in the sunlight and looking like crystals. When my eyes meet his, he looks mesmerizing. His face is more relaxed and at peace.

I smile. "Hey."

He returns it. "Hello."

I just sit there, staring at him, still finding it hard to believe that a merman is right before my eyes.

He flips over and dives into the water, swimming to the deep side. Then he leaps into the air, creating an arc. The sunlight coming in from the window shines on the droplets of water dripping from his tail. They look like rainbow colors. It's one of the most beautiful things I've ever seen. As much as I like him as a human, I have to admit that his merman form is the real him, the person he's supposed to be.

He lands in the water with hardly a splash. He jumps up a few more times before swimming back to me. His entire face is bright and energetic. It's obvious he misses being a merman.

I trace my finger on one of the tiles. "How do you feel?"

"Very well, thank you."

I raise my eyes. "You can't do that in the ocean, can you? Leap in the air like that."

He shakes his head. "My grandfather has told me tales of when he was a fry and had the freedom to soar in the air. But humans can detect us if we were to swim past the surface of the sea. Therefore, leaping is considered highly dangerous and has been banned."

"Fry?" I ask.

He nods.

"What's that?" The only meaning that pops into my head is French fries.

"Young."

"Oh, you mean merkids. Fry." I giggle. "That's really cute."

He smiles.

We grow silent. I feel like I should leave, maybe give him privacy to enjoy being a merman. But just as I'm about to get up, he says, "Join me."

"What?"

He pats the surface of the water. "Join me."

"Oh." That causes my cheeks to flame for some reason. Maybe because swimming together with him while he's in his merman form feels…intimate. "Are you sure?" I ask.

"I am quite sure."

"Okay. Just give me a minute to change."

I exit the pool room and climb the stairs to my room. My wetsuit is slung over a chair. My eyes trek to my closet, to where my bathing suit is stashed. I bought it a few months after Kyle and I started going out. I hadn't worn a bathing suit since I was twelve, when I began surfing. I wore only wetsuits because of surfing and because I felt extremely awkward in bathing suits. But once Kyle and I were dating, I wanted him to see me as something more than a surfer girl—I wanted him to find me sexy. I never got around to wearing the bikini, though.

But now…

I head to the closet and shuffle the contents around until my hand closes around it. The fabric feels soft and foreign against my skin. I pull it out. It's a royal blue bikini Leah swore I look amazing in. I've tried it on a couple of times in my room in front of the mirror, but I didn't feel comfortable. I guess I don't see myself as sexy.

I stand in front of the mirror and hold it against me, studying myself for a few seconds, imagining it on my body. I shake my head and throw it aside, then reach for my wetsuit.

Damarian's swimming when I return to the pool room. He's moving so fast he could probably beat the world record ten times. I drop down to the edge and dip my toes into the water. Merpeople must have acute hearing, because that small movement sends Damarian rushing toward me. When he's only a few feet away, he makes a short stop and sprays me with water. I squeal and cover my face.

He grabs onto the edge of the pool and lifts himself, supporting his weight on his elbows. He grins at me.

I laugh, and something inside me stirs to life. I don't know what it is. I haven't felt this alive in a while, not since I started falling in love with Kyle.

I raise my leg and poke him in the shoulder. "Some people don't like the taste of salt water."

He scoffs. "You live in the sea almost as much as I do." He treads his hands in the water, then falls back and floats, his tail rising in the air. He twirls around on his back and makes a circle. I remember doing that as a kid in the public pool when I just learned how to swim on my back.

I place my palms on the edge and slide into the pool. Damarian flips forward. We're only a few feet apart. I can feel the strength of his tail. It's creating currents in the water.

This is way too intimate. Every part of me wants to run.

Damarian swims a little closer to me. "Now we are in my world."

"Well, almost."

He swims even closer and I feel the heat radiating off his body, despite the cool temperature of the water. It's a good thing we're in the shallow side, because I'm not sure I would be able to stay afloat if we were in the deep.

He takes hold of my hand and gently moves me until I'm behind him. Then he takes my other hand and pulls me to my tippy toes, locking my arms around his neck. "Place your legs around my torso," he says.

I go still, butterflies flapping around in my stomach.

He waits.

I raise my right leg and wrap it around his middle. The contrast between his skin and scales is striking. His chest feels hard and his skin soft, like a man, but his tail is slimy and sticky, like a fish. I slide my leg higher up his back and chest. Then I do the same with my left foot.

I've never been this close to a guy since Kyle and it's sending all my emotions into a frenzy. It's hard to breathe. My body begs to sink into him, but I try to put some distance between us, which isn't easy.

"Do not release your arms and legs."

Before I can process his words, I'm flying in the air. The sunlight bouncing off his tail is so bright it nearly blinds me. I squeeze my arms and legs tighter around him. A second later, we crash into the water. I didn't have a chance to hold my breath and I swallow a ton of the salt water. Damarian leaps into the air again. I gasp for air. When we enter the water this time, I'm ready and hold my breath. We jump two more times, and it's the most amazing thing I've experienced in my life, even better than a rollercoaster ride or bungee jumping.

He floats upright in the water, expecting me to slide off. But my arms and legs are stubbornly locked around him. I don't want to let go.

But I know I have to. I untangle myself from around him and drop into the water. We're in the deep side now, so we're both treading. His tail swooshes against my leg a few times, making it tingle. I tell myself it's normal to be attracted to him despite the tail. It's totally normal. Yep.

His eyes search mine expectantly.

"That was the best thing I've ever experienced in my life."

He smiles shyly. "Yes?"

"Yes."

"I have always wished to do so with my sisters, but we cannot leap in the sea, as you know."

My heart drops into the water. I avert my gaze from his. Sister. Is that how he sees me?

"Let us have a competition," he says.

I'm burning to ask him how he feels about me, but I don't want to ruin the fun we're having. So I brush it aside and say, "You mean a race?"

"Yes."

"No fair. We all know who's going to win."

He spreads out his arms and falls onto his back. "You cannot be so certain. Zarya has defeated me quite a few times. I admit I allowed her to do so twice or thrice, but she is only a fry."

"Zarya. Your sister?"

"Yes."

He's slowly floating farther and farther away from me. I swim closer until I'm at his side. I rest my hands on his chest and heave myself onto him, straddling him. It's only once I'm on him that my cheeks boil. I'm sitting on him like a surfboard. What's wrong with me? This is way too intimate.

He seems shocked with my behavior, too, because a big swallow makes its way down his throat. His gaze travels from his chest, to my legs hanging off his sides.

"I'm sorry," I mumble, turning my head away. "I'll get off."

He touches my cheek with the back of his webbed fingers and forces my face to meet his. "Do not apologize, Cassie."

I can't look him in the eye. "I'm *riding* you. This is so humiliating."

"I do not believe it is, for I know we both very much enjoy it."

My cheeks are still scorching. I don't know what to say or do. My attraction to him is so intense, something I've never experienced before. Things moved so slowly with Kyle. We went from buds to best friends to boyfriend/girlfriend gradually.

His tail bounces. The fin catches my attention. It's sapphire like the rest of his tail, but it's much more translucent and looks like silk. I haven't touched that part of him. I twist around and bend toward it. I didn't realize how long his tail is—my arm is too short. I get on my knees and stretch my arm. My heart pounds as my shaky hand inches closer and closer. I feel Damarian stiffen under me. When my fingers make contact, I spring back. His fin is hard and feels like rubber, and it's sticky like his tail. I can't say I'm not disappointed—I was hoping it felt feather-like—but it makes sense that it feels hard. He's got a lot of bones and muscles there because the fin gives power to the tail.

His tail drops down and I almost lose my balance and fall off. He quickly picks it up. "I am truly sorry, Cassie. I did not intend to hurt you."

It looks as though his whole tail is trembling. Because of me? I swallow, turn around, and scoot toward his chest. "It's okay."

I remain seated on him for a little while, with our eyes locked on one another. I slide off and swim toward the wall, holding onto the edge as my heart returns to a regular beat. I hear him treading in the water behind me.

"M-maybe we should get out," I say.

He's quiet for a few seconds before saying, "Yes, perhaps we shall."

I swim toward the ladder and climb out. I feel his eyes on me, and that causes my legs to quake. I don't want to look at him, because I'm so confused by all these feelings.

But I do know one thing: I don't want Damarian to ever return to the ocean.

Chapter Nine

Damarian is back in his human form. We're sitting on my living room couch, wrapped in towels, although one of us is naked underneath. I shut out any thoughts relating to the fact that he's got nothing on. He's so close to me, and that causes every hair on my body to stand on edge. I wrap the towel closer to my body and shiver.

The doorbell rings.

My heart quickens. The only person who should be stopping by is Leah. But there's always the possibility that it could be someone else.

"Damarian?"

"Yes?"

"Someone's at the door. Um, just in case it's my uncle or my mom, act natural, okay?"

His eyebrows come together. "Natural...you wish for me to return to the pool and reacquire my tail?"

Despite the fear pumping throughout my body, I giggle. "No. I mean, pretend you're a human. Your name is Damian and you're my friend. We met on the beach."

He slowly nods as he digests my words. "I understand. Thank you."

"For what?"

"For concealing my secret."

I want to hug him, but I just punch his shoulder. "Always."

As I head for the door, my knees tremble. *Please don't be Mom.* It's her type to return home early and surprise me, but she'd have a key and wouldn't ring the doorbell. She's been known to "misplace" it, though.

My entire body sags with relief when I see Leah. She holds up some DVDs. "Decided to go with horror tonight," she says, but then she sees my expression. "What's wrong?"

My mouth is shut. I'm too flabbergasted to say anything.

"Oh my God, you have a guy over." She bounces on her feet and stretches her neck to get a look into the house. "Do I know him?"

"Who..." I clear my throat. "Who said I have a guy?"

She squeals. "You totally have a guy over! This is awesome." Her gaze suddenly widens as she looks past me.

I spin around. Damarian is standing in the doorway between the living room and hallway, face curious. And he's still only wearing a towel.

When I turn back to Leah, her face is pale and she's sputtering, "M-m...mer—"

I quickly shake my head and motion with my eyes for her to keep quiet. Damarian doesn't know I told her, and I feel so horrible for betraying his trust. But I didn't know he'd return—how could I have?

She mouths, "Merman," her eyes stunned.

I nod and motion her into the house. She moves in hesitantly, her gaze on Damarian. He looks intrigued, but also wary and terrified. I feel an overwhelming need to protect him, which is stupid because he doesn't need to be protected from Leah. She'd take his secret to the grave, too.

"Damian, this is my best friend, Leah."

She's still staring at him in disbelief, but my words must snap her out of it, because she glances at me with amused eyes. "Damian? Huh."

I give her a pleading face. I can't bear the thought of Damarian finding out I betrayed him. I can't bear the thought that he'd never trust me again, that I'd never see him again.

"Nice to meet you." Leah steps forward and stretches out her hand.

Damarian just stares at it.

"Right. Handshakes. You don't do handshakes." She moves toward me and mutters, "You might want to teach him that."

"Shh," I hiss.

We all stand there looking at one another.

After a few moments, Leah backs away toward the door. "So I thought we were having our Girls' Night In like we usually do on Wednesday nights, but now that I see you have a guest, I'll just make a quick exit and leave you two to enjoy each other's company."

She heads for the door.

"Excuse me for a sec," I say to Damarian and hurry after her. "Leah."

She turns around. "Oh my God, he's back!" She cranes her neck toward the living room. "And he's so, so hot. I almost forgot how hot he is. Mmmmhmmm." She smacks her lips.

She's making my checks, ears, and neck steam. "Leah."

"Why did he come back?"

I bite down on my lip and drop my gaze to the carpet. "Leah…I promised him I wouldn't tell anyone about him." I raise my eyes and see a hint of betrayal on her face. "I know we're best friends and tell each other everything, but he doesn't know you, so he can't trust you. Maybe once he gets to know you and trust you, he'll let me tell you. But for now, you need to pretend that he's a regular guy."

She presses her lips together and folds her arms across her chest, her gaze on anywhere but me. Then she nods. "I totally get it. And I'm cool with it. But." She holds out her index finger. "I still want details. You know, the non-merman human stuff."

"Leah!"

She laughs. "I'm so happy for you, Cassie. You look so different, so much better. It's like you were sleeping for the past few months and have finally woken up."

I chew on my braid.

"It's nothing to be embarrassed about."

"But, Leah. He's a *fish*."

She raises an eyebrow.

I look back to make sure Damarian's not there, then lean close to her. "I'm falling for a fish, for a guy who lives in the ocean. I can't have normal relationships with human guys. What does that say about me? Am I really that screwed up?"

Her eyes soften. "You're not screwed up. These things happen. I mean, they don't really happen, but what I mean is that you and Damar—I mean, Damian—have something special. Different and special. Don't worry about how not human he is. Something really wonderful is happening to you. He's a merman, Cass. A *merman*. Out of everyone in this world, he met *you*."

I swallow.

"That means something, and if I were you, I'd accept it. Embrace it. And live, because honestly, you really need to start living again."

That brings tears to my eyes. I pull her into a hug. "Thanks. I'm just so scared."

She pats my back. "I know. But I'm here for you, okay? Talk to me whenever you need to, just not classified information, you know?"

I laugh.

She waves and closes the door after her. When I return to the living room, I find Damarian flipping through the channels. For a guy who lives in the ocean, he sure knows how to use our gadgets. I flop down next to him. "Sorry. Leah and I usually hang out Wednesday nights."

"Hang out?"

"Spend time together."

He nods. I lean back and watch him search the channels. Nothing seems to interest him, until an image of a coral reef flashes before the screen. His eyes narrow a bit as he scrutinizes the screen. A longing look captures his face.

"You must really miss home," I say softly.

He tears his eyes from the screen and shakes his head. "I have only been on land for a short while."

"It doesn't matter. It's your second time away from home, right?"

He nods.

I grab a couch cushion and pick on a loose thread. "I'll be leaving home in a few months. For college."

His head tilts sideways. "College."

"Higher education."

His eyes cloud with confusion.

"You have schools in the ocean? Places that provide kids with an education?"

"Is that not the responsibility of the parent?"

I place the cushion behind me and rest my back on it. "Well, yeah. It's the job of the parents to raise the kids with morals, teach them right and wrong. But when it comes to the hard things, like how to read and write and math and science, trained professionals take over."

He leans back, too. "Yes, I have heard that humans have other means of communication in addition to tongue."

I reach for one of Mom's fashion magazines sitting on the coffee table and open to a random page. "Yep. Reading and writing."

He takes the magazine from me and studies the images. "Who is this woman?"

I shrug. "A model. Someone who's hired to wear these clothes and jewelry and sell them to other people."

He nods slowly, his attention still on the magazine. Then his gaze moves to the photos of Mom and me hanging on the walls and in picture frames. "I understand humans have the means to capture their reflection."

I nod. "It's like seeing your reflection in the water."

"Yes." He focuses on the magazine. "This," he says, pointing to the words on the page.

"Yeah, that's words. Someone writes them and other people read them."

"I understand."

I smile and take the magazine from him, placing it on the table. Then I look at him. His gaze is on me. I keep my eyes on his for a little bit before they slowly trek to the bottom half of his body—to his towel. I shake my head. "I'm so sorry. You're probably cold, wearing nothing under there."

He glances down at his towel and shrugs. "I am accustomed to not being clothed. And I am afraid it is quite stifling here on land. It is much cooler in the sea."

"Your body will get used to it, just like humans get used to the cold water after being in there for a while."

He nods.

Silence.

I tap my foot on the floor. "Um…so do you want to dress into something or…stay like that?" I nod toward the towel. He might be accustomed to not wear anything, but I sure as heck am *not*. I don't know if I can sit here like this when I know he's got nothing on down there.

He shrugs again. "I am not familiar with the ways of humans. If I am meant to wear a garment, I shall wear one."

"Okay." I stand. "You should probably take a shower before you dress into your pajamas."

"A shower…"

"I know we just came out of the water, but you need to wash yourself with soap and shampoo so that you get cleaned. We humans get dirty pretty quickly."

I bring him to the upstairs bathroom and turn on the shower, showing him how to adjust it to the right setting. "Here's the soap," I tell him. "Rub that over your body. And this is shampoo for your hair." My eyes circle over my strawberry scented shampoo. "Oh…I don't really have any male shampoos." I open the cap and sniff it. It smells really girly.

He leans forward and inhales. "This scent…it is like you. I very much enjoy it."

My body grows rigid. The shampoo bottle slips from my hand, but I manage to catch it in time. Shampoo sprays across Damarian's chest and my hands.

I bring my mortified gaze to his and am about to apologize, but his eyes are filled with humor. After a second, his lips pull into a grin. My body relaxes and I find myself giggling, small at first. Then it grows louder and louder, making my chest hurt. I'm not sure when I last laughed like this.

Damarian wraps an arm around my waist and gently hauls me to his chest. I'm so caught off guard that I jerk away. His eyes grow big and he steps back. "Forgive me." He whips around and touches the water. "I believe the temperature is satisfactory." His voice is low and bothered.

Something gets caught in my throat. I swallow a few times. "Okay. I'll get your pajamas and a towel."

"Thank you."

When I'm out of the bathroom, I lean back on the wall and breathe in heavily through my nose, letting out the air through my mouth. I didn't expect him to grab me like that. I'll admit I liked it—I liked it a lot. I want him to touch me like that again, to touch me more than that, to feel his lips on mine. I wish I hadn't pulled away.

I shake the thoughts out and gather his pajamas and a towel. When I return to the bathroom, I find him staring at the mirror. I stand next to him. He's about a head taller than me. My brain says we look really cute as a couple, but I tell it to shut up.

"The portrayal is quite accurate, more so than in the sea."

I smile. "I can't imagine not having mirrors around." I hold out the towel and pajamas. "Here you go. You don't have to wear the tank top if you don't feel comfortable."

"All right."

"Take as long as you need. Showers can be very relaxing. They are for me." I close the door after me.

I head to the guest room to make sure his bed is in order. Mom and I usually don't have any guests, so everything should be clean. I bend forward and press my nose into the mattress, making sure it doesn't smell dusty. Once I decide it's fine, I fluff up the pillows and lean them against the headboard. Then I fold the blanket back. He should be comfortable here.

The shower is still running when I pass the bathroom. Figuring he must be hungry, I make my way to the kitchen and open the fridge. Damarian only likes fish, but as his designated human tour guide, it's my responsibility to introduce him to the delicious delicacies we, as humans, have to offer.

Standing there for a few minutes, I can't decide on anything. I open the pantry. My eyes settle on a box of pasta. I've been told I make a mean baked ziti...

I grab the ziti and fill a pot with water. Once it's boiling, I add in half the box.

A strawberry-flavored scent attacks my nose. I turn around to find Damarian standing behind me. Wet hair dripping down his chest. His *bare* chest. He's only wearing the pajama bottoms.

When he notices the way I gape at him, he holds out his hands in an apology. "Forgive me." He hands me a crumpled ball of white. I take it from him and realize it's the tank top, split right down the middle. "I did not intend to damage it."

I burst into giggles, grabbing the counter for support. He stares at me with a confused expression. "Sorry," I say. "I guess you need some practice with human clothes." I lightly slap the shirt against his chest. "It's no big deal. You can stay like this for now."

His gaze moves to the pot on the stove.

"Oh, that's a surprise for you. My specialty—baked ziti. If this doesn't turn you human, nothing will," I joke. "You hungry?"

He touches his stomach. "Yes, I believe so. May I be of assistance?"

I mix the pot with a wooden spoon. "Sure. Grab some shredded cheese from the fridge."

He doesn't budge.

I turn back toward him. Then it hits me. "Oh! That is the refrigerator, where we keep food cold so it won't spoil. You'll find a package in there with white strips. That's shredded cheese."

He nods and walks over there. When his head disappears into the fridge, a sudden image hits me. Damarian and me as a couple, living together, cooking together. I quickly shake my head and mutter,

"Idiot."

"I believe this is the 'shredded cheese?'" he asks, holding up the package.

"Yep. Bring it over, please."

He does as I say. I take the pot off the stove, grab a large bowl from the cupboard, and pour the ziti in, along with the shredded cheese and pasta sauce. Then I mix, pour them in a pan, and pop it into the oven. Damarian watches every movement with curious eyes.

"Now we wait," I say.

He nods.

I reach for my gummy worms and lead Damarian to the living room, where I turn on the TV.

"Will you not shower?" he asks.

I bite off the end of a worm. "You'll be okay alone here?"

"Yes. I understand how to navigate this device," he says, nodding toward the remote.

I hand him my gummy worms. "Just don't eat too much. You don't want your teeth to rot, or spoil your dinner." I wink.

As I pass him to leave the room, he takes hold of my hand. Despite him being in his human form, his hand is ice cold. It sends a shiver up my spine. I look down at him.

"Cassie," he says softly.

"Yes?" my voice is above a whisper.

"I very much appreciate your hospitality. Thank you."

I smile. "It's my pleasure to have you here."

When I'm in my room, I rummage through my pajamas to find a decent-looking pair. I can't believe an actual guy is *in* my house. A guy is going to *sleep* in my house.

The bathroom smells like him. Like the ocean mixed with strawberries. I stand still for a few seconds with my eyes closed, enjoying his delicious smell, before turning on the water.

Normally, showers relax me, but not today. My heart is beating in every inch of my body and I keep dropping the soap and shampoo bottle. Once I'm finally out, I brush my hair in my room and check my reflection in the mirror. I've got on a blue tank top and matching blue bottoms with black polka dots. Sexy? Not really. Cute, yes. I'm not sure if Damarian goes for cute, though.

The smell of baked ziti reaches my nose as I make my way to the kitchen. I rush inside and inspect it. It still needs a few minutes. When I stand up, I stumble back because Damarian is standing in the doorway. My hand goes to my heart. "You scared me."

He takes a step forward, holding out his hand. "Forgive me. I did not intend to startle you."

"It's okay." My chest rises and falls. I try to keep my eyes on his face and not his chest, but that's not exactly easy.

He moves a little closer to me, his gaze on my face. Then it slowly moves to my hair. Stepping even closer, he raises his hand toward my face until his fingers intertwine with my hair. "It is no longer bound," he murmurs.

I swallow a few times. When I talk, my voice is shaky. "I don't bother with it. Just let it air dry and braid it in the morning." No matter what I do, I can't seem to get my hair to look good. It's the type that can never look good, no matter what I do with it. Hay hair. That's what the kids at school always called it.

He continues to comb his fingers through my hair. That sends little chills up and down my back, and it takes all my willpower not to shiver. Then he lifts his other hand and does the same. His fingers massage my temple. My eyes flutter closed. After a few seconds, a moan escapes my lips.

My eyes flash open and my cheeks burn.

Damarian is staring into my eyes. "Hair is the most attractive element on a female. It is a shame to bind it."

It's hard to form a coherent thought, let alone a sentence. "Not for me."

He raises his eyebrows in confusion.

"My hair. It's not pretty."

"Certainly it is."

I shake my head. "Not really. I don't think any part of me is attractive. Not like other girls." Definitely not like the mermaids he swims around with all day.

His right hand slides down, caressing my neck. My knees want to give in and I want to melt in his arms. "You are mistaken, Cassie. You are one of the most beautiful females I have ever laid eyes upon."

I look into his eyes, wanting to believe him. But I don't. It's not that I have such a low self-esteem that I think I'm ugly. I just know I'm not very pretty and that I wouldn't be guys' first choice. Of course Leah claims that *I* have a lot to do with that, since I have problems letting people in, but it's easier to put the blame on my average looks than my actual self.

I seriously doubt that out of all the females in the world, a smokin' hot merman finds *me* beautiful. He's just being nice, maybe because he feels like he owes me or something. Maybe he's blinded because I'm his "savior" or whatever.

I clear my throat and turn around, forcing his hands to fall away. "The food's probably done."

After taking out the pan from the oven, I pour some of the baked ziti into two plates and place them on the table. Damarian and I sit down across from each other.

"Careful, it's hot. You're not used to hot dishes, so be extra cautious."

When I blow on the ziti, he copies me. I watch how he slowly takes a bite, his eyes going from hesitation, to wonder, to delight. "Like?" I ask.

"This is quite delicious." He dumps some more in his mouth.

"Careful," I remind him.

I feel all giddy that he likes my baked ziti. Once again, an image of him and me cooking together flashes before my eyes. I blink it away and focus on eating. When I bring my gaze to Damarian, I find that he finished everything on his plate.

"More?" I ask.

"Yes, please."

I take his plate and add another serving. Damarian digs in. I grin as I watch him devour it, feeling giddy again. I try to shake it off and not make a big deal out of it, but I can't help how good I feel. How good he makes me feel.

When we're done, he offers to help me with the dishes. Like a real gentleman. I put him on drying duty while I rinse. We work silently and efficiently, and I find myself smiling like a dork.

Damarian pushes some hair away from my face. "I enjoy seeing you smile," he says.

I hand him my plate. "Thanks. You sound like my mother."

"Does she not see you smile often?"

I hold a glass cup under the faucet for a bit, unsure of how to answer without spilling my life story. "It's a little…hard to be happy and smiley around her."

"Why?"

I glance at him, at his sincere eyes and caring face. Opening up has never been easy for me, especially with a guy, but Damarian is different. Even if he returns to the ocean one day and I never see him again, I still feel like he's someone I can let in. My body deflates as I think about never seeing him again, but I don't want to think about that for now. I don't want to worry about what lies ahead. I just want to live in the present and enjoy whatever this is.

"It's kind of a long story," I say, laughing lamely.

"I am willing to listen."

I puff out some air. "Okay. After we're done with the dishes."

We finish working in silence. I put popcorn in the microwave so that I can busy myself with something while I bare my soul. Once it's ready, we sit down on the living room couch. I cross my legs underneath me and face him.

"So…my father left me and my mom when I was ten."

Both his eyebrows lift. "Left?"

I pick some popcorn and play with it. "Yeah. He met a woman online and fell in love with her. I guess my parents' marriage was already failing if he went snooping around online. He and the woman met secretly for a while until my dad finally had the balls to tell my mom. He was cheating on her for about eight months. He walked out the next day. He didn't even, like, kiss me goodbye or anything. It was just a pat on the head and a promise to keep in touch. I wasn't that young, but I was pretty naïve and innocent, so I thought Daddy would always come back. I didn't want to be one of *those* kids, the one with the divorced parents. He and I hardly spoke, and when we did, it was because I reached out to him. We lost all contact after he and his new wife had their kids. Now he wants to reconnect." I shake my head. "I can't bring myself to do it."

I slowly raise my eyes to his. They're a bit confused. "Cheating," he says.

I stare at him for a few seconds. "You're telling me merpeople don't cheat? Husbands and wives don't leave each other for other mermaids or mermen?"

He's looking at me like *I'm* the mythical creature who washed up ashore. "One never leaves his mate."

"Never?"

"It is not done."

I grab some more popcorn and squeeze it between my fingers. No way. He's telling me that cheating isn't even a thing in the merworld?

"You stay together forever," I say.

"Yes."

"Do you know how amazing that is?"

Now he grabs some popcorn and smashes it between his fingers. "It is most certainly not amazing."

I just look at him.

His focus is on his fingers. "If one were to mate with one he does not wish to mate with, he is…"

"Trapped," I finish.

He nods. I open my mouth to expand on this, but his face shines. "I very much enjoy having conversations with you."

I pull on a loose thread on my pants. "Thanks. Me, too."

He takes a handful of popcorn and shoves it into his mouth.

"Wanna do something fun?" I ask.

"Yes."

I shuffle back a little. "Take one and aim it at my face."

He plucks one out of the bowl and throws it. I catch it in my mouth, producing a laugh from him. I munch on the popcorn, pumping my hands in the air. "You're looking at the world's popcorn-catching champion. Okay, maybe not the world, but I like to think so."

His eyes flash with glee. "I must attempt this."

I take the popcorn bowl from him and toss one at his face. When he misses, we both roll around laughing. I try a few more, but he keeps missing them. He grabs a handful and launches them at me. Soon the carpet is covered with popcorn, and I'm laughing so hard tears run down my cheeks.

Somehow, he and I have inched closer to one another. As my laughter dies down, I lightly shove his shoulder. "Who exactly is going to clean all this up?"

I now notice that tears cover his face as well. He rubs his left cheek and examines his fingers. "Water," he says.

"You don't see tears in the ocean," I say, the realization hitting me.

"I know tears," he says, still fascinated by the liquid on his fingers. "But I did not know they were as so."

"Taste them."

He does and his eyes widen. "Salt."

"Yep." I get down on my knees and gather the popcorn in a pile. I straighten up and look at him. "Damarian?"

"Yes?"

"I…" My gaze drops to the floor. "I haven't really had this much fun in a while."

Our eyes meet. "Neither have I," he says.

That causes a warm feeling to pass through every cell in my body.

I reach for the small garbage bin in the corner of the room and throw the popcorn inside. Damarian joins me on the floor. "I am exhausted," he says.

"Yeah, it's been a long day. We'll head to bed after this." I freeze. "I mean, we'll each head to our own beds, because…you know, we both have our separate beds…" My voice trails off when I realize how silly I sound.

"Of course," Damarian says.

I don't know why my body fills with disappointment. Was I hoping he'd ask to bunk in with me? This guy—well, non-guy—is affecting me in ways I've never been affected before. We go from having awkward moments, to great conversations, to throwing popcorn at each other. I don't know what to make of all of it. It scares the hell out of me, but it also makes me feel really excited. And alive.

He follows me upstairs to the guestroom. As soon as he walks in and looks inside, he says, "The royal bed." His gaze treks to me. "I am to sleep here?"

I fluff up the pillows again. "Yep."

"And you?"

"I have my own bed in my room."

He runs a hand through his hair. "I am not fit for a royal bed."

"It's okay. I already told you it's not for royalty. You'll sleep really comfortably here. You're my guest and I want to make you feel at home. If you need anything, my room is right down the hall. Just knock on the door. Okay?"

"Yes. Thank you."

I feel like the appropriate thing to do is to depart with some gesture. A hug or something. That would be weird, though. I give him a smile and close the door behind me.

My room is down the hall, but it might as well be on the other side of the planet. I climb into bed and tuck my blanket under my chin.

I toss and turn for a few minutes, but sleep just won't come. My mind is too active, filled with thoughts and memories of Damarian. From the moment he saved me, to the moment I closed the guestroom door.

Rolling onto my side, I feel my mouth curve into a smile.

Chapter Ten

The first thing to enter my head when my eyes shoot open is Damarian.

I spring up in bed and glance at the time. 7:15. Work starts at nine. I climb out of bed and head to the guestroom. The door's open, which means he must be up already. I peek inside and see the room is empty.

Noises come from the kitchen. The sounds of cupboards being opened. He must be hungry.

When I get down there, I stop short. The kitchen is a complete mess. Food and wrappers clutter the table and floor. My eyes search the room until I find Damarian on his knees, bending into one of the bottom drawers.

"Good morning."

He bumps his head.

"Sorry," I say.

Rubbing the spot on his head, he gets to his feet. "Good morning, Cassie." He gestures to the mess on the table. "Forgive me for the disorder. I have tried locating the delicious fish I ate the other day, but I cannot seem to find it."

I feel bad. He's probably been up for a while. I search through the pantry, but there aren't any sardines left. "I guess you finished the last one. Sorry. I can make breakfast, if you want. Scrambled eggs?"

It's obvious by his face that he has no clue what that is.

I open the fridge and take out three eggs—one for me and two for him. By the size of those muscles, he definitely needs more than one.

"May I be of assistance?"

I grab an onion and a knife. "Thanks. I'd ask you to cut the onion, but I don't want you using the knife." I open the drawer and take out the whisk. "You can whisk the eggs."

I crack the eggs into a bowl, tell him to add a bit of salt, pepper, and milk, and then to whisk them all together. He seems fascinated as he watches the eggs blend together. Eyebrows scrunched, he lifts the whisk, and the eggs ooze into the bowl. He opens his mouth and is about to let the eggs drip inside, when I say, "No, don't eat that. We need to fry them first."

I grab a pan, add oil, and turn on the stove.

"You use this…heating device often," he says.

I nod. "Can't live without it."

Once I finish making our breakfast, we sit down at the table to eat. I watch Damarian pick at the eggs with his fork before hesitantly bringing them to his mouth. He chews for a while before swallowing. "This is…strange. Nothing like I have tasted before."

"You like?"

"It is all right."

I bite into my eggs. "Any plans for today?"

He shrugs.

"I have my surfing class in an hour. Do you want to come with me to the beach?"

He nods.

I scoop some more eggs onto my fork. "I was thinking last night. It might be best for you to swim in the pool twice a day, once in the morning and once at night. That way, we'll be assured you'll be okay."

He thinks it over for a bit. "That is a smart solution. Thank you." He smiles, his entire face shining. My stomach flutters. He really knows how to make me feel appreciated.

We finish eating and put our plates in the sink. When I turn around, I ram right into his chest. Slowly, I raise my eyes until they meet his. He twirls a lock of my hair between his fingers. "You have not bound your hair."

My throat dries up. When I talk, my voice is hoarse. "No." *Not since you told me how pretty it looks like this.*

"Thank you for all you have done for me," he says softly, his warm breath tickling my cheek. "For providing me with a bed fit for a king. For this magnificent breakfast. For your kindness."

I can't think over the loud hammering of my heart.

"I enjoy being near you," he says, his voice above a whisper.

My eyes drop to his lips less than a few inches from mine. Wrapping his hand around my waist, he backs me up against the sink. His lips close over mine.

The sink digs into my back as he presses into me, his lips moving against mine in desperation, as if this has been building up inside him for days. My arms snake around his back and slide upward. I bury my fingers in his hair, tugging and hauling his face closer to mine. His lips are warm and taste like the ocean, and I feel like my mouth is exploding. A soft moan escapes my lips. Heat pools all over me, making it hard to stay upright. It's a good thing my body's leaning against the sink because there's no way my legs would support me.

Just as I feel myself melting into him, he jerks back.

I blink a few times, my chest huffing and puffing, my head spinning.

Damarian looks as though he accidently killed someone. "Forgive me," he mutters, turning around and raking his fingers through his hair. "Forgive me, Cassie. That was most inappropriate."

No, it was wonderful.

He whips around. Did I say that out loud?

His worried and ashamed eyes soften for a second, but then they turn a little hard. "Perhaps we shall head for the beach."

Every organ in my body slides down and dissolves into a puddle around my feet. Am I a bad kisser or something? Do I disgust him? Does he regret what he did? Because I don't. Not at all.

Tears threaten my eyes, but I shove them away. "Yeah. We should go." I glance at the time. I need to be at work soon.

I collect the rest of the dishes and dump them in the sink. He stands on the side with his arms crossed, his eyes anywhere but on me. Something cold prickles my skin, causing goose bumps to pop up all over my arms and legs.

Trying my hardest to ignore the negative feelings starting to consume me, I go upstairs to change into my wetsuit. As soon as I reach my room, I close the door and sink down, pulling at my hair and burying my face in my palms. I don't understand what happened. Why is he acting so strange, so cold and rude? He kissed me, a real one this time. It was the most amazing thing I've ever experienced in my life. Granted I don't have a lot of experience in this department, but it breaks the top-ten-awesome-things-that-have-happened-to-me list. In the short moment when our lips were attached, I felt something deep. Something beyond the physical and emotional. It's like we were connected spiritually, as if the universe told us we're meant to be together.

It's easy to forget he's a merman. So easy.

A few tears seep out. I wipe them and change into my wetsuit. When I return to the kitchen, I find Damarian washing the dishes. The sight makes my heart warm up, but I close my eyes and throw those feelings away. I clear my throat, and he turns around. "We need to leave soon. Want to go for a swim in the pool?"

"Yes." He shuts the water and walks over to me. His hand slowly lifts toward my face. I close my eyes as I feel the back of his fingers brushing my cheek, so light, like the touch of a feather. "Forgive me for my behavior, Cassie," he murmurs.

My eyes flutter open. I bring my hand to his cheek and do the same. "It's okay. I'm glad you kissed me again." I feel the blush all the way in my toes.

His gaze drops to my lips for a second before returning to my eyes. "I am glad as well."

***

After Damarian finishes his swim, he pulls himself out of the water in his merman form. He dries off with a few towels to speed up the process because I'm running late for work. He shifts into a human, and now we are on our way to the beach.

All I'm thinking about is how I want those lips on mine again. He walks silently next to me, studying the scenery around him.

The beach is quite full. I lead Damarian to the spot where I have my class. When I turn to him, I find him gazing out toward the ocean, a longing look in his eyes. I slide my fingers through his and squeeze. His eyes find mine and his features soften into a smile. We stand side by side, our hands interlocked, staring out at the beautiful ocean.

"Miss Cassie!" Eight-year-old Timmy runs toward us, towing his surfboard behind him.

I squeeze Damarian's hand again. "My kids are arriving. You can wander around the beach if you want. Check out the shops. My class will be done in an hour."

Damarian sweeps his hand toward the sand. "I shall remain here and observe you, if that is all right."

"Okay. Just make sure you don't get too close to the water." We do *not* want the tail at this time.

When my class is done and the kids disperse, Damarian gets up. "May I observe you sailing on the sea?"

"Sure." I grab my surfboard off the sand and race into the ocean.

Usually when I surf, I don't pay any attention to spectators. It's just me and the ocean. But now that Damarian's watching, I'm nervous. I want to prove something. I'm not sure what. Maybe...if I surf well in the ocean—his home, his life—maybe I'm worthy enough for him.

The waves are decent today. Not amazing, but pretty good. As I wait for a wave to hit, I take a deep breath and let it out, telling my mind to focus on nothing but the sparkling blue and green water. Next thing I know, I'm surfing on a semi-huge wave.

And I totally nail it.

I run back to Damarian and press my towel into my face, grinning at him, who's grinning back. Then I catch sight of a guy a few feet away, wearing a wetsuit and holding a familiar-looking light blue surfboard. Kyle. My hands freeze mid-wipe. Damarian, seeing my expression, spins around. Then he looks back at me. "Are you all right?"

I tear my gaze away from the Ex. "Yeah. I'm cool."

As I dry off the rest of my body, I see Kyle headed our way. "Damn," I mutter.

He stops right before me. "Hey, Cass."

I continue wiping my legs. "Good morning, Kyle." Anyone with half a brain could sense how stiff and cold my tone is.

Kyle scans Damarian up and down. "Who's this?"

Keeping my eyes on my work, I say, "Why do you want to know?" Immature of me, yeah, but I'm not exactly liking the way he's looking at my fishman.

Kyle holds out his hand to Damarian. "Hey, I'm Kyle. Cassie and I used to be together."

My head springs up. Seriously?

Damarian looks confused by Kyle's outstretched hand, but he must remember Leah doing this, because he brings an uncertain hand to Kyle. Kyle shakes it hard, like to prove who's more of a man or something. "What's your name?" he asks.

Damarian's eyes meet mine. I nod to him, mouthing "Damian." Damarian quickly nods. "I am Damian."

A small smirk captures his face. "Damian." He steps back a bit and glances from me to Damarian. "Cute couple."

I throw my towel to the sand. "What do you want?"

He circles Damarian, taking in every part of his body.

"What the heck, Ky—"

He claps Damarian on the shoulder. "Well, see you two around."

He winks to me, then takes off toward the ocean with his surfboard. I stare after him and feel Damarian do the same. When I bring my eyes to him, I see the puzzled look on his face. I shrug. "Yeah, we used to date." I look back at the ocean and see him riding a wave like a pro, totally showing off. I roll my eyes and take my towel and surfboard. "Let's go."

I lead him toward Misty's Juice Bar, and we sit down at the counter. When Leah sees us, she waves and rushes over. "Hey, Cass." She nods to Damarian. "Damian."

"Hello."

"So I'm thinking something wild for him," I tell her.

She nods. "I got just the thing."

As she turns toward the machine in the back, I say, "We met Kyle a few minutes ago."

She twists her head back. "Uh oh."

"Mhm. And he acted like a total jackass in front of Damar—I mean, Damian."

She lays Damarian's smoothie on the counter and presses down a lid. "Jackass how?"

"Checking him out. Poking fun. Calling us a cute couple. I even think he dissed Damian's name."

Leah waves her hand. "He's just jealous. Ignore him."

"Jealous how? I mean, he's the one who broke up…" My mouth snaps shut as I catch Damarian studying me. "Never mind. We'll talk about this another time. Sorry, Damian." I rub my hand down my face. "That guy drives me insane."

"It is not a problem, Cassie."

Leah grins as her eyes move from between us. "You guys do make a cute couple, though."

I give her a face, my cheeks warming.

Leah sticks a straw through the cup's lid and slides it to Damarian. "Here ya go. Our bestseller this month."

"Thank you," Damarian says. He eyes the cup for a bit before raising his confused eyes to me.

Leaning closer to him, I whisper. "You put it in your mouth and drink." I grab another straw and slide it in, demonstrating how to drink. Damarian nods and does the same.

"Oh my God, he's delicious," Leah hisses.

I scan the shop. A few girls have their eyes on him, some are whispering and pointing. For a few seconds, I feel threatened. I know how ruthless girls can be. But when Damarian lifts his head to me with that special look in his eyes, it disappears.

"How's the smoothie?" Leah asks Damarian.

"Scrumptious."

106

"He's a keeper," she half-sings. "What do you want, Cassie?"

I wave my hand. "I'm good."

"Would you like to share with me?" Damarian holds out the cup.

Leah sighs in her "how cute" way.

My hands tremble. Drinking from the same cup as him feels intimate. Yet, I want to do it. "Okay, thanks."

I slide my straw inside and drink. Damarian bends and drinks, too. I feel the heat of his body jump onto my skin.

When the liquid's gone, I pay for the smoothie. Leah says, "Call me sometime, okay? I need to talk to you about something."

"Is everything okay?"

"Yeah, yeah. Just." She wipes the counter with a rag. "My thing with Frankie is kinda..." She runs her index finger across her neck.

"What? You guys are done?"

She continues wiping the counter. "Yeah. It's like whatever. We've never really gotten along that well, anyway. I mean, there's more to a relationship besides sex, you know."

"Leah!" I hiss, my face scorching.

"Sorry." She holds out her hands in a what-can-I-say way.

I can't help but shake my head and laugh. "So, did any smokin' hot dudes catch your eye?"

Leah's gaze drops to the counter, her face turning a light shade of red. I sit up. Leah hardly ever blushes. The last time I saw her blush was when... "The guy from the beach! The day we recused..." I look at Damarian. "Sorry."

"I am confused," he says with furrowed eyebrows.

"Sorry. This is what we call 'girl talk.'"

"Girl talk."

"Yeah. When girls get together and talk about guys and clothes and things that would drive a guy insane."

He nods as recognition enters his eyes. "I am familiar with this concept. My sister and her friends engage in this activity quite often."

I feel something inside me when I hear those words. I guess I love hearing how many similarities we have. It makes our…whatever we have, more possible.

"Sister," Leah breathes, her tone full of disbelief. I'm guessing she's been hit with the reality that there are others like Damarian in the ocean. It's hard to fathom.

"Want to check out some sights?" I ask Damarian.

He finds a sudden fascination with his pants pockets. "May we return to your residence?"

"Okay. Sure." I'm game with spending time alone with him. The thought sends my blood into a frenzy.

"I'll call you," I tell Leah.

"Uh uh. You spend time with your friend." She raises her eyebrows suggestively.

I give her a face before grabbing my surfboard and towel and leading Damarian out of the shop.

He's quiet as we walk home. Each step I take has a small bounce to it. I'm so excited for what awaits once we get to my place, but I'm also nervous as hell. I feel Damarian stripping away every bit of armor I built as an emotional shield. But I'm ready to shed it all—for him. The fact that I'm falling so hard and fast for a guy—well, a merman—makes me want to dig a hole in the ground and hide in there forever. But it also makes me want to jump onto a table and dance until the early hours of the morning.

"Well, here we are." I open the door to my house and we walk in. I chuck my towel on the floor and rest my board against the wall. "So what do you want to do? We can swim in the pool. Maybe watch a movie? I can show you the Net—"

"I am afraid I must return to the sea."

My mouth snaps shut. I stare at him, feeling my heart crash to the floor. "W...what?" My voice is so low, I barely hear myself.

He turns his back on me and sweeps his hair to the left. The sun peeking in through the window reflects off it, making it look even more golden than usual. I feel a pang in my chest and want to bang my head into the wall. That's what I get for falling hard over someone I just met. Of course he's going to go back to the sea. That's his home. It's where his family and friends are. It's where his *life* is.

But why did he come back in the first place, then? He must be running because he hated the kiss. No, it wasn't the kiss. He's not that shallow. But what if it was the kiss?

Damarian whirls around and drops down on his knees in front of me. He grabs both my hands, staring up at my face. "Cassie."

Where did he learn to do that? I shake my head. Tears enter my eyes. I quickly blink them back and bite down on my bottom lip. I'm not that pathetic to cry because a guy is leaving me. I'm stronger than that.

But I'm not. Not really. In the few days that I've gotten to know him, I've grown so attached. He can't just leave me like this. He *can't*.

His face changes. I guess he sees my tears. I yank my hand out of his and swipe them away. He gets to his feet and envelopes me in his arms, hugging me close to his chest. His hand rubs the back of my head. I want to push him away, yell at him, accuse him of playing me, for making me fall for him. But I don't. Because I want to stay in his arms forever.

"Cassie," he whispers, running his hand up and down my back. "Do not fret. I shall return."

Wait. What?

I pull out of his arms and look at him. "You're not leaving for good?"

He shakes his head. "No. I wish to visit the sea for some time before returning to you. I worry my family may be concerned of my whereabouts. I do not wish to cause them heartache." He rubs the side of my face. "I cannot leave you, Cassie."

My heart swells. I feel like an idiot now. It might have been a good idea for him to have mentioned that little detail two minutes ago.

Filled with relief, I find myself laughing. Damarian's eyes fill with laughter, too. When he pulls me to his chest again, I wrap my arms around his neck and hug him close. "You're driving me insane," I say into his ear.

"You drive me insane." His soft breath tickles my cheek.

Chapter Eleven

It's three AM and Damarian is all set to go. I hand him a baggie filled with gummy worms. "I hope you guys have dentists down there."

Munching on one, he says, "I believe Zarya will love this dearly."

I'm not sure if they will taste good down there, but Damarian is willing to risk it. I wish I could go with him, but I know that's impossible, so I'm not even bringing it up. I'm pretty sure his dad and king would behead him. Not that they do that…as far as I know.

I also wish I could meet Zarya. Damarian clearly has a lot of love for her, and I want to be part of that area in his life. But again, I know that's impossible.

"I am ready," he says.

Linking my hands through his, I lead him out the door and toward the beach. On the way, I squeeze it and give him a small smile. Unlike last time, I'm not surrounded in a black cloud. I know he'll return.

As soon as we enter the beach, I peer to my right and left to make sure no one's around. I tighten my hold on his hand and race toward the rocks, lugging him along. He must not be used to running, because he trips over his feet and flies to the sand, bringing me down along with him. I topple onto his chest.

We both laugh. The moon casts a soft glow on his face. I brush some hair away from his forehead and just stare at him, etching his features into my mind. There's always a chance he won't make it back. Anything could happen. I want to make sure I remember how he looks like for the rest of my life. Because I know I will never meet anyone like him.

He takes hold of the back of my head and gently pulls me forward until our noses touch. "Every second we are apart, I shall miss you terribly." Next, I feel his soft, warm lips on my temple.

My voice above a whisper, I say, "I will miss you every second, too."

His arms come around me, enclose me, until our chests nearly fuse together. I bury my head in the space between his neck and shoulder, inhaling his exotic smell. We lie like this for what feels like an eternity, but is probably only a few minutes. Damarian worries we might run out of time, and we reluctantly get up and head to our spot by the rocks.

It's a bit windy today. Standing near the edge of the rocks, I hug my upper arms and stare down into the ocean. The waves seem violent. Maybe a storm is coming. I glance at Damarian. "Will it be safe for you?"

He's looking down at the waves, too. "I have swam in more dire conditions."

I hug myself even tighter.

We stand here for a few minutes. I open my mouth a couple of times to say something, but shut it. I don't want him to go, even though I know he needs to.

After a little while, Damarian faces me. I don't meet his eyes. I don't want to. He said he's coming back, but what if he doesn't? I don't want to look at him for the last time. Because I don't want him to leave me.

His thumb and index finger touch the bottom of my chin. He lifts it until I'm forced to meet his gaze. "I do not wish to go," he says softly. "But I must."

I nod, my throat tight.

"I shall return early the next morning," he says. "Will you be here?"

I caress his cheek with the back of my fingers. "I'll be waiting for you."

He wraps his hands around my arms and pulls me to his chest. My arms come around him, and we're clutching on to each other as if we want to merge into one person so we can spend every second of every minute of every hour together. "It may not be wise to do so, but it is what I wish to do."

I don't get what he means, until he raises me a few inches off the ground and swallows my lips with his. I wrap my legs around his waist and tangle my fingers through his hair as I kiss him. What begins as a slow and gentle kiss deepens with the desperate longing that hangs between us, leaving my chest heaving from its intensity. As we push ourselves even closer, our lips melding into each other, Damarian wobbles. In the back of my mind, a little voice tells me to be careful, that we're standing on rocks and we can fall and hurt ourselves. But the voice is muffled by a pulse going through every inch of me, focusing deep in my stomach.

When Damarian sways again, my eyes pop open and my lips unlatch from his. I lower my legs to the ground and take a step back. My chest rises and falls heavily, and his does, too. I can't see his face clearly, but I don't need to. I know the fire burning in his eyes, the yearning conquering every cell in his body. The heat between us is so thick, I can feel it.

"Wow," I mutter. Those are the mind-blowing kisses everyone always talks about. I've exchanged passionate kisses with Kyle, but not like this. I want to haul Damarian back to me and plant my lips on his again, to spend the rest of the night in his strong, protective arms, and feel what he feels for me through his tender and wild kisses.

"I am afraid we must part, Cassie," he says.

A lump forms in my throat. I nod because I can't speak.

He sets the bag of gummy worms on the rocks before unzipping his khaki pants and pulling them off. I look away as his underwear comes next. Then his T-shirt. I gather them in my arms and hug them close, inhaling his unique Damarian scent. The smell won't fade, not for a while. Holding them in my arms will give me comfort, will make me miss him less.

Knowing he's naked makes it that much harder to look away. But I do. Until he tucks his fingers under my chin again and lifts it upward. He bends forward and pecks my lips. "I shall see you early the following morning."

"I wouldn't miss it for the world."

He picks up the bag of worms and turns to the ocean. But then he faces me, like he can't bring himself to dive in.

"I wish I could come with you," I say.

He doesn't say anything. I see the pain in his eyes, the worry and doubt. Is this how we're going to live? To part and say goodbye? Is he going to travel between both our worlds forever? There's no witch who can give me a tail. And even if there was, I wouldn't give up being a human. I'd never ask him to give up his merman life.

He places both hands on the sides of my chin. "Let us not be concerned over what shall or shall not happen." He runs his lips across my cheek. "When I sleep tonight, my dreams will be filled with the beautiful human girl I long to hold in my arms."

I've been trying so hard to hold in my tears, but I feel them sliding down my cheeks. Damarian rubs them away with his thumbs.

"It's getting late," I say as I notice the sky growing lighter. "I don't want anyone to see you."

He nods. Then he moves closer to the edge of the rocks, staring down. He looks back at me. I wave with a trembling hand. He gives me a quick nod before diving into the ocean.

I fall onto my knees and bend forward, tears blurring my vision. The waves hit the bottom of the rocks more violently, and then his sapphire tail shoots up in the air. A second later, it's replaced with his head.

"Cassie." His voice drifts over the waves in a soft whisper that caresses every centimeter of my skin. Then he dives back into the ocean.

"Damarian," I whisper.

Chapter Twelve

Leah and I are huddled together on the sand, wrapped in towels. It started to drizzle a while ago. We stopped by early to go for a surf, but it looks like the rain will get heavier soon. I might cancel my class today and head home, but I need to first get the details on Leah and her new crush.

I shiver. "We should go somewhere warm."

"Yeah, we should."

Except, we're both too lazy to get up. The rain plops on Leah's wavy, dark brown hair, and for a few seconds, I'm filled with a drop of jealousy. I've always wished to have hair like her. As a kid, I used to imagine that she was Belle from *Beauty and the Beast*. I'd get jealous that she was the prettiest girl in town, and that she got to break the spell on the beast and help him return to being a handsome prince. And of course I envied the gorgeous golden gown she danced in.

I finger my hair. It reminds me of Damarian. He's the only guy to call my hair beautiful. Thinking about him creates a black hole in my stomach. It's sucking in all my energy. He's only been gone for a few hours, but I feel like half my soul ran off with him. That just shows how attached I've grown to him. It scares me to feel so dependent on a guy. But yet, it makes me feel really good, too.

116

Leah tugs her towel tighter around her body. "I met him on the beach a few days after we rescued your merboyfriend."

"What's his name?"

"Jace. My shift ended and I wanted to go for a swim. He was with those same guys. He asked me if my friend was doing okay. Then we started talking a bit. He's into art, which is cool, and he has a weird fascination with action figures. He has a huge collection in his basement."

I raise an eyebrow. "He collects action figures?"

She shrugs. "I know I don't go for guys like that, but I don't know." She shrugs again and looks out into the ocean. "I just feel something, you know?"

I nod because I know *exactly* what she means. Damarian and I come from two different worlds, are two different species. Science would claim our kinds shouldn't mix, just like a zebra and a bird would never work out. Yet, there's something that pulls us together. With so many differences, we still have a lot of similarities.

My leg twitches. I need to think of something other than Damarian. He'll be back tomorrow morning. I can wait that long. I need to have a life outside of him.

"So you broke up with Frankie?" I ask.

"Yeah. Our relationship was never headed anywhere. I think it's time I go out with someone I actually can have a future with."

To be with someone she can actually have a future with. The words ring in my ears. I shove them out of my head before they can settle in and attack my mind. I won't think about it. I *won't.*

"Has he asked you out?" I ask.

She shakes her head. "I think I'll ask him out tonight."

"Oooh." I punch her shoulder playfully. "You go, girl."

She smiles.

We sit in silence for a few seconds before she says, "How are you holding up?"

"Fine."

"Uh huh."

I dig my finger in the sand. "I feel like half my heart's been sucked out of me and thrown into the ocean."

She nods. "Love will do that to you."

My gaze snaps to her. "*Love?*"

She shrugs. "Like-like?"

I punch her shoulder again.

"It's okay to miss him," she says.

I sigh. "But to miss him *this* much? It hasn't even been five hours."

"My parents have been married for twenty years and whenever my dad goes away on business, my mom is a complete mess. Even now. When you care about someone, it's hard to be apart."

"Says a lot about my independence," I mutter.

"Hey, look at me."

I do.

"You are an independent person. You've had to fend for yourself many times growing up when your mom was working late. Now you have someone to lean on, at least on an emotional level. It scares you."

It does. I *have* come to lean on him, in many ways. That makes all of this even harder.

"Hey, we should totally check out a movie tonight," Leah says. "Gotta squeeze out as much as I can of you until lover boy returns from the sea."

Guilt eats away at me. "I'm sorry we haven't been spending a lot of time together."

She waves her hand. "I care more that you met a guy and that you're happy."

I lean forward and hug her. "You're a really good friend, you know?"

She grins. "I know."

The rain splats down on us. I cover my face. "How about we head back?"

"Good idea."

***

Leah and I are curled on the sofa, watching the number one romance movie of the year. We've seen it over ten times, but it's the kind of movie that never gets old, the kind that brings me to tears and moves something deep inside me.

Watching it when I didn't have a guy in my life made me yearn to experience what the girl on screen did. To have a guy love her so much he'd do anything for her, even betray those he holds dear. Even after my breakup with the Ex, I watched the movie. It didn't repulse me like I thought it would. In fact, it made me realize that kind of thing could never happen to me, so I lived vicariously through the main character.

But things are different now. Now, a guy washed up on shore, into my arms. Instead of living vicariously through the girl on screen, I close my eyes and imagine what could lie in store for me and Damarian. It makes me love and appreciate the movie in a way I never did before.

"Fantasizing?"

My eyes snap open. Leah's looking at me with a teasing smile. I kick her. "Shut up."

She laughs.

My phone rings. When I glance at the screen, I see my mom's name. "It's my mom."

"So answer it."

"I don't know..." Lately, it's been hard to have a normal conversation with her. She tends to gush how awesome her job is, which means her new life is awesome. Her life without me.

"You haven't spoken to her in a while."

She's right. It's been a few days—since the night before Damarian showed up at my house.

She pokes me with her toe. "Well, go on. Want me to pause the movie?"

I wave my hand. "It's okay. I've seen it too many times. Lower the volume, please."

Like the last time, I feel the excitement leaping off my mom. "Hey, how's my favorite daughter doing?"

"I'm your only daughter," I mutter.

"You doing okay, Cass Bass?"

My fingers squeeze the phone. "Why would you call me that?"

It was Dad's special nickname for me. He and I used to go fishing when I was eight or nine, and unlike a lot of the other girls, I wasn't afraid to touch the bait or the fish. Actually, I *loved* unhooking the fish. That's why he named me Cass Bass. It made me feel so special.

"Sorry." Mom's voice is above a whisper and full of regret. "I thought it would invoke happy memories of you and your father. I understand you didn't call him."

I don't say anything because I don't *want* to say anything. I know perfectly well that I'm acting like a spoiled brat. Boo hoo that my dad left me as a kid. Lots of people would kill to have their fathers reach out to them. I don't know what it is. It's like this whole thing with my dad is locked up deep, deep inside me, and something is blocking me from letting it out. The thought of rebuilding a relationship with him makes me want to hide in a cave and never come out.

Mom sighs. "I can't make you call him. I wish you would do that on your own."

"When are you coming back?" As soon as the words leave my

mouth, I regret them. I want to change the subject, but I don't want my mom to come home. Not when I need the pool to supply a merman with seawater so he won't die. Going back and forth to the beach with so many people around is risky.

Mom sighs again, except this time, I sense the guilt. "Not for some time, honey."

I feel relieved, but also hurt. Damarian's a great distraction—hopefully, more than that—but the fact still remains: my mom sort of abandoned me.

"I promise that the next time I'm home, I won't fly out for at least two weeks."

I believe her for a second, and that makes me smile. But my lips turn upside down when I remember she said the same thing the last time. "It's okay, Mom." I shrug. "Take all the time you need. I mean it."

She's quiet for a little bit before saying, "I'll talk to you tomorrow, okay?"

"Okay. Goodnight, Mom."

"I love you."

"Love you, too."

As soon as I hang up, Leah says. "You okay?"

"Fine."

She taps her finger on her thigh. "Was that about your dad?"

"Yeah."

"Are you going to call him?"

I hug my upper arms. "I don't know. I want to. I really do. But the thought scares the shit out of me. I wish I were up to the point where he and I already have a relationship. Taking the first step…"

"Is very scary," she finishes.

I nod.

She wraps her arm around me and yanks me close. We bump heads in the process and yell "ouch!" at the same time. Our eyes connect before we burst into laughter.

Leah pulls me to her again and hugs me close. "Taking the first step is the hardest. It'll only get easier after that."

I twist my mouth because I'm not sure I believe her.

"Think about it," she continues. "He wants to have a relationship with you. Half the work is already done."

She makes it seem so simple, and I know it can be. I just need to push myself to do this. The worst that could happen is that he'll reject me. I survived it the first time. I'm pretty sure I could survive it again.

Except, I don't know how true that is. Getting rejected by my dad again? Could anyone survive that?

"Your fishman should be coming back soon."

My entire body lights up. For a second, I completely forgot about Damarian. Picturing him makes my heart dance. I glance at the time. Nine thirty. Only six hours until I'll see him again. Until I can bury myself in his arms.

"When are you going to ask Jace out?" I ask.

Leah grabs some potato chips from the snack bowl. "I don't know. Not yet."

"Why not?"

She shrugs.

I study her. She's munching on the chips, her gaze on the rug. "Are you *nervous*?"

She snorts. But I see the unease in her eyes.

I touch her arm. "Hey, it's okay to admit you're scared."

She picks up the remote and pauses the movie. Then she shifts over until she faces me. "You're right. I *am* nervous. But I don't know why."

"Maybe because Jace is the type of guy you can settle down with. You've never had a serious boyfriend before." Her relationships usually last no more than a few months. It's not that she's afraid of the commitment or that she'll get her heart broken. She's afraid to settle down and start the next chapter in her life. Just like I am.

I wrap my arms around her. "The first step is the hardest, remember?"

She rolls her eyes. "This is the first time someone's using my advice against me."

"I'm not using it against you. It's really great advice."

She waves her hand.

"Really. You should start an advice column."

"Uh huh."

We watch the rest of the movie. When it's over, Leah sends Jace a text to see if he's awake. When he responds, she disappears in the kitchen to call him. As soon as she returns, I see the light shining in her eyes.

"I'm guessing he said yes?" I ask.

She leaps onto the couch and covers her face with her hands. "He said he was *just* about to call me." She uncovers her face and squeals. "We're like telepathically connected."

I laugh. "So he said yes?"

She nods eagerly. "Yep. He's taking me out tomorrow afternoon. He told me he wished he could talk more, but he had to cram for a test."

"So he's in college."

She squeals again. "I'm officially going out with a college guy!"

Her enthusiasm makes me bounce on the couch. "Hey, we'll be college girls in two months. Please, it's not *that* impressive that you're going out with a college guy."

She grabs a couch cushion and rams it into my face.

"Oh, no you didn't."

She shoves it into my face again.

I retaliate by hitting her with two cushions. Somehow, the snack bowl flies off the couch, and the potato chips and pretzels scatter the carpet.

"You are so cleaning that up," I tell her.

"No way. You started it."

"You started with the hitting!"

"Seriously, are we five?"

"Yes, you are definitely acting like a five year old."

She leans back on the couch and lays her legs on my lap. "Cass, what am I going to do without you?"

I stare at her. "What do you mean?"

She looks straight at the blank TV. "You're going to school in Texas. I have no idea where the hell I'm going. Nothing will be the same anymore."

Lifting her legs off me, I scoot closer until my shoulder bumps hers. "I've never really sat on that. It's always been pushed to the back of my mind. I guess I've never wanted to face it."

She puffs out some air.

"People do it all the time," I say.

"Yeah, and they grow apart."

"That won't happen to us."

She moves her gaze to mine. "How can you be so sure?"

I don't answer because that's just it—I'm not sure. I'm so focused on comforting her that I don't even know if I'm telling the truth. We all hear how college is the best years of your life, that you make long-lasting friendships with people. Leah's a social girl and makes friends easily. If anything, she's the one who might outgrow me.

Merman's Kiss

I rest my elbows on my knees and place my forehead on my palms. "With my mom and my dad and Damarian and college, I think I might explode."

She sighs. "Who said life gets easier after high school?"

I shrug.

"Because he's one big liar."

Chapter Thirteen

.

I'm standing on the rocks by the beach.

The wind blows my hair into my eyes, blocking my view for only a second. The waves hit the bottom of the rocks in a steady rhythm. My hands tighten on the shirt, pants, and towels I brought with me. When I push the light on my watch, I see it's well past 3:30 AM. He's late.

I lower myself onto the rocks and cross my legs, hugging the clothing and towel to my chest. Merpeople don't have a sense of time like we do. The fact that he's late shouldn't worry me.

But it does. I'm worried he's hurt, that he got caught. That he decided not to return.

Raising my gaze from the ocean, I scan my surroundings. No sign of anyone. A sigh of relief escapes my lips. If only he'd get here already.

After another ten minutes, I see movement near the rocks. I scramble to my knees and peer over. Something splashes in the water. My heart soars when I see the familiar sapphire crystals. It blinds me for a second. Then his head pops out of the ocean.

Time stops. Damarian, with his beautiful blue eyes and sexy golden hair, looks like the god of the ocean. Lame, I know. But seeing him in there, knowing he's my guy, it stirs something in me. I can't help but smile like a love-struck teenager.

Merman's Kiss

He waves his webbed hand, then dives back in the water. I follow his movement in the ocean. He's heading toward the shore. I gather my stuff and hurry down the rocks to meet him. As soon as I reach the sand, Damarian has already pulled himself out of the water. I rush toward him, and when he sees me, he holds out his arms. I launch into them and wrap my arms around him, squeezing him to death. A rumble travels down his chest as he laughs. He whispers into my ear, "Oh, how I have missed you, Cassie."

Those words ignite something warm in me. It travels through every cell in my body. I press my cheeks to his. "How I've missed you."

We stay in each other's arms for a while. As the minutes tick by, I know we need to get moving. It feels so good to just stay like this, but he needs to be safe.

I reluctantly pull out of his arms. "We better get you dried off."

I unfold the mint green towel I brought. It's the largest one we have in the house. I wrap it around his tail and start drying him off. "Use this to wipe yourself." I hand him the smaller towel.

Working my way down the length of his tail and fin, I can't help but marvel at how stunning it is. I glance up at Damarian and find him watching me. "You're beautiful," I say.

He puts his hands on either side of my waist and gently hauls me toward his chest. I fall into him, inhaling that ocean scent that makes me feel protected. "You are beautiful, Cassie," he murmurs.

"I'm so glad you're back," I say into his chest. "I don't know if I could have survived another day."

He runs his hand up and down my back. "Your feelings match mine."

I tighten my arms around him. I can't believe how close I feel to him right now. It's like we've known each other all our lives. A tear pricks my eye. I can't lose him. I don't know what I'd do.

"The shift," he says, his voice weak.

I look up at him.

His eyes shut before springing open. "It is beginning."

I quickly get off him and rest my hand on his back, lowering him to the sand. A grunt escapes his mouth and his eyes close. I back away a little and watch as his body convulses. I press my knuckles to my lips. It hurts so much to see him suffering like this.

His sapphire scales slowly fade into legs. His fingers are no longer webbed. When he stops shaking, I edge closer and stroke the side of his face. His eyes flutter open. He smiles softly.

"I hate watching that." I run my fingers through his hair.

"It eases me when you are here." His voice is faint.

I adjust the towel and crawl closer, lying down on him and folding him in my arms. "We can rest here for a bit. Swimming and shifting must have tired you out."

He says something, but his voice is so weak that I don't hear. I raise my head and glance at his face. His features that were contorted in pain a minute ago are now relaxed. I slide my fingers through his and bring his hand to my mouth, pressing my lips on the back of it. "I'm so glad you're back," I tell him again.

***

The sun beats down on my back. When I move, I feel something hard and soft beneath me. My eyes fly open. The right side of Damarian's face is buried in the sand. The grains stick to his lips.

It's really hot today. I glance at my watch and see that it's past ten AM. I lift myself off Damarian. Stretching, I search the area. The beach is full. Little kids play in the sand while their parents work on their tans. The ocean is filled with people.

I look back at Damarian. He's out cold. I brush some hair away from his eyes. Then I bend toward his ear. "Hey, we need to get up."

He moans and his eyes slowly open. When he sees me, he smiles. "It was not a dream. I am here with you."

I lock my fingers with his. "It's too good, I feel like it *is* a dream."

He sits up and studies the beach and the people. "Is it safe?"

"We're okay. But a few hours have passed and you might need seawater. Let's get you into my pool just in case." I reach for the pants and jeans. "Dress into these in the changing room. I'll show you where it is."

As I get to my feet, I realize how stiff I am. I slept in a really bad position. At least tonight Damarian will be in my house, sleeping in the guest room next door, and we won't have to worry about him changing on the beach or someone seeing him.

I take his hand and swing it as I lead him to the changing room.

Damarian smiles. "You are cheerful."

"I'm so happy you're here."

He squeezes my hand. "As am I."

He enters the changing room and I wait outside. As I turn away, I catch sight of Kyle standing next to a group of guys by the ice cream shop. At first, I think he's studying the area behind me, but then I realize his eyes are on *me*. When he notices me looking, he smirks and lifts his hand in a small wave.

I cross my arms over my chest. What exactly is his problem?

The door to the changing room opens and Damarian steps out. My eyes land on his chest, at how good he looks in that shirt. Then they travel lower, to his khakis. Mmm, those pants definitely do him justice.

"Come." I link my arm through his. "Let's get you in the pool, and then I want to take you out for breakfast."

As we walk away, I look back at Kyle. He takes a sip from his water bottle, his gaze on us. A chill runs down my spine. I don't like the way he's looking at us.

***

We return from breakfast and settle down on my couch. I scoot closer and climb onto Damarian's lap, clasping my hands around his neck and gazing into his eyes. "Tell me about your world."

"My world?"

"Yeah. You know so much about humans, but I don't know anything about merpeople. Other than they are half man and half fish." I laugh.

He places his hand on the back of my head and lowers it to his chest. He plays with my hair. "I wish to tell you all, but I am concerned—"

"I promise I won't tell anyone. Not a soul. Not anything living or non-living. I swear."

He gazes down at me. "I believe you." He leans forward and brushes his nose against mine. "I wish for you to be part of my world."

"Me, too."

With his eyes still on me, he says, "We are of five clans. The Sapphires, the Violets, the Emeralds, the Rubies, and the Diamonds. Our tails represent which clan we belong to. I, as you know, am of the Sapphire clan."

I poke him in the chest. "I think your color is the prettiest."

He laughs. "The Violets are the ruling clan. They live in Eteria, our capital city."

"That's interesting. I'd think the Diamonds were the ruling clan."

He shakes his head.

"So is there a castle in um…the capital city?"

"Yes."

"Cool. Have you ever been there?"

"Once or twice," he says. "It is most beautiful."

"So there's a king and queen? I know we spoke about it a little bit, but I didn't get a chance to ask you anything specific."

His gaze moves to me. "Yes. King Palaemon and Queen Lamara."

"So they rule the rest of the clans."

"Yes."

I snuggle closer and smile up at him. He only told me a little about himself, but I feel so much closer to him. "Thanks so much for sharing this with me."

He wraps his arms around me and hugs me close. "It gladdens me to."

My fingers tiptoe up his arm, his neck, and tangles in his hair. "How many brothers and sisters do you have?"

A faraway look captures his face. His eyes get unfocused. Then he blinks and laughs, shaking his head. "How I miss them. I have only returned."

"It's understandable. I miss my mom like crazy, even though I'm sort of glad she's away."

He runs the back of his fingers down my cheek. "Your mother is away?"

I nod. "She has a job where she needs to travel a lot."

His eyes soften. "I had not realized. I presumed you reside alone. I am sorry."

"It's okay. It's good for her, and I need to learn to be independent, anyway. I'll be away at college in two months."

He nods slowly, and his gaze drops to the carpet. My heart lurches. If I go to school in Texas, I won't be near the ocean. I won't see Damarian. *Two* months. That's such a short amount of time.

My mind runs with the different options I had. I applied to some local colleges here, hoping for a scholarship, but my grades weren't that great and I'm not a pro surfer. The only school I got into is in Texas.

Damarian shifts on the couch and pulls me closer to him. He bends forward until his breath tickles my cheek. His lips are only a few inches away. "I have three brothers. Kiander, and Syndin and Syd, who are twins. I have two sisters. Doria and Zarya." He smiles at the blank TV screen. "How I miss Zarya." His eyes sparkle. "She very much enjoyed your gift of worms."

I grin. "I'm glad. Do you have a mom? You've only mentioned a father."

"Yes."

"What are their names?"

"My father is Syren," he says. "My mother is Kiandra."

"You all have such pretty names. I'm sorry you miss them."

He shakes his head, placing his finger on my lips. "Please do not be sorry. My only wish is to be with you." His lips graze my cheek and ear. "Only you."

A million butterflies flap around in my stomach. My heart races and my breathing is heavy. "Me, too," I whisper.

He takes hold of my waist and backs me up against the couch's armrest. Lowering his lips to my neck, he trails kisses down my throat. A soft moan escapes my mouth. His gentle, warm lips sweep a little lower, to my collarbone. My head rolls back and I moan again. His mouth leaves my neck, and a second later I feel them on my lips. When we break apart, he mutters, "Cassie, please forgive me."

He makes a move to back away, but I grab his hand. "Forgive you for what?"

He runs his fingers through his hair. "I feel things. Things I have never felt as a child of the sea."

I cup his chin and force his eyes to meet mine. "It's okay. It's probably human hormones that you're feeling. I guess they're more intense than your merman hormones." I stroke his cheek. "It's perfectly normal to feel this way."

He presses his forehead to mine. "Do you feel what I feel?"

"Yes."

His body is heavy against mine, but not too much that it hurts. "I am not accustomed to this. It is overwhelming. I have desires…"

I swallow. "What kind of desires?"

"I do not know. I do not understand them."

I enclose him in my arms. "It's okay. Let's take one step at a time."

Two months. The words ring in my head. I shut my eyes. I won't think about it. I can't.

Damarian rests his forehead on mine again, and I open my eyes. "Thank you," he says. "You are very understanding."

We lie in silence for a few seconds. Then I say, "Do you want me to give you a tour of the city?"

"I would very much enjoy that."

Chapter Fourteen

Damarian and I drive around. We stop at a few seafood restaurants so he can try some of our goods. While he likes them well enough, he claims nothing beats catching them with his bare hands and eating them while swimming in the ocean.

The weather is extremely hot today, and I worry he might need water, so we cut our trip short. After he takes a swim, we sit on my couch. He insists on wearing his towel, since he feels more "free." I don't object, even though it makes me uneasy.

A sci-fi thriller is on TV. Damarian seems intrigued, especially when the robots come on the screen. I take a few minutes explaining.

His eyes grow wide. "The human world is quite fascinating. I could not have imagined so."

"Your world's pretty amazing, too. I've always been blown away with whales. They are so cool."

I remember seeing pictures of size comparisons between humans and whales. The humans were ants compared to the some of them.

He smiles.

A few silent seconds tick by.

"Um...are you tired?"

"Yes, I am exhausted."

"Let's get ready for bed."

I grab his pajamas and hand them to him. Before he closes the bathroom door, he wraps an arm around my waist and hauls me to his chest. When his lips touch mine, they are almost savage-like, like he can't get enough of me. He's not hurting me, but it's intense enough to stir something in the pit of my stomach.

He releases me, and I'm left reeling, barely standing on my own feet. He disappears into the bathroom and I stumble to my room. I take care of some personal things, like answering emails and texts, and then it's my turn to hit the shower. When I'm done, I find Damarian asleep in his bed, the blanket gathered by his feet. I slide it out from underneath him and pull it up to his chin. It can get pretty chilly at night, since we have central air conditioning.

I stand there for a little while, watching him sleep. His chest rises and falls in a steady, calm rhythm. He's not snoring, but his mouth falls open occasionally. His hands curl and uncurl at his sides.

My heart fills with something, something deep and intense. Love. But it can't be. I've only known him for a week. I'm not the kind of girl to fall for a guy that quickly. But as much as this scares me, I feel a sense of peace. Because I know that I trust him. I know he won't hurt me like Kyle did. Like my dad did to my mom and me.

My gaze travels down his body, to his feet sticking out of the blanket. I sigh. He's a merman—he lives in the ocean. Can we have a future together?

As I study him, something dawns on me. I'm willing. I'm willing to do whatever it takes to be with him. If that means I need to wait for him every other day at the beach at three AM, I will. If it means I'll live near the beach my whole life, I will. If it means I'll have to provide him with a pool of salt water, I will. Because I've never felt this way about anyone, and I'll do whatever I need to have a future with him.

I turn to leave. Damarian clasps his hand around my wrist. "Cassie?" he says sleepily, squinting up at me.

I kneel down. "I'm here. Are you okay?"

"Must you sleep there?" His eyes flutter until they're open and staring at me.

"W-what?"

"Sleep…here?"

My stomach muscles clench.

"If it is all right with you," he says.

It's such an intimate thing to do. Almost every single part of me wants to flee to the safety of my room, but the part of me that wants to stay is the authority figure now—my heart.

I nod and walk over to the other side of his bed. Taking a deep breath, I lift the blanket and slide in next to him. My leg brushes against his. It's warm and soft, and it sends a jolt of electricity up my body. Damarian flips onto his other side so we face one another. We're only a few inches apart. I can smell him, and every so often I feel his breath on my cheek.

"Hi." My heart is beating nervously.

He touches my ponytail. "Hello, Cassie. May I unbind your hair?"

I nod.

He drags off the pony holder. Once my hair is free, I feel it fall down my shoulders and back. Damarian combs his fingers through it. Every hair on me stands on edge. I shiver.

"Are you cold?" He takes me in his arms and hugs me close. I feel the heat radiating off his body.

"For a guy who lives in cold temperatures, you sure know how to keep a girl warm and toasty."

He laughs and pecks my temple. "I wish only to protect you."

His words wrap around me and lift me in the air. I shut my eyes and sink into the bed and pillow, releasing a relaxed sigh. I open my eyes and find his on mine. We gaze at each other for what feels like an eternity.

Damarian says, "Cassie, may I hold you closer in my arms?"

Our arms are wrapped around each other and our legs are intertwined. I don't see how we can get any closer. But I nod and shift over. Our chests are nearly glued together. I close my eyes and let go of my fear and insecurities. I lower the wall I built around myself and am completely vulnerable, at his mercy. If I'm going to risk my heart with someone, I want it to be Damarian.

He dips his head, and our lips meet. His fingers dig into my skin as his mouth moves over mine. I clutch the back of his head as his lips devour mine as though he's dying from thirst and I'm the spring of water he desperately seeks. When he moans, it fuels the energy inside me. I yank his hair and immerse myself in this kiss, in this feeling, in the magic sparking between us. His hands explore my body, and mine explore his. It feels as though my molecules are dispersing and I'm floating up and up. I don't feel anything except for the heat bouncing between us and the throbbing in my body.

"Damarian," I breathe.

"Cassie."

His lips are roving down my throat. I throw my head back and moan as ripples of pleasure pass through me. I try to lift my arms and touch him, to feel his smooth, hard flesh beneath my fingers. But they are so heavy.

I whisper his name as he touches me, caresses me, kisses me, brings me to oblivion and back.

"What I feel for you," he says softly. "I do not wish for it to end."

It takes a few seconds for his words to enter my fuzzy mind. "Me, either."

Chapter Fifteen

Something knocks into my face. My eyes open. Damarian's hand is blocking my view.

Waking up next to him feels really, really good. His face is smashed into the pillow. I wonder how he looks when he's in his merman form and sleeps in his oyster shell with seaweed.

As if he senses me watching him, he slowly opens his eyes. He smiles, then shifts onto his back.

"Good morning," I say. "How did you sleep?"

"Good morning. I slept very well. Thank you for sharing the bed."

I slide closer and rest my head on his chest. "Can I ask you something?"

"Certainly."

"The morning I found you washed up on the beach. What were you running from?"

His eyes that were full of life a second ago now turn dark. He tears his gaze from me and stares straight ahead.

I place my hand on his arm. "Sorry. I see I touched a sensitive topic. Do you want to talk about it?"

He puffs out some air. "Father and I...we quarrel often."

"What do you fight about?"

He's quiet for a little while, his expression serious, his breathing heavy. I rub circles on his arm, hoping to soothe him. This discussion clearly upsets him.

He shakes his head. My heart sinks. I'm slowly opening up to him, but it doesn't seem like he's doing the same. We share such deep, emotional moments together, have amazing, passionate kisses. But he won't let me in.

"Damarian, please. You can talk to me."

"We quarreled that night," he says and shakes his head. "I should not have been swimming in the storm."

I'm about to ask more, dig more, but he sits up, dragging the blanket with him. The cool air of the air conditioner blows on me, and I shiver. When he realizes, he quickly untangles it from around his body and throws it over me, wrapping it around me and lifting me toward his body. His lips graze my cheek. "Humans and children of the sea are alike in many ways. I have issues with my father as well."

"Another thing we have in common."

He nuzzles my nose. "Yes."

I won't pry. He'll tell me when he's ready. I guess it doesn't matter whether it's a human guy or a merman—men don't like to share their innermost feelings.

"How about some breakfast?" I ask.

The door to the guestroom springs open and a woman gasps. My head whips around. Mom stands there, a suitcase handle in her hand.

"*Mom?*"

"*Cassie?*" Her wide, shocked eyes trek from me to Damarian. She blinks and steps back.

"What are you doing here?" I want to bury my face in my hands, but my body is wrapped in the blanket like a cocoon.

She stares at the two of us, her mouth slightly ajar. After a few seconds, she gathers herself and holds her hand out to Damarian. "I'm Joanie."

"Damian." He shakes it like a pro. I sigh in relief that he remembers his human name.

"What are you doing home?" I ask.

"I feel so bad for always leaving you. So I spoke to my boss and got a few days off."

I'm glad to hear that, but at the same time, I feel disappointed. I want my mom here with me, but she has rotten timing. How can I hide a merman in my house when she's around?

I clear my throat. "Um, Mom, can you please give us some privacy?"

"Oh, sure." She walks backwards to the door. "And you and I are going to have a talk," she says to me.

She shuts the door after her. My cheeks are burning. Damarian unwraps the blanket from around me. "You resemble your mother."

I push some hair away from his eyes. "Yeah. You know what this means?"

He raises his eyebrows.

"You can't...I mean, the swimming pool..." The words get stuck in my throat.

He nods slowly. "I cannot shift into my merman form."

I nod.

His lips form a straight line.

"I'm so sorry, Damarian. I didn't know she'd be back—"

"It is all right. Do not fret." He smiles, but I know it's forced.

I take him in my arms. "We'll think of something, okay?" I bite my lip so I don't offer to tell my mom. That decision is up to Damarian. I doubt he'd want to tell anyone else about his true identity.

We sit in silence for a long time.

After a while, I ask, "Do you feel okay?"

"Yes."

He would have gone into the salt water by now. I don't know what to do. What if he cries out like a dying whale? I would rush him to the pool ASAP. Mom would know everything. I need to find a way to get him to the ocean. But how can I with so many people around?

"What is the matter?" Damarian asks. I realize my eyebrows are scrunched.

"I'm just thinking."

He places his hands on my shoulders and looks into my eyes. "Please do not fret."

I need to. I feel responsible for him. After all, this is my world. He's been on land for quite a bit, but he's still an alien. His safety depends on me.

An idea flashes in my mind. I sit up. "We can take a boat and ride deep into the ocean where no one else is around. No people, no boats."

Relief washes over his features. "Are you certain it will be safe for you to be so far out in the sea?"

Maybe. I don't know. But I'm not thinking about me. Damarian's health is my priority right now. "I don't have a lot of experience in sailing, but we'll be okay."

He nods.

A few silent seconds tick by. I hug my knees to my chest and lay my chin on them. This will cause a major shift in our relationship. We've both grown so used to Damarian changing in my house. It became his second home. But now...

What if I won't be able to see him again?

"When are we to head to sea?" he asks.

I notice his face is a little pale, and I jump to my feet. "You're feeling sick?"

"A bit."

"Come." I take his hand. "Let's go."

When I open the door to my room, I get a whiff of the smell of pancakes coming from the kitchen. Guilt chokes my throat. Mom's making breakfast. She's not one to cook a lot, especially breakfast. This must be a special treat for me and Damarian.

He breathes in the aroma. "The smell is divine."

"My mom's making breakfast. Pancakes."

He nods.

We're about to head down the steps, but then I realize we're still dressed in pajamas. "Oh." I gesture toward his outfit. "It might be a good idea to change."

He returns to his room and I go to mine. I change into a T-shirt and jeans as fast as possible. I don't know how long Damarian has left. I'm not sure what causes his need to change. There doesn't seem to be a pattern. My guess is a lot has to do with the temperature and what's going on in his body. It could be a million factors.

We meet at the foot of the steps and climb down. Mom's standing over the stove, wearing an apron. She only makes pancakes on special occasions, like birthdays and holidays. I remember sitting on the counter as a little girl and marveling at how the pancakes were made. Seeing my mom like that brings me back to that time, when my dad was around. When we were still a family.

I blink the memories away and step inside.

"Hey, kids," Mom greets.

"You're making breakfast."

"Yes, I am." She smiles.

I glance at Damarian. "Um…Damian needs to run. Family emergency." I peer closely at him to see if he's getting worse, but he seems to be fine. Unless he's fighting it.

Mom's face falls. "I thought we can eat together. Catch up. Get to know one another."

"I am afraid I must take my leave."

Mom lays the spatula on the counter and moves closer to Damarian. "Where are you from? I'm trying to pinpoint your accent."

His eyes flit to mine, all flustered. I tug on his hand, leading him to the door. "We'll talk later. Okay, Mom? We really need to run."

As soon as the door shuts after us, I say to Damarian, "We need to work on your speech."

"I agree."

I smile and squeeze his hand. That means he still wants to see me. We'll figure something out. We *need* to.

I bring him to the marina, where we meet up with Leah's cousin, Ian. He rents us a boat for half price. I help Damarian inside, then start the engine. After a few minutes of sailing, Damarian bends over the side of the boat to sweep his hand through the water, but I yell, "No, don't!" I'm not sure how much salt water needs to touch him before he'll change into a merman. We're still in public.

Damarian jumps back. "Forgive me. I have forgotten. The sea calls for me."

"It's okay. We're almost there."

I take us as far away as possible. I'm freaking out because I have no idea what lurks here. There could be sharks and whales and who knows what. But it calms me to know Damarian will be safe here.

He's leaning over the side of the boat, his eyes mesmerized by the water. I tap his thigh. "Feeling okay?"

"I feel a bit ill."

When I think we're far enough, I kill the engine. I scan the area to make sure no boats are in the distance. I don't see any around, but that doesn't mean they won't show up, though. I face Damarian. "Are you ready?"

His face is paler than before. His knees tremble. He brings a shaky hand to my cheek. "I do not wish to part with you."

I rest my hand on his. "We won't stay apart for too long. We'll figure something out. But you need to get into the ocean first."

He nods reluctantly. I check the area one more time to make sure no one's around, then nod. Damarian leans forward and closes his mouth over mine. I grab onto him, yanking him to my chest. He loses his balance and we crash to the floor of the boat. Our lips continue to push against each other, melting into one. It's like we're putting everything we have into this kiss because we're not sure when the next one will be.

When he pulls back, he buries his face in my hair and inhales. "I shall miss you, Cassie. Very much."

I clutch him. "Me, too."

He presses his lips to my temple. "I love you."

Hearing those words makes my heart thump. I feel it all over, as if his love touches every part of me, body and soul.

"I love you, too," I whisper.

"Meet me tonight," he murmurs, his lips grazing my ear. "At the rocks. I will wait for you."

My clutch on him tightens. "I'll be there."

He pulls back and gazes into my eyes. "I cannot bear to live without you."

I slide both my hands into his. "I feel the exact same way. Tonight?"

"Yes."

He looks at the water. Then he takes my hand and presses the back of my fingers to his lips. I feel his tongue tickling my knuckles, and it ignites a flame inside me.

He drops my hand and gets to his feet. The boat sways a bit. He glances at me for a second before raising his arms and diving into the ocean. The water splashes into the boat and onto me. A puddle forms at my feet, drenching my sneakers.

I look over the side of the boat and find the water bubbling, as if it's cooking. I want to reach down there, to feel him.

A second later, his fin protrudes out of the water. He quickly pulls it in, and then his head pops up in its place.

I stretch my hand toward him. He stretches his webbed one. When our hands connect, I feel whole again. He lifts his hand and runs it up my arm, making goose bumps appear all over me.

"I shall see you tonight," he says.

I nod. "Enjoy your time with your family."

"Yes, thank you."

He drops his hand and makes a move, but then he whips back around and rests my palm against his cheek. "Parting with you is so difficult."

A lump bigger than the boat lodges in my throat. Tears prick my eyes. "I know, but we'll see each other soon."

I may be wrong, but I think I see tears in his eyes. I bend over the boat and kiss the top of his head. "Don't go meeting other human girls," I joke.

A small smile forces its way onto his face. "Never. I do not wish to be with anyone but you."

That causes the tears I was battling to rush down my cheeks. He wipes them away with his finger. Then he touches his own tears. He brings his hands together, mixing our tears. "I am only a sea away."

I smile sadly. "Bye, Damarian."

"Goodbye."

He turns around, then looks back at me. We gaze at each other until he dives into the ocean. I see his backside and tail before he disappears for good.

The tears come in full force. I wipe them away, feeling like an idiot for crying like this. I guess this is what being in love feels like. That you can't bear to be apart, not even for a few hours. It creates a deep hole in your heart, and nothing can fill it. Absolutely nothing. Only the arms and heart of the special one.

My eyes examine the surface of the water. It's calm. No sign of movement.

I start the engine and head back to shore. Ian asks me if I'm okay. I must look pretty messed up. I nod and somehow make it back home. A stack of pancakes sits on the kitchen table. Mom's leafing through a magazine, sipping coffee.

When she sees me, she says, "Where did you find him? He's *gorgeous*." But then she takes one look at me and her expression changes. She stands and envelopes me in her arms. I sob onto her shoulder, and I don't even know why. A whirlwind of emotions race through me. I'm so glad Mom's home—I miss being in her arms.

My heart hurts from parting with Damarian, but there's also a sense of calm because I know we didn't say goodbye for good. I will see him tonight. But as much as I try to ignore it, something lurks underneath, something that's been worrying me ever since I started having feelings for him. That he and I could never be. I've always pushed it aside, told myself it didn't matter as long as we wanted to be together, but who am I kidding? I can never be with him. It's naturally impossible.

I don't know if I can stand getting my heart broken again. But I don't know if I can stand being away from him, either.

Mom rubs my back. "Oh, honey. What's wrong?"

"I don't know." I pull back and wipe my face with my shirtsleeve.

"Did he break up with you?"

I shake my head, swatting more tears that drip down my cheeks.

"Then what's wrong?"

"I really like him, Mom. Like really, *really*." I bite down on my lower lip. "I'm so scared."

Mom twirls a strand of my hair that's hanging in front of my eye. "Relationships can be very scary. But they are so, so worth it."

I study her. This is coming from a woman who's had her heart ripped out her of chest and crushed into a million pieces. The same woman who hardly spoke about my dad after he left and who's avoided the topic of relationships until this point. "You still believe in love?" I ask. "I mean, after what Dad did—"

"Honey, you can't let one mistake ruin your life. I don't regret meeting your dad. For starters, you wouldn't be here, and I wouldn't trade you for anything. And two, everything happens for a reason. I learned a lot about myself and what I need in a relationship."

I drop down on one of the chairs and stare at my nails. My father leaving my mom affects her more than she lets on. "You don't go out," I say.

She walks over to the fridge. "I'm thirsty. Do you want orange juice?"

I watch her bustling around the cabinets in search for a glass cup. She's pushing me to pursue a relationship with my dad when it hurts her. She knows having my father in my life will be to my benefit. She and I are not as different as I thought. She deserves to run off and live the life she's always dreamed of. She doesn't need to sacrifice for me anymore.

"When will Damian return?" she asks from the counter.

I chew on my thumbnail. "I don't know."

She turns around and leans back, the glass of orange juice poised at her lips. "I didn't get a chance to know him, but I can tell he's the right guy for you."

I stare at her. "How do you know?"

She takes a sip from her orange juice. "The way he looks at you. The chemistry I see between the two of you. It's obvious he cares deeply about you. Unlike Kyle."

I feel my defense shield rising. "You're saying Kyle never cared about me?"

"I'm saying he had a crappy way of showing it."

Anger fills me. Not at my mom or Kyle, but at myself. I thought Kyle was the perfect guy for me and treated me well. But Leah and Mom don't seem to agree. I must have a lousy taste in men. Which means what exactly in regard to Damarian?

Merman, a voice says in my head.

"But Damian," Mom continues. "Now he's a catch. Where did you meet him?"

"At the beach," I mutter absentmindedly. She doesn't know how true her words are—that he literally *can* be caught. "Mom?"

"Yeah, honey?"

"What if I told you Damian was…different?"

She arches an eyebrow. "Different?"

"Yeah. Not like everyone else."

She eyes me closely. "What are you trying to tell me?"

My body fills with fear and dread. I've said too much. I can't have Mom prying. I can't betray Damarian.

"Never mind." I get to my feet. "My class will start soon."

"Let's go out tonight," she says. "Maybe catch a movie."

I smile. "Okay."

***

I devour my strawberry mango smoothie.

"He's back in the ocean?" Leah whispers.

The high school guy sitting next to me at the counter asks her for a refill. She nods impatiently, then turns her attention back to me. "I don't understand how you can live with that." She shakes her head. "He is hot, though."

I slap her arm.

She laughs. "Just kidding. Seriously, though, how are you doing?"

I play with my straw, my gaze on the cup's lid. "It's killing me. But I'm glad he gets to go home and see his family. I'm really happy about that." I lean in close and say, "I'm so worried someone will see him. It's almost like…" I sigh. "Like I'm being selfish by wanting him to come back."

I place my elbows on the counter and rake my fingers through my hair. I rest my forehead against my palm. "If he gets caught, it's over. His whole life is ruined, not to mention the lives of all…his kind."

"I'm still waiting for my refill," the high school guy says.

Leah quickly refills his cup, then bends closer to me. "What's life if there's no risk? Damarian knows what he's doing. He wouldn't do it if he didn't want you."

"He said he loves me."

"Oh my God! Did you say it back? *Do* you love him?"

I shut my eyes for a second and nod. "This feels like a warped version of *Romeo and Juliet*. My life should be called *Romarian and Cassilette*."

Leah bursts out laughing. "But *Romeo and Juliet* is like one of the best romances ever."

I cock an eyebrow. "You do know how their story ends, right?"

She rolls her eyes. "Shakespeare is fiction."

"And my life's a fairytail. Mind you, that's fairytail with a t-a-i-l."

Leah laughs again. "You're funny when you're grumpy." She

glances at the guy. "Are you trying to *eavesdrop* on our conversation?"

He gives her a cheeky grin. "Nope. You girls aren't making it easy. I can't seem to take my eyes off you, though."

She groans. "Pay for your smoothie and get the hell out of here."

He drops a folded piece of paper and winks. "Call me."

He's gone, and Leah groans again, tossing the paper into the trash. "My love life has reached rock bottom if a high school kid is hitting on me."

"Are things not working with Jace? How was your date?"

She shrugs. "A little awkward. We don't have a lot in common."

I sip my smoothie. "Give him a chance. You never know, right? Look at me. I'm dating a fish."

Her lips lift. "Yeah. You're making out with a creature that lives in the ocean. And I thought I have problems."

I slap her shoulder.

"You must miss him like crazy. You can't even call or text to see how he's doing."

I don't want to think how true that is. Anything could happen to him during his trips between land and sea. He's not meant to come to the shore. What if he gets caught in a fisherman's net? My chest aches at the thought. If something were to happen to him...

"I'm meeting him tonight at the beach," I tell Leah.

She nods. "That's good."

My throat is dry. "Except for the fact that the beach is a public place and anyone can drop by."

"Who'd be nuts enough to go to the beach at three o'clock in the morning?"

"Other than drunks? A girl who's meeting a merman?"

She points at me and grins. "Exactly."

I check my watch. "Mom wants to go shopping. She claims that since I have a guy now, I'm in desperate need of new clothes." I shrug. "But I'm really glad she's back and we can spend time together. At the same time...I sort of want her to leave so that I can spend time with Damarian. Does that make me selfish?"

Leah takes the orders of a group of middle-aged women who just walked in. When her focus is back on me, she says, "Hey, choosing between a hot merman and your mom? I think that answer is obvious." She lays her hand on mine. "You're an adult now. It's time to live your life. It's okay to go after what you want."

I nod and get up. "But I still want to spend time with my mom, too. Good luck with Jace. Give him a chance, okay?"

She salutes me. "Yes, ma'am."

As soon as I leave the smoothie shop, my eyes immediately sprint toward the ocean, as if I'll see Damarian. But I only see the many people swimming around. I glance at my watch. Only a few more hours until we're together again.

Chapter Sixteen

He's late.

I pace around on the rocks, although there's not a lot of room for pacing, not to mention it's dangerous. I press the button on my watch. 4:29.

After Mom and I returned from shopping, I took a shower and went straight to bed. I want to be wide awake when I see Damarian. But what if he doesn't show? What if he ditched me?

Or worse—what if he got caught?

I take out my phone and go online. I do a search for breaking news about mermaids, but I don't find anything. My fingers plow through my hair. If every one of our meetings will stress me out like this, I don't know if I can take it.

Squinting at the ocean, I don't see any crystals, only the dark water. I collapse on the rocks and bury my face in my knees. I think I might die from worrying.

I must have dozed off, because the next thing I hear is splashing. Looking over the rocks, I nearly leap into the ocean. He's here. He's actually *here*.

I grab the bag I brought with me and race down the rocks. Damarian is still in the ocean. I bop up and down on the sand as I watch him swim closer. The moonlight reflects off his tail, illuminating his face. "Damarian!" I call.

Mid-swim, his head springs up. He waves and swims faster. As soon as he reaches the shore, I grab his hands and pull him onto the sand. Then we fall into each other's arms.

His hand closes over the back of my neck and he pulls my mouth to his. Our lips open and close over each other's. Every inch of me is on fire. I crawl on top of him and press his body into the sand as my mouth devours his. I feel the stickiness of his tail beneath my legs, and that's when I'm yanked back to reality.

I climb off him and grab my bag. "I got a blanket to cover you." I move my head right and left, my eyes searching the area. No one's around. I unfold the blanket and throw it over him. Then I hand him a towel, take one for myself, and we get to work. I go under the blanket and wipe his tail. Damarian lifts the blanket and looks down at me. He smiles, and my heart swells.

When he seems mostly dry, I slide up his body and wrap my arms around him. "I want to comfort you during the change," I whisper.

His fingers brush through my hair. "You do not have to do so."

"I want to. It hurts me so much to see you in pain."

"It is all right. I have grown accustomed to the pain. It is more bearable now."

As soon as the words exit his mouth, his eyes roll back and he groans. His tail flaps around from underneath me. I clutch him tighter and rest my cheek against his. His whole body trembles.

He moans again, this one harsher than the last. I press my lips to his temple and murmur, "It's okay. You'll be okay."

"The...pain..." His eyes shut. "It is not any more bearable than in the past."

My heart cries. Everything he's doing—the agony—it's all for us.

For me. Guilt washes over me, almost knocking me to the ground. His lower lip quivers and sweat breaks out on his forehead. I brush some hair away from his head as I continue to whisper comforting words. After a few seconds, it's over.

I take a towel and dab at the sweat. Damarian looks up at me with weak, pained eyes. But then his lips pull into a smile. "Thank you."

I lie on him, feeling his chest rise and fall heavily. His hands are clamped into fists on the sand. I reach for one and flatten it out. He threads his fingers through mine. I'm very aware of his lack of clothes. He only has a towel wrapped around his waist. I swallow as heat rushes through my body.

He must feel a change in me because he touches my hair and says, "Cassie?"

"How do you do it?" I blurt. Then I mentally kick myself.

His hand stills. "Do what?"

My cheeks burn. Why did I even bring this up? "Well...you know..."

He brings his hand to my cheek and tilts my face so our eyes meet. "I am afraid I do not understand."

I puff out some air. I don't know why I'm embarrassed. I love this guy and feel like I can be totally open with him. But this topic has never been easy for me. I clear my throat and mutter, "Sex."

His eyebrows crease. "Sex?"

I stare at him. Wait a second. Is he trying to say he doesn't know what that is?

His eyebrows rise higher. "What is sex?"

I shift on his chest. I thought it would be years before I'd have the birds and the bees talk with someone. I clear my throat again. "So...um. Well, when two people want to have a baby..." Okay, this is really, *really*, awkward. "You guys do have babies, don't you?"

His eyebrows relax. "Are you referring to mating?"

"Oh, yeah!" I hit my head. "Of course. Mating."

"Certainly we mate," he says.

I think back to his tail. I'm pretty sure I didn't see anything there. "So how exactly...?"

Damarian laughs softly. "The scales move aside when the child of the sea is...excited."

I stare at him. Then I get it. "Oh. Yeah."

He laughs softly again. "Why do you ask?"

"No reason," I quickly say. "I guess that's one of those things a human might wonder about a merman..."

He leans in close and whispers in my ear. "I think about it."

My blood zooms through my veins. I become immobile.

"I wish to mate with you."

My heart is thumping so hard and fast, I think I might faint. My mind is spinning and I want to say so much. But I can't move my mouth.

Damarian takes hold of my waist and flips us over so that he's on top of me. His legs press down on me, but not too hard to hurt me. "As a human, I feel it more," he murmurs.

I don't feel anything, other than the heat pooling over me.

He grazes his finger across my cheek. "Have I upset you?"

I shake my head. "No...not at all," I breathe. "I'm finding it hard...to do anything."

"The emotions overwhelm you?"

I nod.

He gets to his knees and gathers me to his chest. He sweeps his hand under my knees and lifts me in his arms. He sits on the sand with me on his lap. "We cannot, Cassie."

"Why?" I whisper.

But I know why.

"I am not certain what...what shall be the result," he says.

I want to yell, "Nothing! Nothing will happen," but I know that's not true. He's not human. I'm not a fish. True he's a human now, but that's not who he really is. What if I get pregnant? Will she or he be a half fish?

"So what do we do?" I ask. But what I'm really asking is, "Is there a future for us?"

He doesn't say anything, just wraps his arms around me and holds me close. We sit like this for a long time, with Damarian occasionally skimming his lips across my cheek, my throat, my collarbone. My head snaps back and I moan. Maybe I don't need more. The passion and pleasure this merman gives me can satisfy me forever. It's enough to just be in his arms.

"My beautiful Cassie," he says against my neck.

Don't leave me. Please. Just don't ever, ever leave me.

"You are the light of my day. I did not know I could feel this way."

"Me, either." I rub his cheek. "I have such a hard time trusting people, Damarian. You changed that."

I rest my head on his shoulder and he lays his against mine. Our chests rise and fall in unison, our hearts beating as one.

The sky grows light. Damarian lifts his head. "Cassie."

He tries to pull away, but I grab him. "No. You can't go. Please."

"I do not wish to go." He buries his face in my neck. "How I wish I could take you with me."

Tears fill my eyes. I blink and they roll down.

Damarian wipes them away with his thumbs. "Do not fret, Cassie."

"It's not enough. I want to be with you. This isn't fair." I sob onto his shoulder. "It's not fair."

"The boat," he says. "Meet me in the ocean. Where we parted this morning."

I move back and look into his eyes. If we're as far away as possible from everyone, maybe we *can* meet. I touch his cheek. "It's so dangerous. I can't let you risk your life and expose yourself to the world. Your people won't be safe."

"I cannot lose you. Please. Meet me."

More tears splash down my cheeks and drip down my chin, onto my shirt. "After my surfing class. I promise."

He presses his cheek against mine. "We must part now before I am discovered."

My hands are wound tight around his middle. I can't let him go.

He kisses me. The warmth from his lips travels down my body, cooling the ice that's starting to form inside me. "It's so hard to see you go," I say.

"I know." He lifts my chin so we see eye to eye. "Walk with me to the sea?"

I nod.

Hand in hand, we head toward the shore. As soon as the tide hits Damarian's legs, he starts to shake. I give him a quick hug, then a slight push. He dives into the water. A few seconds later, he's deep in the ocean. I stand on my tippy toes and blow him a kiss. He raises his tail in the air and waves it around. Then it disappears into the water.

I walk home, fresh tears blurring my vision.

Chapter Seventeen

I stare at my reflection in the mirror. The blue bikini looks just as awkward on me as it did the last time I tried it on. Like it doesn't belong on my body. I grab my wetsuit and pull it over me.

Mom's lying on the living room couch, flipping through the TV channels with her feet propped on the coffee table. I take my surfboard. "What's the plan for today?" she asks.

I freeze in place and shut my eyes. Mom's dying to spend time with me. It feels like the tables have turned—that I'm the mom running off to live her life while the daughter stays at home, desperate for some bonding.

I turn around to face her.

She holds up her hands. "No, don't say anything. You're meeting Damian. You better run off, then."

"He lives far," I mumble. "Sorry, Mom."

"Nonsense." She waves her hand. "Go. Enjoy. I'm so happy to see you with a guy."

I shift from one foot to the other. "What about you?"

"Hmm?"

"When are you going to date again?"

She sighs. "When are you going to call your father?"

"Eventually…"

She purses her lips. "Life goes on, Cassie. Soon it might be too late. He'll devote himself to his new family. And one day, you'll wish you took the time to build a relationship with him."

I know she's right. Like Leah always says, there ain't no time like the present.

I move toward the door, clutching my surfboard. "I'm going to be late."

"Just a phone call, sweetie."

Letting out a breath, I nod and close my fingers over the doorknob, pulling it open. I head to the beach and start my class.

When it's over, I leave my board with Leah, who promises to take very good care of it. Then I make my way to the marina. When Ian sees me, he smiles and walks over. "Here to rent another boat?" he asks.

"Yep." I try to muster a smile, but I'm sure I fail. My nerves are driving me insane.

He helps me get settled and I start the engine. My heart pounds and my knees tremble. When I reach the place where Damarian and I departed yesterday morning, I kill the engine. Silence fills the area, except for the waves hitting the boat. I lean over the left side. I don't see anything but the beautiful ocean. Then I check the other side. Nothing. Leaning back in the boat, I cross my ankles. I rub my sweaty palms on my wetsuit. Then I uncross my ankles.

Something hits the back of the boat. I gasp and whip my head around. The sound continues toward the right side. A shark. Am I getting attacked by a shark?

Damarian's head pops up, and I fall back, knocking my elbow onto the side of the boat. His eyes widen in alarm. "Cassie."

I sit up, rubbing my arm. "You scared me."

"I apologize."

"It's okay." I move closer to him and rest my hand on his that's touching the boat. "How did you know it's me?"

"I know."

I stare down at him and he looks up at me. "How are you?" I ask.

"Magnificent, now that you are here."

I smile shyly, dropping my gaze.

"I know of a location," he says. "Where we will be alone. Follow me."

I start the engine and follow him deeper into the ocean. I scan the area to make sure no one is around. After a few minutes, Damarian stops before a sandbar. His webbed hands grab the side of the boat and his head pops up again. "Is it all right?"

"It's perfect."

I steer the boat to the sandbar and climb out. Damarian swims over, placing his hands on it. My legs dangle into the cool water. It feels good against my skin.

He runs his hand down my leg, sending chills up my body. He plays with my toes and grins. "They intrigue me."

"My toes?"

He nods. "The more I look at them, the more I find it peculiar to have fingers on your legs."

He's tickling me and I giggle.

He smiles. "I very much enjoy your smile."

"You're one of the only people who can make me smile for real."

My gaze skims down his body, from the top of his head, down his chest, to the scales I see through the water. Here, Damarian is in his natural environment. It's amazing.

I stand and unzip my wetsuit. Damarian's expression is surprised as I shimmy out of my suit and toss it into the boat. I'm left in my bikini. His eyes rove over every inch of me. I'm not used to having a guy study me when I'm half naked. I try not to flinch under his gaze.

"You are beautiful," he says.

My cheeks blaze.

I stand at the edge of the sandbar and jump into the ocean. The cold water pricks my skin. When my head breaks the surface, I find myself face to face with Damarian. I wrap my arms around his neck and my legs around his middle. "I've always dreamed of swimming with you in the ocean."

He nuzzles my nose. "As have I."

I feel the strength and power of his tail as he pumps it. His arms around me are so strong that I know I'll be safe in them.

The waves hit us, occasionally spraying salt water into my eyes and mouth. Damarian strokes the side of my head. Then he bends forward and slowly, so slowly, trails soft, warm kisses down my neck. My stomach muscles squeeze together and I moan. The water cools the heat crawling all over my body. I'm hot and I'm cold. My limbs are numb. If not for Damarian's arms holding me to his chest, I would drop right into the water.

His lips graze the top of my bikini. A hiss escapes my mouth. His mouth sends ripples of pleasure throughout my body. My arms and legs lose their energy, and I slide down his body, into the water. It jolts me awake and I thrash around.

Damarian tugs me to his chest, wrapping his arm around my waist. "I very much enjoy the way you react when my lips touch your body," he whispers.

My blood pounds. My legs are too weak, and it's hard for me to tread in the water. Damarian tightens his hold on me.

"You turn me into jello," I rasp.

His lips rub against my jaw. "I do not know what that is."

He puts his hand under my knees and lifts me in his arms. Then he swims with me to the sandbar and sits me down so that my legs hang in the water. He rests his hands on either side of my waist. It burns there.

I open my mouth, but snap it shut when I see something in the ocean. My head is still fuzzy, so it takes a few seconds until it clicks in my head.

A gray fin.

"Shark!" I scamper to my feet. "Damarian, a shark!"

His head twists toward the direction of the shark. I expect him to swim away—after all, he's half human, and sharks eat humans. But instead of getting as far away as possible from the creature that can sever his arm with just one bite, he swims *toward* it.

"Damarian!" I yell.

When he's a few feet away, Damarian stretches his hand toward the shark and pats the top of its head. I see now that it's a great white, but small. Maybe a baby.

They float together like that, with Damarian's hand on its head, his eyebrows furrowed in concentration. The last time I saw him do that was when we were at the pet shop and he spoke to the fish.

He's talking to the shark.

After a minute or two, they swim toward me. No, no, no. I stumble back as far as I can, but the sandbar isn't that big.

"Cassie," Damarian says, gesturing to the shark. "This is Fiske."

I just stare at him, dumbfounded.

The shark bobs its head. *Bobs.* I've seen enough movies to know that animal is *not* my friend.

Damarian holds out his hand toward me. "Do not be alarmed. Fiske will not hurt you."

I hug my upper arms and shake my head. When I was a kid and just learned to surf, I heard of a horror story about a kid who got attacked

162

by a shark. He lost his leg.

Damarian's gaze is on the shark. Then he brings it to me. "Fiske is intrigued by you."

"Are you sure he doesn't want to eat me?"

His lips form a straight line. "It is his nature, Cassie. But he will not hurt you."

"I don't get it. Shouldn't he eat you? You're half human."

He shakes his head. "Sharks are our sworn protectors."

I raise an eyebrow. "They protect you?"

"Yes. Every clan is protected by a species of shark. The great white sharks guard the Sapphires. Hammerheads protect the Violets. Blue sharks protect the Diamonds. Tiger sharks protect the Emeralds. Bull sharks protect the Rubies."

Again, I stare at him at a loss of words.

"When humans swim too close to our colonies, our sharks eliminate them."

I gape at him. "*Eliminate?*"

He shrugs helplessly. "It is their nature, Cassie."

I hug myself tighter. This…I don't know what to make of it. I should be scared shitless—it's a freakin' shark. But Damarian's chasing away a lot of that fear.

"You may touch him, if you would like," he says.

I think I'd rather not.

"Do you not trust me?"

My arms fall to my sides. "Of course I trust you. But—"

"Then come." He holds out his hand. "Please."

I eye it. What if this is some ploy to feed this shark dinner? I shake my head. Damarian wouldn't do that. Right?

"I will hold you, if that eases your mind."

I let out a breath. I trust Damarian. He won't feed me to this shark.

This actually is pretty cool, to get this close to a shark. I could never experience this anywhere else.

I get down on my bottom and slowly slide into the ocean. Damarian's arm comes around me. He hauls me to his chest. "I wish for you to be a part of my world," he says softly. "Fiske is not like others of his kind. He will not attack you."

I look at the shark. It's just floating there, its eyes on me. I don't know if it looks like it wants to eat me, because I don't know sharks' expressions. But he doesn't seem hostile.

Damarian slowly swims closer to the shark. He takes my hand and extends it toward the shark. "If he attacks you," he says into my ear. "He will attack me as well."

The shark doesn't move as our hands edge closer to him. When they're only a few inches away, my hand curls into a fist. Damarian flattens it out and brings our hands to the top of the shark's head. It feels rough, like sandpaper.

The shark inclines its head as though it's accepting my touch. Then it swims around, circling us. After a few seconds, I feel it nudge my side, and I yelp. Damarian chuckles. "He wishes to play with you."

This is insane. I'm swimming right next to a shark.

"Are you frightened?" Damarian asks.

"Mhm…"

"He will not hurt you."

"Why is that?" I glance at the shark, who's just floating there, staring at me, then back at Damarian. "Why doesn't he want to eat me?"

He shrugs. "I do not know. Fiske wishes not to harm humans."

I reach my hand toward it. It rushes to meet me, knocking its head into me. Then it falters back, like it's sorry. I find myself laughing. Damarian smiles.

"Come." Damarian grabs onto its fin. "Take hold of Fiske."

I must be losing it. I do as he says, and the next second, the three of us are swimming together. The shark's not moving very fast, but it's fast enough to give me a thrill. We first swim above water, but then we slowly dip inside. I quickly breathe in a gulp of air. My eyes open in the water, but I can't see much.

We break the surface, and the shark continues to swim. I love this feeling. Sailing through the peaceful ocean, the wind blowing in my hair, the salt water touching my lips.

When we stop at the sandbar, I say, "That was amazing." Fiske inclines its head again. I laugh and tap it. "Thanks. You're a cutie."

Damarian touches the top of Fiske's head and looks into its eyes. A few seconds later, he turns around and swims away. Damarian tows me toward his chest. "Did you enjoy that?"

"Yeah. Thanks so much." I lock my arms around his neck.

His lips sweep under my ear. "You are very welcome."

I wrap my legs around his torso and gaze into his eyes. "Damarian."

"Cassie."

"I really love you."

He caresses my cheek. "And I love you."

I unhook my legs from around him and swim toward the sandbar. I hear him follow. I heave myself onto it and hug my knees to my chest.

His hands enclose over my ankles. "Are you all right?"

I rest my cheek on my knees. "I've never felt this way about anyone. It really scares me."

His hands slide up and down my legs. A spark goes through my body. "What frightens you?" he asks.

"I don't know what's wrong with me. I guess ever since my dad cheated on my mom and left us, I find it hard to trust people.

Especially men."

He nods slowly. "I understand. Do you trust me?"

I nod. "I've never trusted anyone like I trust you. Except for my mom and Leah."

He massages both my feet. "Do you not speak with your father?"

I shake my head.

"Why?"

Tears gather in my eyes. I usually don't get too emotional when I discuss my dad, but it's different with Damarian. Because I know he truly cares. "I'm just scared," I whisper.

He takes hold of my waist and gently pulls me off the sandbar, into the ocean. Into his arms. I smash my face into his chest, mixing my salty tears with the salt water of the ocean. "It is all right," he says tenderly.

"That's what it comes down to," I say into his chest. "I'm just afraid of getting hurt."

His hand traces circles on my back. "It is all right to be afraid."

I know. But sooner or later, we need to face our fears. I don't know when I'll be ready.

"Do you wish to speak to your father?" he asks, his lips skimming across my ear.

"Yeah. I'm just scared to."

"I understand." He tucks his finger under my chin and lifts my face toward his. "I can be with you, if you would like."

That's so sweet of him. "Thanks. Maybe you can sit with me when I call him?"

He cups my cheek. "Of course."

I'll call him when my mom leaves and Damarian can stay over again.

I hike my legs up his body and wrap them around his waist. "What about you?"

"Yes?"

"You and your dad. Have you guys been arguing? You spend more time at home now."

"Yes," he mutters, his gaze staring off in the distance. "We quarrel often."

I already know that, but I wish he'd expand and tell me *what* they fight about, how he feels about it. But I know this is a topic he doesn't like to talk about. Maybe he needs time. I can give him that.

"Oh, I almost forgot!" I swim back toward the boat and reach for my bag. "I brought you a present."

When I produce a bag of gummy worms, Damarian laughs. "I have missed them." He takes three and dumps them in his mouth. His eyes crinkle as he smiles. "Why do you have such a love for these worms?"

I take a worm and bite off its head. "They remind me of my childhood."

"How so?"

"Well, my dad used to take me fishing when I was a kid. I didn't squirm like the other girls when I had to put the bait on the hook." I shrug like I don't care, but a lump forms in my throat. "My dad nicknamed me 'Cass Bass.' The day after our first fishing trip, he took me to a candy store and bought me a jar of gummy worms." I finger the worm in my hand. "I was really happy back then."

He holds my hand. "Are you happy now?"

"Very much."

Damarian plucks a worm out of the bag and dangles it in front of my mouth. I laugh before opening my mouth. He sticks it inside, and I bite into it. Then he pulls it out while my teeth are still lodged on it. The poor worm is sliced in half.

"You murderer," I tease.

167

"*I* the murderer? I believe you have eaten his head."

I laugh again and punch his shoulder. He spins around in the ocean, splashing water everywhere. I push away and splash him. His expression is surprised. "You have splashed me."

"Don't act so surprised. We humans know how to have fun in the water, too."

"You cannot outswim me," he says, a challenge gleaming in his eyes.

I snort. "Sure, I can." Even though I know that's sure as hell not true.

"If I catch you, I will lay you on the land and kiss you until your body cannot withstand it."

My stomach flutters. I feel it all the way in my toes. "And if you don't catch me?"

He grins. "I shall."

"Cocky, just like a human guy. Okay, fine. Are you ready?"

"Yes."

I count to three, then zoom off. Two seconds later, arms wrap around my waist and haul me back, until I hit his chest. His lips tickle my ear. "I win. Now for your reward."

He brings me back to the sandbar and does just as he promised.

Chapter Eighteen

When I get home five hours later, I find Mom packing her bag in her room.

I step inside. "Mom?"

Her head springs up. She gives me an apologetic smile. "Hey."

I sit down on the edge of her bed. "Didn't you say you're staying for a week?"

She takes a shoe and lays it in her suitcase. "I was so worried about you. Uncle Jim called to tell me how upset you were when I left for Philadelphia. As soon as I was able to, I hurried back." She picks a loose strand of hair off my forehead. "But I see you're okay. You're not lonely."

I'm at a loss for words. When she left two weeks ago, I felt abandoned, betrayed, alone. But I don't feel that way anymore. Not since I met Damarian. "I guess I don't need you as much as I thought I did. I mean, of course I *need* you, but—"

Mom squeezes my knee. "You're growing up, sweetie. You're learning about yourself and the world around you. You're learning about love."

I stare down at my lap. "I'm sorry. I made you drop everything and come home."

"No. I didn't drop everything. I know I haven't always been there for you when you were growing up. I want to fix that. But that doesn't mean you can't start your own life. There will be plenty of time to spend together. You'll be going off to college soon, and then you'll move away and start a career. Maybe get married. We'll still be close."

I lay my head on her shoulder. "It's time for you to start living your life, too. Meet guys, Mom. Have fun."

She laughs. "Okay, okay. I promise I will try to meet a guy in New York."

"New York? Cool. How long this time?"

She plays with my hair. "I'm not sure. But you can visit if you want. I'll be getting an apartment there."

I raise my head. "That long?"

She bites down on her bottom lip. "It's a possibility."

I smile. "I'm happy for you. You're finally living the life you've always dreamed of. Now all you need is a man."

She bursts out laughing. "Did you spend the evening with Damian?"

My cheeks heat up. "Maybe…"

She laughs again. "Without me around, he'll be living here?"

I swallow. "Is that a problem?"

"Just as long as you're being responsible."

I nod, my cheeks growing warmer.

"Call whenever you need me."

I smile again. Part of growing up is accepting change. Mom spent the last eighteen years of her life taking care of me. I'm an adult now and can take care of myself. Embarking down that road is very scary, but that's part of life. It's Mom's turn to take care of herself.

"Just buy me a really good gift from New York," I tell her.

She laughs and kisses my forehead.

Merman's Kiss

***

Damarian stares down at me with something shining in his eyes. Love. He tucks a strand of my hair behind my ear. I can't describe how happy I am to have him here with me—to have him lying in my bed. With Mom's plan to stay in New York for a while, Damarian and I have all the time in the world to spend every second together.

He ducks his head and traces his lips from under my chin to my collarbone. His hands explore every inch of my body while mine trek over his. They slide up his chest and hook around his neck. I inhale his unique Damarian scent. "I wish I could get even closer to you," I whisper.

His lips meet mine, then go upward, to my nose, my forehead, and then back to my lips. "We cannot, Cassie. As much as it pains me, and as much as I yearn to, we cannot."

Tears of frustration and disappointment stab my eyes. He notices, because he kisses the tips of them. "Please do not be upset." His mouth moves to my ear. "Children of the sea mate for life."

As his lips brush the bottom of my neck, I finally understand what he's trying to say. Why he and I could never take our relationship to the next level. Because merpeople mate for life. If he and I "mate" and break up, Damarian will be stuck. He'll never move on.

"I understand," I tell him, trying to hide how hurt I feel. When I see how hurt *he* is, the guilt on his face, that he wants it just as much as I do, I rest my lips against his, letting him know it's okay. Things are never this simple. We don't always get what we want, do we? That's what Mom's always told me.

"Forgive me, Cassie." He lowers his head a bit, causing his hair to fall into his eyes.

I push it away and put on a smile. "It's okay." I hold either side of his face and look into his eyes. "It's enough that we're together, that we're in each other's arms. We both know how easily we can lose that."

My words cause his face to relax and brighten. He lies down and lays me on top of him, running his hand up and down my back. "When I am in the sea," he says, his breath tickling my cheek. "I think of nothing but you. I have difficulty eating. I do not sleep. You are constantly on my mind."

I love how he whispers romantic things in my ear. When I was a teenager and fantasized about having a boyfriend, I imagined him being a sweet, kind guy who'd whisper romantic things as we cuddled together. Kyle is definitely not a romantic guy, so I figured the guy of my dreams was just that—in my dreams. But as Damarian continues to whisper and make me feel things I didn't think I would ever feel, I realize dreams *can* come true.

But a little voice in the back of my head starts to talk. It warns me that I'm making myself too vulnerable to this guy who isn't even a guy. It tells me to be practical, that I'm living in a love bubble, and that I'll have to face the reality soon. That the bubble will burst and so will my heart, and that I will get hurt in a way I've never been hurt before.

I look at Damarian. I see the love he has for me gleaming in his eyes. I feel the love he has for me as his lips swallow mine, as they make their way down my throat, sending pulses throughout my body.

And I know that voice is just my insecure self trying to resurface.

***

I finger my cell phone, my heart pounding. All I need to do is press a button—that's all. But it feels like this button is a detonator for a bomb. A bomb in my heart.

Damarian wraps his arms around my stomach and kisses my temple. I'm lying on him on the living room couch. Being in his arms makes me feel protected and like I can take on the world. But it doesn't provide me with the strength to call my dad.

"Your father cares deeply for you," he says.

I know. At least, that's what Mom's been telling me. And deep down, I know it's true.

"If all fails," Damarian continues, "I am here. I will never hurt you."

I twist my head back. "Do you promise?"

His lips touch mine. "I promise."

I inhale a large gulp of air, then let it out slowly. Damarian tightens his hold on me and lightly coats my face with kisses.

I press the "call" button.

After two rings, a male voice answers. "Hello?"

I freeze. That voice. It hasn't changed. It's the strong, masculine voice I've always distinguished as my dad's. As familiar as it sounds, it only makes me feel more distant from him.

Damarian says softly, "Cassie."

I clear my throat. "Hi, uh, Dad." That word rolling off my lips doesn't sound like it belongs to me.

I hear him intake a breath. He pauses. Then movement, like he grabbed a pen or something to play with. "Cassie?" he finally asks.

My lower lip trembles, a sign that if I don't get hold of my emotions, I'll turn into a human fountain. I close my eyes and regulate my breathing, taking control of my emotions. He's just my dad, the guy who donated his sperm to create me. That's all. "Yeah," I say, my voice shaky. "It's me…Cassie."

Another pause. My heart rate speeds up. He's mad I called, that I disturbed his new, perfect life. I should hang up.

"I'm so glad you called, Cass Bass."

At the sound of my nickname, I feel my eyes tear up. "You are?"

"Yes. I've wanted to talk to you for so long."

I didn't know that. I thought it was a recent thing, a result of his mid-life crisis or something. "You have?" I ask.

"Yeah. I guess I was too…scared." He laughs like he's embarrassed. "Scared of my teenage daughter."

I don't know what to say. I never expected to hear this.

"I'm so sorry I left you, sweetie. I…" His voice cracks. "That's the biggest regret of my life."

Tears pour out of my eyes. Damarian reaches for a tissue from the coffee table and hands it to me. I give him a thankful smile. "Why did you leave me?" I ask.

He sighs, although it trembles, probably because of his tears. "I was in a bad place. My job, your mom. I…" He sighs again. "Can we meet and talk?"

I freeze again. I thought this conversation would go south, that I'd spend the rest of the day sobbing all over Damarian and drenching his shirt while gorging on gummy worms and ice cream. But my dad wants to *meet* with me. I'm so thrown off.

I glance at Damarian. He nods encouragingly.

"I…" My voice is hoarse. "I guess I'd like that."

"That's great." The relief in his voice is profound. I never imagined how scared he'd be. I guess I wasn't the only one wanting to rebuild our relationship but terrified to actually do it. "Can we meet for coffee? I have a meeting that will take up the whole morning, but after that I'm free."

A meeting? Growing up, my dad was a fisherman. I knew it didn't bring us a lot of money, because Mom and Dad constantly fought over that. Hearing he's most likely an executive in an office makes me feel more at ease. Because he turned his life around. Maybe it's about time I be a part of it.

"Coffee sounds good," I say.

"Great." His voice is even more relieved. "I'll text you the address of the café."

"Okay."

"Bye, Cassie. And thanks so much for calling."

I hang up, completely dumbfounded. I sit still, staring at nothing in front of me, the conversation replaying in my head. It's not until Damarian shifts in his seat that I snap out of it.

My hands shake a bit. He lowers his on them. "How do you feel?" he asks.

My heart is still beating fast and my palms are a little sweaty, but overall..."I feel really good."

He smiles. "I am glad. I feel proud of you. I understand it was not easy."

I rest my head on his shoulder. "No, it wasn't. But it's just about to get harder. I'm meeting him for coffee."

He lays his head on mine. "It will go well. I believe in you. If you would like me to accompany you, I would love to."

"Thanks." I reach to kiss him. "You're amazing."

***

Leaving Damarian in the car, I enter the café. It's practically empty. The only customers inside are a young couple—probably newlyweds, since they have that honeymoon glow—and a middle-aged man wearing a plaid shirt and dark pants. His hair is graying at his sides.

My dad.

He looks just as I remember him. A few years older, though. But he's still the same. He's got my nose and my lips, and some people say my ears, although I refuse to believe that, since his are large and stick out of his face. I searched him online a few years ago out of curiosity and was glad to discover he still looked the same as when I was a kid. I worried he changed his look because he hated the man he used to be, the man that used to be my father.

I muster my courage and head toward his table. He's drinking a cup of coffee as he scrolls through his phone. As I get closer, he raises his eyes. He stares at me.

I stare back.

He gathers himself and clumsily gets to his feet. "Cassie." Before I can blink, I'm in his arms. His scent enters my nose, the same scent I remember growing up. His favorite cologne.

He steps back and studies me. "You've grown into such a beautiful young woman."

It's the typical thing a man in this situation would say to his estranged teenage daughter. But still, it fills my heart and makes me feel good. "Thanks."

He gestures to the table. "Please sit down. I already ordered my coffee."

We sit down and he calls for a waiter. My stomach buzzes with nerves, and I'm not sure I could put anything in my mouth. I order a glass of water.

We're quiet for the first few moments. Dad has his eyes on me, but I have trouble looking at him. I knew the meeting would be awkward, but it's *really* awkward.

"How's your mom?" he asks.

"Fine. She's in New York."

He nods. "I'm glad to see that she's happy."

I nod.

Quiet again. Dad leans back. Then he leans forward. Then back again.

I trace the wooden table with my finger. I'm bursting with questions, but I'm not sure it's the appropriate time to ask them.

"I heard you're going to school in Texas," he says.

I've been contemplating applying to the community college here so

I can stay close to the ocean—close to Damarian. But nothing's final yet, so I just say, "Yeah."

"I'm very proud of you."

Small talk sucks. "Why did you leave?" I ask.

His expression changes from cheerful to anxious. He must not have been anticipating me asking this question right off the bat.

He rubs his hand down his face. "Business was bad," he says. "I was stressed. I know that's not an excuse."

I bite down on my lip. I'm not sure I want to hear this, but I know I need to. It's the only way I can forgive my dad and get past this.

After I nod for him to continue, Dad says, "We were having problems before that. I said one thing. Your mom said the opposite. We never were able to compromise." He shakes his head and sighs. "We got married too young. We grew apart. When I met Sheila, I started being happy again."

"You left me," I say, trying to keep my voice from shouting accusations, but I fail. "I get why you and Mom split up, but I was your daughter."

I see the regret on his face. This man's not putting up a show. He places his hands on the table and staples his fingers. "I know." He shrugs like he has no excuses. "It was a big mistake. I admit that. But I'm willing to fix it. Whatever I can do." He slowly reaches out his hand and lowers it on mine. "I want to start fresh. Do you think you can forgive me?"

It's so easy to say no. To throw this man out of my life and pretend he never existed. It would make me forget about all the hurt. Reject *him* before he can reject me again. But I don't want to do that. He made a mistake. Yeah, it sucked and screwed me up, but the important thing is that he's trying to make amends.

I slide my hand away. "Maybe. I don't know."

He tries to mask his disappointment, but I see his face fall. "I'm glad you're being honest."

"I need time. Maybe after a while, I can learn to trust you again."

He nods, smiling a little. "That's more than I hoped for."

I raise an eyebrow. "What did you hope for?"

"That you'd actually show up at the café."

I find myself laughing. His face relaxes and he laughs, too.

"I'm willing to try," I tell him. "It'll take some time, but maybe we'll get there."

The waitress arrives with my water. I take a sip, then get to my feet. "Thanks for opening the door. I'm grateful you're trying to make me part of your life."

He stands up, too, and hugs me. "Maybe we can meet up some time later this week."

I nod. "I'd like that."

"Maybe go fishing like we used to."

"Yeah, maybe."

He hesitantly kisses my cheek. "See you around, Cass Bass."

"See you around…Dad."

I leave the café and head toward the parking lot. Damarian is sitting in the passenger seat. When he sees me approach, he waves and opens the door for me. I slide inside. I'm not sure what expression I'm wearing on my face, but if it matches what I'm feeling inside, I look confused, comforted, relieved, and happy.

"I gather the meeting with your father went well?" he asks.

A smile creeps onto my face. "Yeah. It went well. Better than I expected."

He rests his hand on mine. "I am glad."

"Me, too."

"Do you want discuss it?"

"I want to spend some time with you."

He laughs. "All right."

"Seafood restaurant?"

"Perhaps we shall taste that 'pizza' you constantly speak of?"

"You're gonna love it." I start the engine. "After one bite of pizza, you won't want to ever step foot in the ocean again."

"I feel that way when I am with you."

Our gazes lock. We bend forward and touch our lips. "Same with me."

Chapter Nineteen

Damarian springs up with such a force I nearly roll off the bed. I rub the sleep out of my eyes. "What's wrong?"

He stares at the door. "It cannot be."

"Damarian?"

He blinks and his eyes snap to mine. "We must dress."

He gets up, and I follow him. The expression on his face—it's a mixture of shock, fear, confusion, and worry. He's scaring me.

We get dressed. He takes my hand and we climb down the stairs. Damarian walks over to the door and just gazes at it. I step forward, reaching for his hand, but his fingers start opening the locks. After taking a deep breath, he opens the door.

Two people stand there. A guy and a girl. They have golden hair and striking dark blue eyes. Identical to Damarian's. They're beautiful, with translucent skin and broad shoulders.

Damarian's brother and sister.

The girl's wearing a male's plaid shirt the wrong way and a male's trunks. The guy has jeans on and no shirt. The muscles on his chest would make any girl melt at his feet.

"Kiander," Damarian says, his voice laced with shock. "Doria."

He ushers them inside and quickly shuts the door. I gape at them.

Mermaids. Well, a mermaid and a merman. Three merpeople in my house.

Doria looks at me with hostile eyes. Kiander's eyes aren't friendly, but I don't feel like I need to run as I do with his sister.

"Who is this, Damarian?" she demands.

It feels like a chunk of sand is lodged in my throat. I swallow a few times, but my throat is as dry at the beach on a scorching day.

Damarian comes to stand near me, wrapping his arm around my waist. Doria's face fills with disappointment and rage. "I cannot believe this! *She* is the reason you have not been home? All this time you have been living on *land*? As a *human*?" She says the last bit with such disgust that for a second I'm ashamed to be a human.

My eyes slowly move to Damarian. He hasn't been going home? Where has he been all this time when he returned to the ocean?

Kiander steps forward and holds his hands up, as if making peace between the two of them. "Remain calm, Doria."

"Father is most upset," she mutters. Her gaze flashes to Damarian. "King Palaemon—"

"I understand," Damarian says.

Her eyes narrow. "No, you do not understand! Father is upset that you have fled."

"I did not flee," he mumbles.

"Have you not?" She looks at me. "A human," she scoffs.

"Doria," Kiander warns.

"How have you located me?" Damarian asks.

Doria folds her arms. "Did you not wish to be located?"

"We have sensed you," Kiander explains. "We worried you had been injured."

"You must come home at once," Doria says. "Do not waste your time with a human."

Ouch. Okay, I definitely do not like Doria.

"I promise I shall return home tonight," Damarian says.

"Tonight? The ceremony—"

"Tonight," Damarian stresses with a finality in his tone. Doria purses her lips.

Kiander turns toward the door. "We shall take our leave now."

"You cannot," Damarian says. "You must wait for nightfall, when the humans are asleep."

Doria's hands drop down to her sides. She fists them. "I do not wish to wait until nightfall."

Damarian glares at her. She glares back.

"We can use a boat," I offer.

Doria now gives me the death glare, like I'm forbidden to talk. I try not to shrivel under her gaze, but I've never been good with confrontations.

"We can," Damarian agrees. He nods to me and takes my hand. I feel the disapproval leaping off his sister. I ignore it as I grab my bag and lead the three of them to the marina. People stare at us as we pass. They look mesmerized at the three beauties. When we approach Ian, his eyebrows skyrocket. I push the unease out of my mind.

He grins. "Another boat, I gather?"

I nod. Doria is glaring at him while Kiander's face is emotionless. Damarian's is tense. The "what the hell?" look is evident on Ian's face.

We head to the boat. After Damarian helps his brother and sister inside, the two of us settle in. I start the engine. The boat is quiet, save for the sounds of the ocean. All three merpeople gaze at the ocean, their lifeline.

When we reach the sandbar, I kill the engine. Damarian nods to his siblings, and the two of them dive into the ocean. I watch, amazed, as their clothes tear into shreds and identical sapphire crystal tails spring up in the air. Doria's head and the top of her torso pop up. Sapphire crystals—just like the ones on her tail—splatter her chest. It seems like they trail down to her tail. Kiander's head breaks the surface. The sun beats down on them, causing their hair to look more golden.

"Return with us," Doria calls.

I glance at Damarian. His eyes meet mine. I notice he has an internal battle going on. He knows the right thing to do is go back with his siblings. To talk to his father. But I know how much he wants to say with me.

"Go," I tell him.

He locks his fingers through mine and brings the palm of my hand to his lips. "I do not wish to go."

"You'll come back."

He doesn't say anything.

I touch his arm. "If you go, you won't come back?" I ask. His eyes shut tight. Tears fill my eyes. "Damarian…"

He opens his eyes and faces his siblings. "I shall return tonight."

Kiander nods while Doria's lips are pulled into a firm line. Damarian waves. "I assure you, I shall return."

Kiander turns around and dives into the ocean. Doria keeps her gaze on us for a few seconds before following her brother. After a bit, the splashing stops and the water stills. The area grows silent. I can't bring my eyes to him. I don't want to face any of this. That bubble I talked about? I think it's about to burst.

"Cassie," he says, touching my knee.

I pull my leg away. "You lied to me. You haven't been going home."

The guilt on his face makes it hard to be mad at him. But the one thing that really causes me to lose trust in a person is when he lies to me. The fact that Damarian did makes my chest slice open and my heart plummet to the bottom of the boat. Tears threaten my eyes, but I force them away.

"I did not lie to you, Cassie," he says softly, this time reaching for my hand. I pull it away, too. "I do not feel happy at home. That is the reason I have not returned."

"For how long? Since the beginning?"

He shakes his head. "Since the day your mother returned."

"Why didn't you tell me?"

His gaze falls to his hands before creeping back to me. "I do not wish to discuss unpleasant things with you."

"Why not?"

"I wish only to make you happy."

The anger seeps out of me and is replaced with understanding. Damarian's not keeping me in the dark. He just doesn't want to drag me into the crappy parts of his life. I cover his hand with mine. "But I want to talk about the unpleasant things in your life. That's what makes me happy—to be able to talk about your problems and help you get through them."

His eyes drop back to his hands. They stay there for a bit, like he's contemplating my words. They then trek to mine. "Yes, you are correct. However…" His voice trails off.

"What is it?" I ask.

He shakes his head.

"Please, Damarian. You can talk to me."

He takes in a sharp breath. "I am a disappointment."

"Who says that?"

"Father."

I reach up and push some hair out of his eyes. "Why does he say that?"

He shifts in the boat, clearly uncomfortable. I squeeze his hand reassuringly. "Father does not approve of my lack of maturity."

My eyebrows shoot up. Compared to many guys his age, he's *very* mature. "Why does he think that?"

"The day I returned home—after our first encounter—I played squid wars with Zarya, Syd, and Syndin."

"Squid wars?"

"It is a game we play. Zarya and I were partners. The twins were partners. We each held a squid and he who shot ink at the opponent first was rewarded a point."

I nod. Squid wars sound just like paintball. It's crazy how our species are so similar. "What happened?" I ask.

"The twins were winning. Zarya was most upset. She is not one to accept defeat easily." The corners of his mouth lift a little. "As twins, Syd and Syndin possess a special connection, one I do not share with Zarya, despite how attached we are." He looks down to his lap, then at me. "Father was furious. He does not approve of my playing with the little ones. He wishes for me to be mature. To find a mate."

My heart collapses. "Find a mate?"

He nods, his eyes pained. "I am the eldest. I must set an example for the others."

"What do you mean by set an example? It's not like your siblings are going to run off with humans. What's your dad worried about?"

Damarian shrugs. "This is our life. We are born, we grow up, we mate, we produce offspring."

To ensure the survival of their species. Like any specie, they could become extinct. I'm guessing there aren't that many of them.

I place my other hand on top of ours. "I get it. Whether you're a human or a merman, parents just don't get their kids."

Damarian nods. "I understand Father wishes only the best for me. But I do not wish to mate and have fry. I wish to explore the ocean and learn."

I rub his hand.

"I do not enjoy the manner in which Father behaves toward me. As if I am a failure."

I reach for him and gather him in my arms. Damarian buries his head between my neck and shoulder. "When I met you, Cassie, I did not know such a sweet being could exist." His lips press down on my skin. "I worried at first and returned to my family. Father was upset and wished to know my whereabouts, but I concealed the truth. When I returned the next time, Father was furious and once again wished to know my whereabouts. I claimed I visited my companions in the Ruby colony. We quarreled. I decided not to return home. It was difficult to part with Zarya, but my choice was final."

He sniffs, which means he's crying. I hold him tight against me. "What about your mom?"

"Mother tells Father that I have time. He does not listen to her." He lifts his head and runs the back of his hand across his eyes. "Please, Cassie. I do not wish to discuss this further."

The pain in his voice is overwhelming. Biting my lip, I nod and change the subject. "Was it dangerous living away from the colony?"

"Fiske has protected me."

I now have much more appreciation for that baby great white shark.

Damarian stays in my arms for some time. The clouds move aside and the sun peeks out, bathing us in its heat. Damarian will need to be in seawater soon.

"I suppose I am to return to the sea tonight," he says, his lips grazing my throat. "I must speak with Father."

I brush my hand through his hair. "I wish I could come with you. Just like you came with me."

He raises his hand, leans forward, and gives me the most intense kiss he's ever given me. Everything he's feeling comes through this kiss. His frustration, fear, desperation for his father's acceptance, the love he feels for me. I fall back as his lips rove over mine, sucking and swallowing, sending jolts throughout my body.

I fall flat against the bottom of the boat as our hands roam over each other's bodies, claiming one another as our own. His hands slide down my thighs and his fingers dig into them. His name escapes through my lips and my back arches. "I want you," I rasp. Our mouths slide over each other in unison and our bodies rock in the same motion. It's as if our souls are connected. Damarian softly bites on my bottom lip as my nails dig into his back.

He sits up and runs his fingers through his hair. "How easy it is to lose myself in you."

My chest rises and falls speedily. I raise weak, shaky hands to the sides of the boat and lift myself. Damarian pecks my forehead. I want to ask him why he doesn't want to lose himself in me. That's what I want—desperately. I don't want anyone other than him, and I'm pretty sure I will never want anyone but him. My heart cries for him to lose himself in me so that we could be mated for life, and that nothing, absolutely nothing, would keep us apart.

He touches the side of his head. "I feel a bit ill."

I'm about to start the engine to take him home to my pool, but then I remember we're in the middle of the ocean. "Jump inside and swim around for a bit."

He nods and stands, staring down at the water. "How am I to return to a human?"

He has a point. Getting him dry won't be easy. I'd have to help him onto the boat or sandbar. "Maybe you should go home now and we can meet tonight."

He sits down and shakes his head. "I do not wish to return now. I wish to be with you."

"Are you sure?"

"Yes."

"Can you hold off until we get to my pool?"

He nods.

I start the engine.

Chapter Twenty

After Damarian goes for a swim, we head to the theater to catch the latest sci-fi movie. He's really into them. We share popcorn, our hands touching a few times. A spark travels from the tips of my fingers, up my arms, and into my chest. A few couples make out as the movie runs, but we don't copy them. Damarian's concentrating hard on the movie. I know he's trying to distract himself. I know he wants to get closer to me, but it's not so simple for him. Sex is a big, big deal for humans, too, but it's like a binding contract in his world. One he can never take back.

I wish he were willing and ready to go down that road with me. But maybe he needs time. Maybe once we spend more time together, once we declare ourselves lovers for life, he'd be willing to take that step. I'll wait an eternity. Okay, maybe not that long, but I'll give him as long as he needs.

When the movie's over, Damarian sits back in his seat and smiles at me. "I very much enjoyed that."

I smile.

We stop at a fast food restaurant and order burgers and fries. Damarian's never tasted anything like this before. We settle down on my couch with our food and watch TV.

He munches on his burger. "This is delicious."

"Mmm."

Sometime during the show, we end up in each other's arms. Everything around me disappears as I lose myself in his kisses and caresses.

***

"Cassie."

Damarian's shaking me. I open my eyes and find him staring at me. "I must return to the sea. Are we too late?"

I moan, stretch, and check the time. It's nearly three AM. "We need to move."

The TV is still on. After I turn it off, we head for the beach. I feel myself pout. I don't want Damarian to leave, but that's so selfish of me. He hasn't seen his family in days. He must miss them terribly. He's prepared to talk to his dad. I can't keep him locked in my bubble forever.

When we reach the beach, Damarian takes my hand and drops to the sand, taking me with him. I cross my legs. He catches a strand of my hair that's blowing in the warm wind and twists it between his fingers. He doesn't say anything, but I can read it on his face.

Tears clog my throat. "You won't be back?"

He flattens his palm against my cheek. "Of course I shall return."

I swallow the wave of tears. "What if your father doesn't let you? What if...he pressures you to find a girl...?"

He shakes his head. "You are the only girl for me."

I put my hand on his that's resting on my cheek. "Then prove it. Get closer to me."

He pulls me into his arms. I shift until I'm on his lap and I wrap my legs around his waist. "How I wish," he murmurs against my ear. "That is what I desire most, Cassie."

Numbness travels to every one of my limbs. I squeeze closer to him.

"I do not wish to harm you, my love."

"You won't," I say.

His hands wrap around my waist and dig into me as he closes his mouth over mine. Then they move down my thighs.

"Please?" I ask.

He gently lifts me off him and lies me down on the sand. Crawling on top of me, he lowers his lips to my ear. "It pains me to refuse you." His fingers stroke my cheek. "I wish only to make you happy."

"Then tell me why we can't. Please."

His lips trail down my cheek. "I am not certain of the result. I would die if something were to befall you."

Something like what? I don't understand.

"I apologize, Cassie, but I must return to the sea."

I grab his shoulders. "Don't leave me, please."

He twirls my hair around his index finger. "I shall return. I promise we will be together shortly."

"When?"

"Tomorrow night."

He presses his lips to mine before lifting me to my feet and raising me off the ground. He hugs me close.

"Farewell, Cassie." He kisses his fingers and places them on my mouth. Then he runs toward the ocean and dives in.

I turn away just as he disappears into the waves.

Chapter Twenty-One

Leah and I sit side by side at the beach, me in my wetsuit and she in her bikini. The weather's so hot it could melt my skin right into the sand. Our feet rest by the tide that cools us off every time it hits.

Leah whistles. "That sounds pretty intense."

I draw shapes in the sand with my index finger. A triangle, a circle. A sad smiley. A fishtail. I rub it away. "I just don't get it, Leah. He refuses to talk to me about anything personal. And he doesn't want to sleep with me. You should have heard how I begged him last night." I shake my head. "I feel so stupid."

Leah lays her hand on my arm.

"What does he want from me? Am I just his shiny new toy or something? If he's not in this for long term, why am I wasting my time with him?" I bite down hard on my lower lip. "Why did I fall for him?"

She scoots closer and throws an arm around me. "He loves you, Cass."

"How can you be so sure?"

"The way he looks at you. He can't be putting up an act. And for what? What would be the point of him playing you?"

I don't know the answer to that. Maybe the merpeople are not a magical, fantastical fairytale-type of people. Maybe they are the demonic ones you'd find in a horror movie. Maybe he's on a mission to seduce me and kidnap me and lock me up in the ocean's abyss.

"He told you he loves you," Leah says.

I nod. "And he makes me feel so…sexy. And loved. He makes me feel like I'm the most important person in his life."

"And he's risking his life and the safety of his people to spend time with you."

She has a point. "Then why not commit to me?"

She digs her toes in the sand. "Commitment is a big step. Human guys have problems committing—imagine a guy having to commit to someone who's not his kind? It'd scare the crap out of me."

"So you're saying he needs time?"

"I think you should give him a chance."

I pull my knees to my chest and rest my chin on them, staring off at the ocean. "Who am I kidding, Leah? I can't have a future with a merman. He can't live on land for more than twelve hours straight before needing salt water."

"Then what do you want to do?"

Pressing my cheek into my knee, I say, "I don't know. What am I supposed to do? I can't go into the ocean. That means Damarian will have to live on land. How often will he visit his family? There's no way they'll accept me. And what do I tell my parents? Mom and Dad, this is my boyfriend, Damian. By the way, he's really half fish." I emit a fake laugh. "And what if he gets caught?" I bury my face in my knees and shut my eyes. "If we have sex, Damarian will be tied to me for life. What if we realize some time down the road that we can't have a future together? I'd ruin his life."

Leah's arm tightens around me. "You guys can make it work. If you both love each other and want this, nothing should stand in your way."

"Maybe I should break up with him."

"What?" Her arm slips off my shoulder. "Cass, you'll be heartbroken. He'll be heartbroken."

"Maybe I'll be even more heartbroken if we stretch this out much longer."

She slides her arm through mine and rests her head against my temple. "Think long and hard before you make any rash decisions. Think of how Damarian makes you feel. Think of how you'd feel if he's no longer part of your life. Do you think you could ever get over him?"

My vision grows blurry. "No."

"But if you see you have no future, then maybe the best thing is for you to break up. Only you can decide."

Tears drip down my cheeks. I wipe them away. "I know. Thanks for talking me through this."

She hugs me. "Anytime."

"I'm having lunch with my dad."

"I'm so glad you finally called him."

I nod. If not for Damarian, I'm not sure I would have. Mom pushed me, Leah pushed me. But it was Damarian who gave me the confidence to do it. Having him in my life changed me for the better.

But maybe it's time to say goodbye.

***

I enter the beach and head for the rocks. My knees knock into each other, but not because I'm cold. It's because I plan to have a long talk with Damarian. I don't want to be the kind of girl who gets pushed around by the man she loves. If he won't give me what I need—a lifelong commitment—I can't have a future with him. As much as I love him, and as much as it pains me to admit it, it might be best for us to go our separate ways.

Merman's Kiss

My feet stop dead in their tracks when I see someone in the distance. It's not Damarian. He's much shorter than him and has short hair. Jet-black, short hair. A chill runs down my spine.

Kyle.

He steps closer to me and smirks. "Look who's here."

I swallow, my heart racing, my breathing growing heavy. "K-Kyle." I square my shoulders to appear calm and collected. "What are you doing here?"

I want to scan the area to see if Damarian showed up, but I don't want Kyle to get suspicious. What if Damarian swims out of the ocean? Hopefully he'll stay there when he sees I'm not at the rocks.

"I can ask you the same thing," Kyle says, folding his arms. "But that would be useless. See, I know your little secret."

My heart races so fast I sway a little. I can feel sweat gathering on my forehead and other parts of my body. "Secret? What are you talking about?"

He snorts, rolling his eyes. "You know exactly what I'm talking about. Your boyfriend? Fishtail? Fins? Gills?"

My entire body freezes. No, this can't be happening. Kyle knows. He *knows*. Oh my God. How could he know? He must have seen us.

Squaring my shoulders again, I say with the best confidence possible, "What the hell are you talking about?"

He steps forward, and I automatically stumble back. "Don't play dumb, Cassie. I see it all over your face."

Oh, God.

He smiles a sinister smile. "Who would have thought that merpeople live in the ocean! I must alert the media."

My whole body shakes uncontrollably and it's hard to breathe. But I force out a snort. "Merpeople? Are you serious?" Now I force out a laugh.

"I'm dead serious."

Panic conquers every inch of me. "W-what exactly are you going to tell the media?" I force out another laugh. "Think they'll believe you?"

With a grin, he reaches into his pocket and pulls out his phone. "I have proof."

I'm frozen in place. I'm not sure if I'm even breathing.

Kyle takes a step toward me, holding out his cell phone. He has a video. My heart sinks to the bottom of the ocean.

But a sudden thought calms me. Kyle must have seen us on the beach in the middle of the night, when it was so dark you could hardly see a thing. There's no way he could have gotten a clear recording of anything.

He hits play.

My heart sinks even deeper into the ocean. He must have used some sort of effect on his phone, because I can see myself and Damarian clearly. The image has a bluish color, but I can definitely make us out. I see myself running toward Damarian as he swims to the shore. I see myself grabbing his hands and hauling him out of the water. Damarian's beautiful tail rises in the air. There's no way to miss it, not with the way the moon reflects off it, basking it in a strong glow. As real as it looks, I'm pretty sure a lot of people would call it a hoax. My heart slows down a bit. But then I see myself throwing the blanket over Damarian. I see how I wrap my arms around him and hold him close as he convulses. His movements are so jerky that the blanket slides off. His transformation is as clear as day. The tail slowly fades into legs.

There's no way anyone could have faked that, unless he used special effects.

But Kyle's not done yet. He swipes to another video, one where Damarian and I are standing on the rocks. Damarian dives into the ocean, and a few seconds later, his tail shoots out of the water. Then it slams down and his head appears. A little while later, his tail replaces it and he swims away.

That doesn't look fake at all. Tears enter my eyes.

Kyle slips his phone back into his pocket. "If the media won't believe me, I can always post these videos online. Imagine, you'll be an online sensation." His eyes gleam. I don't like how evil he looks. Kyle might be a jerk, but to be this evil?

I don't understand how I didn't see him lurking in the shadows. I thought I was careful.

He turns to leave. I grab his hand. "Kyle, you can't! Please, don't do this."

He jerks his hand away.

"Why would you do this?" The tears blot my vision.

He doesn't say anything, just walks past me, bumping my shoulder.

I whirl around. "Did you ever love me?"

He stops in his tracks.

"Did you?!"

He nods.

"*You're* the one who broke up with *me*. Do you have any idea what that did to me? How long it took me to get over you? I finally met a guy I love and who's really good to me. Why would you hurt me like this?"

He slowly turns around to face me.

"Are you jealous, Kyle? You can't do this to me. You can't rip my heart out of my chest and then deny me happiness."

His eyes turn hard. "This isn't about jealousy."

"Then what's it about?"

He shakes his head and walks away.

I spring to him and grab his hand again. "Kyle, please!"

He pulls it away and marches off, leaving me to fall down to my knees, the tears practically blinding me.

I sit here like this for a little while, before jumping to my feet and rushing toward the rocks. I don't climb up. Instead, I dive into the ocean.

The moon's not full today, so I can barely see anything. The waves are a little violent. They crash into me, into my mouth, nearly choking me.

"Damarian!" I call.

My arms and legs kick like crazy, but they're starting to get tired. Where is Damarian? I can't let him step onto land. Kyle could be there with a camera—or worse, he could call news stations.

It seems like the waves have gotten more violent. I go under, swallowing a lot of water. When I resurface, I cough all the water out. I don't have a chance to take in more air when I'm pulled under again.

I tumble around in the ocean. My lungs are about to burst. This is it. I'm going to die tonight.

Arms wrap around my waist. A second later, air enters my lungs. I open my eyes and find myself face to face with Damarian. He's holding me close to his chest. "Cassie, what is the matter?"

I grab hold of his arms. "You need to swim away! He saw you and has it on video. He's going to expose you."

"Who?"

"Kyle. It's not safe for you here."

He moves me over so that I'm on his back. "Take hold of me."

I do as he says.

"I am to swim under," he calls over his shoulder. "Take in air."

I nod and breathe in a big gulp. As he starts to go under, my legs wrap around his middle. We're submerged in the water. I can't see a thing, only darkness, but I feel a lot. His powerful tail swooshes behind me, sounding like a washing machine. He's swimming very fast.

When we break the surface, I gasp in as much air as I can.

"One more time," Damarian says. "Are you prepared?"

I nod.

My lungs are not as strong as before. My whole body twitches as we swim in the ocean. Damarian speeds up, as if he senses that I'm about to pass out. Soon, the area around me gets lighter. Next thing I know, oxygen enters my nose and mouth.

I scan the area. We must be in some sort of cave because the water reaches my neck. I'm paddling, but my limbs are so weak. Damarian hooks an arm around my waist.

"Where are we?" I sputter, still coughing up water.

"It is a cave not too far from land. We shall be safe here."

I'm freezing. That along with my weak limbs make me feel like I'm going to faint. My teeth clatter.

Damarian runs his hand up and down my arm, trying to warm me up. "I must return you to land soon. Cassie, what is the matter? Who is going to expose me?"

I tell him what happened earlier at the beach when I met Kyle. Damarian's eyes widen. Fear clouds his face. "I'm so sorry," I say.

He keeps quiet. He probably doesn't know what to say.

"I guess…" I start. "I guess…"

"No. We shall not say goodbye."

I touch his cheek. "What can we do? I won't let you risk your life."

"He is but one human."

"But if he gives it to news stations or posts it online…I need to talk to him tomorrow. I need to convince him not to tell anyone."

He caresses my cheek. "Do you think he will listen to you?"

I think back to our encounter. Kyle was so determined to inform the world that merpeople live in the ocean. But he also admitted that he loved me once. That has to count for something. I'm the only one who can save Damarian now. I need to try to talk some sense into Kyle.

Damarian squeezes me close to his chest and kisses my temple. "I cannot bear the thought of parting with you."

I lock my arms around his neck. "Me, either."

"We shall meet tomorrow night," Damarian says. "Wait for me on the rocks. If I do not see you in the distance, it is a sign that it is not safe to come to land."

"Okay." I pull back and look into his eyes. "This is crazy, Damarian. We're risking your life. The lives of your people. I can't make you do this."

"My love for you surpasses all."

"Let's wait a few days. Maybe a week."

He lays his head against mine. "I wish to be with you now. I cannot bear being apart." His hand runs up and down my back. "I see the way you tremble. The sea is not for you. I must come on land."

He has so much love for me that he's willing to risk *everything* just to be with me. Tears enter my eyes. No one has ever cared for me as much as he does. For his own sake and for the sake of his people, I need to end things with him. The secret of the merpeople ends here. I won't come to the beach tomorrow night. I won't wait for him. Not tomorrow night, not the night after, or the night after.

I press my lips to his. "I love you."

"I have never loved anyone as I love you."

I bite down on my lip so I don't cry. This is goodbye. I'll never see him again.

"You must return to land," he says.

I ride him piggyback again. He brings us out of the cave and toward shore. I see the docks in the distance and tell Damarian to drop me off a few feet away, far enough where I can swim and far enough where no one will see him.

"Tomorrow night," he says.

I lean forward and kiss him like I've never kissed him before. He's about to pull me closer, but I swim away. I don't look back, because I know I'll lose all my nerve.

When I reach the docks, I use all my energy to climb up. I glance back, but I don't see him. Tears run down my cheeks. "Goodbye, Damarian," I whisper.

Chapter Twenty-Two

I down the blended fruit like it's my alcohol. Leah watches me, concern floating in her eyes.

"Kyle's a jerk," I mutter.

"No, shit."

I slide my empty smoothie cup toward her and nod. She refills it.

Every other minute, I find myself about to grab Damarian's hand and fasten my fingers through his. Then the realization dawns on me. The disappointment overwhelms me. Damarian's not here. He never will be again.

"Wait a second..." Leah's eyes are locked on the entrance to Misty's Juice Bar. I follow her gaze, but don't see anything.

She unties her apron and throws it onto the counter. Then she marches to the door.

"Leah?" I call, bolting after her. That's when I see him, standing near the tide with his surfboard and chatting with his buddies. Kyle.

"I'm going to give it to him."

I try to grab Leah's hand, but all I get is air. She charges toward him like a pissed-off bull. I hurry after her. She'll punch him. I know she will.

I finally catch up to her. "Don't get involved."

"Jackass," she mutters, not stopping.

"I can handle it. You don't have to protect me."

My words zoom past her ears. Kyle's eyes flit in our direction. He looks surprised, then smug. Forget Leah—I'll punch him myself.

She stands before him, hands on her hips. "You have some nerve," she snarls.

Kyle tells his buddies he'll catch up with them later. Once they leave, his gaze moves lazily over my face. "Hey, Cass."

I narrow my eyes.

"Who do you think you *are*?" Leah yells.

Kyle crosses his arms over his chest, smirking. "Are you her bodyguard?"

Her nostrils flare. "Only when she's around creeps like you."

His lips lift in another smirk. "Ah, I gather you know about her secret boyfish." He shrugs. "I'm not surprised. You don't keep anything from each other."

Leah's hands fist at her sides. "I've never really liked you."

"I'm glad you feel that way. Because I've never really liked you, either."

They glare at each other.

"Please don't do it," I plead, hoping he'll have the heart to listen to me. "You have no idea what he means to me. Kyle, please."

I can see the sympathy on his face, but it vanishes a second later. "Don't tell me you're *sleeping* with him?"

Gritting my teeth, I fist my own hands.

His nose twitches. "That's disgusting."

I lunge at him, but Leah's arms come around me. I kick the sand, throwing some on Kyle's feet. He steps back, holding out his hands. There's no denying the satisfied grin on his lips.

Leah moves closer until her face is in his, their noses only a centimeter apart. "If you hurt Cassie, I will ruin you. I will crush you. You will curse the day you took your first breath on this world."

I blink at Leah. I've never seen her this way, and I have to admit she's pretty scary.

Kyle rolls his eyes. He grabs his surfboard and runs into the water.

Leah folds her arms over her chest. "He won't tell anyone."

I raise an eyebrow. "How can you be so sure?"

She sighs. "He cares about you. Even though he's being a dick about the whole thing, it's obvious he doesn't want to hurt you."

"Then why is he being such a jerk?"

"I don't know."

***

At three AM, my mind forces my body to wake up. Pulling my blanket up to my chin, I order my eyes to shut, blocking the ache nestled in the pit of my stomach. Damarian. My mind, body, and soul yearn for him. My heart cries at the thought of him waiting for me day after day. I know it's for the best, but it hurts so much. And I miss him. Oh, how I miss him.

My hand touches the empty space near me, the space that was occupied by my merman only a night ago. "Damarian," I moan, my fingers running across the bed.

***

A few days have passed since I ended things with Damarian. I've spent a lot of time with my father and even met his wife and kids. They're not too bad. I'm not promising we'll get along great and be one big happy family, but I'm glad to have the opportunity to get to know them. Now that I don't have Damarian, a void has grown in my heart, sucking out most of the joy of life.

I finger the sand castle left over by a kid. What I'd give to be a kid again—pre-divorce. To not have any worries on my head. No heartache. Relationships suck. Either you fall for a guy who stomps on your heart or you meet the right guy, the guy of your dreams, but you can't be with him.

A shadow looms over me. I raise my head, expecting to see Damarian, hoping to see him, but it's Uncle Jim. He slowly lowers himself near me. "I've noticed you've been down these past couple of days."

I don't say anything, just wring my hands in my lap.

"The kids love you," he continues. "I don't know what I'll do when you leave for college."

A few days ago, I contemplated dropping by the community college and asking for an application. I wanted to stay close to the sea. For Damarian. But now that we're over, Texas is still on. Life continues.

Uncle Jim pats my shoulder. "You're gifted with kids. Got any ideas what you're going to major in?"

I shrug. My mind and heart are still reeling from my breakup with Damarian. I can't even think about college right now.

"Consider being a teacher," Uncle Jim says. "You'd love it."

I nod absentmindedly. I need to move on with my life and not let my breakup crush me. I know that. Maybe one day.

"Cassie?"

That voice. That ocean scent. My head shoots up. He's standing before me, dressed in tan shorts. I stare up at him, surprise, shock, delight, and guilt flowing through my bloodstream.

Uncle Jim pats my shoulder again. "I'll talk to you later."

As soon as he's gone, I clamber to my feet. My eyes soak him in, every inch of him. His golden hair, his mesmerizing blue eyes, his broad shoulders and strong legs. "What are you doing here?"

"You did not wait for me."

The betrayal in his eyes is so strong I fear it might leap out of him and wrap around me, squeezing me to death.

I swallow the guilt. All I want is to jump into his arms and hold him close, crush my lips to his and tell him how much I love him and that nothing could ever keep us apart.

"I'm so sorry, Damarian," I whisper.

He takes a step forward, prompting me to step back. "Please, Cassie. Do not abandon me. You are my Cassie. How I love you so."

The tears come. I shake my head, forcing them at bay. "This is already hard. Don't make it any harder. You belong in the ocean. It's not safe for you on land."

Tears enter his eyes. My heart stings and is so heavy I feel my body is going to collapse into a pile of rubble. "No," he says, the tears surging down his cheeks. "I will not accept this."

"Look who washed up on shore," a voice says from behind me. I spin around. Kyle.

My body fills with rage. I can't believe I once loved this guy.

His eyes travel between Damarian and me. "I'm sensing a bit of tension."

I want to yell the most bitter, angry yell I've ever shouted in my life. I want to slap him across the face.

Damarian's chest expands. A hiss escapes his lips. It looks like steam's about to shoot out of his ears. He takes a step forward, glaring at Kyle. "You are the cause of this."

Kyle moves back. He spreads his arms out and raises them over his head, bringing them together, like he's about to dive. He keeps his arms like that and lowers his head. "Forgive me, Damarian, my king."

My mouth drops and my heart lurches. His name. How can he know Damarian's real name? And why did he call him "my king?"

A relieved laugh brews at the base of my throat. Kyle's just being a jerk and screwing around.

But as I take one look at Damarian, my body grows cold. He's staring at Kyle as though he's pointing a gun at his face.

Kyle lifts his head, but his hands are still in the air. Like in submission.

Damarian is still staring at Kyle, a horrified look on his face. "Who are you?"

Dropping his head again, Kyle says, "Kyler, of the Emerald clan."

Damarian moves his mouth, but no sound comes out. His eyebrows crease.

I gape at the two of them. Kyler of the Emerald clan? As in the merpeople Emerald clan?

Damarian finally finds his voice. "The one who was banished twenty four moons past?"

"The very same."

A breath breaks out of Damarian's mouth.

"You're...you're a merman, too?" I ask.

He grins. "Funny, isn't it? The only guys you've slept with are fish."

Damarian advances toward him. "Do *not* speak to Cassie in such a manner."

Kyle bows his head once again. "Forgive me, my king."

"Why does he call you his king, Damarian?" I demand.

Kyle's eyebrows lift. "She doesn't know?"

Damarian purses his lips, glaring at Kyle.

"Damarian?" I ask.

He won't meet my gaze. My heart tears open. Stabs of betrayal prick every inch of my skin. Is this the thing he's been holding back from me? That he's the king of the merpeople? But how could he be when he spends so much time here?

Seeing I won't get answers from Damarian, I turn to Kyle. "You're human. You're always in the water, and you've never grown a tail or gills."

He presses his lips together. "I'm banished."

"What's banished mean?"

He clenches his jaw. "Two years ago, I fell in love with a human girl. I thought I could speak to my king. I thought he'd understand me." His eyes blaze with fury. "He stripped me of my tail and banished me to live on land, never to enter the ocean as a child of the sea. I couldn't see my family, my friends, my home. I could never have my tail again." His rage-filled gaze goes from me to Damarian, then back at me. "Do you have any idea what that feels like? To be banished from the only life you've ever known?"

His eyes flash to Damarian. Damarian lowers his gaze to the sand. Is he claiming Damarian banished him? I can't believe he'd do something like that.

"At least I had the girl I loved," Kyle continues. "Or so I thought." He laughs bitterly. "She dumped me the minute she discovered I no longer had my tail and fin." His lower lip quivers. "I was alone. Completely alone. I had to learn how to live as a human, without help from anyone."

We're all silent. I just stare at him, not believing what I'm hearing. Damarian's face is expressionless.

Kyle's eyes burn at him. "And *you*. You've been seeing a human girl for weeks. Yet you're not banished. What is it? Does King Palaemon favor you over the many other children of the sea?"

So Damarian is not the king? I'm so confused.

Damarian waves his hands toward Kyle, as if telling him to shut up this instant.

Kyle's mouth widens as he looks at Damarian. "She doesn't know, does she? You haven't told her." He laughs bitterly again. "Of course you haven't told her."

My eyes move from one to the other. "Told me what?"

"Tell her how the crown rightfully belongs to the Sapphire clan, to your family. Tell her how you are the true heir to the throne. That you are betrothed to Princess Flora and will become the rightful king."

My heart pumps ice throughout my body. The world spins. "Betrothed?" I croak.

Damarian's eyes fill with pain. "Cassie…"

"What is he talking about?" I ask, my voice rising an octave. "You're *engaged?*"

He shuts his eyes, letting out a breath. When he opens them, they are filled with tears. "Yes, Cassie," he says, his voice defeated. "I am to take the throne. I am indeed betrothed to Princess Flora, daughter of King Palaemon. Since I was a fry."

"To unite the five clans under one crown," Kyle says. "To return the kingdom to the rightful heir."

Tears burst out of my eyes. I shove Damarian. "How could you?" I shove again. "I trusted you! You're engaged—you're going to get *married* and rule the merpeople. You never intended to have a future with me." I shove a third time. He just stands still, the pain in his eyes magnified by a million. "What have you been doing with me? Was I your distraction? Your bachelor party before you settle down and rule your people? You said you wouldn't hurt me. You said you'd never, *ever* hurt me."

He makes a move to take my hand or touch me, softly saying, "Cassie," but I shove him another time. "I never want to see you again. Go back to the ocean. Don't ever come out. I don't want to ever lay eyes on you!"

I turn around and run.

Chapter Twenty-Three

Leah rubs my back. I'm lying flat on my bed, my face smashed in the pillow. It's hard to breathe this way, but I don't really care.

My heart is bleeding into my lungs, my liver, my intestines, and the rest of my organs. My head pounds so hard it feels like it's going to explode into ashes.

He lied to me. He made me open up, made me bare my heart, my soul, my everything. Then he took a hammer and smashed me to bits.

"It'll be okay," Leah says. "You'll get through this."

"Why do I let this happen to me?" I sob into the pillow, fisting my hands around the blanket and squeezing tight, blocking my blood flow. I gasp and sputter and choke. Turning my head to the side, I take in a big gulp of air. I feel my face caked with tears.

Leah touches my shoulder. "You don't let these things happen to you."

"I fell for two mermen, Leah. Two fish. The only men I've ever fallen for. What the hell is wrong with me?"

"Nothing's wrong with you."

"I trusted him," I mumble over and over again. "How could he do this to me?"

She talks, tries to comfort me. But nothing and no one can comfort me. I need the memories of the past two weeks to be sucked out of my head. I need to forget about him. Forget his expressive blue eyes. Forget the feel of his body so close to mine. The feelings he invoked in me. How he made me feel so alive.

"Talk to me about something," I beg her. "Anything. I can't stand my head now."

The bed creaks as she shifts on it. "Cassie, it's okay to be upset."

New tears soak my pillow. I fist my hands even harder, feeling my nails digging into my palms. Why did I let myself fall for him? Why did I give him the ammunition to hurt me like no one's ever done before? "Men suck," I say into the pillow. "Love sucks. I feel so crappy." Like I'm going to throw up my organs. "I don't think I can survive this."

"You *will* survive this," Leah says. "You're a strong person."

I shake my head. I'm not a strong person. Not at all. If I was, I wouldn't be such a hot mess right now. I wouldn't feel like my stomach is scraping against my ribs.

"You can't let your bad experiences make you think every relationship is like that."

I raise my head. The sunlight coming in through the window blinds me for a few seconds. "I'd rather be single for the rest of my life than go through this again."

"What's the phrase? 'Better to have loved and lost than never to have loved at all.' This happened for a reason, Cass. It'll make you even stronger. And when you do meet the right guy, everything will be worth it."

I smash my face into the pillow. As much as I want to believe her, I'm not sure I can. What's the point in falling in love if I'm going to end up with a broken heart? When Kyle dumped me, I took it hard, but not as hard as I'm taking it now. Will that mean that my next heartache will be worse? And the one after that?

All I see before me is his face. And every time, it feels like someone's cutting my heart open with a sharp knife. I moan and roll back and forth on my bed. I chew on the corner of my blanket. I can't take this anymore. I just can't.

"Talk to me about Jace," I say.

"Are you sure? Won't it—"

"Please. I don't care what you say. I need to be distracted. I can't stand these thoughts and memories playing in my head."

"Cassie—"

"Please."

She's quiet for a few seconds before taking in a breath and letting it out. "We went miniature golfing yesterday. It was fun."

I sense she's trying to hide the excitement from her voice. "Who won?" I ask.

"Who do you think?"

The answer's obvious. Leah's one competitive girl. "Will you go out with him again?"

"Cassie, are you sure you want to talk about this—"

"Will you?" I press.

She sighs. "Yeah. We're going out tomorrow night. I'm looking forward to it."

The room grows silent. My head fills up. I start my rocking again, more moans slipping out of my mouth.

Leah touches my arm. "You'll get through this. One day you'll meet a great guy and you won't give two craps about...you know who."

"That's what you said the last time." I turn onto my back and stare at the ceiling, tears sliding into my ears. "You have no idea what this feels like."

"I've had my share of broken hearts."

"Have you ever felt such a strong, emotional, and spiritual connection with anyone?" When she doesn't answer, I say, "I'm talking about being in so much love that he makes you feel things you've never felt before. True love, just like they have in fairytales. It's killing me." My eyes shut tight. "I don't know how I'll get through it."

"At least you've experienced it," Leah says, her voice rising an octave. I open my eyes. A little bit of pain fills her face. "That love they talk about in books and movies? I've never experienced that before. You may be heartbroken, but at least you've had a taste of it." She grabs my smaller pillow and hugs it to her chest. "I'd like to experience that one day, even if it'll hurt me."

I blink at her as her words enter my ears. Leah's been in a few relationships, but she's never been in love. Really in love. I drag myself to a sitting position and reach for her hand. She gives it to me. "I'm sorry," I say.

She shakes her head. "There's a bit of good in everything, even in the hardest parts of our lives. I'm not saying you shouldn't cry. I know you're hurting. But you need to believe that you'll meet the right guy one day. You can't know until you try."

I scoot closer to her and pull her into my arms. "You're right. I'm sorry. It just hurts so much."

She squeezes me close. "I know. Just promise me you won't let this break you."

"I don't know if I can, but I'll try."

Chapter Twenty-Four

It's been exactly a week since I ended things with Damarian. I lie awake, replaying the memory for the hundredth time. My heart longs for him. It tells me to forget what he did and forgive him, that he must have a reasonable explanation. But a week passed and I haven't heard from him. I thought he'd return the day after I told him I never wanted to see him again. I thought he'd fall to his knees and beg me to hear him out. To tell me there's been a misunderstanding and he's not engaged. That he loves me and wants to be with me. I would have fallen into his arms, would have forgiven him. The fact that he hasn't shown up confirms one thing. That everything is true.

When the sun peeks into my room, signaling that morning has arrived at last, I sit up and strain my ears. No knocking on the door. I want to slap my aching heart. How much longer will I cry for him?

I'm trying so hard to not let this break me. But it hurts too much. I hope one day I can look back on this and realize it was worth it. All of it.

I drag myself out of bed to get ready for work. I tie my hair into braids, swallowing the lump in my throat. Every little thing reminds me of him. When I untie my braids, I remember the feel of his hands as they freed my hair and ran through the strands. I haven't touched my gummy worms for days because the thought of putting one into my mouth makes my stomach churn.

The kitchen—specifically the oven—reminds me of when we cooked together. I haven't stepped foot in the pool room or the guestroom. He's not the one who has to live in a house with his ghost.

I put on my wetsuit, grab my surfboard, and head for the beach. If not for my class, I wouldn't come anywhere near here. I can point out every spot I shared a moment with Damarian. Every memory attacks my mind, my heart, and I feel like I'm going to shatter into a million pieces.

"Cassie?"

I blink and realize I've walked deeper into the beach, standing right in the center of a kid's sandcastle. He looks up at me with tears in his eyes. Kyle stands next to him. He lays a hand on my arm. "Cassie."

I blink again. Then I pull my arm out of his grasp and march away.

"Wait," he calls.

I continue to march. I don't know where—just away from him. He catches up and stands before me. I try to step around him, but he blocks the way. He sets his hands on my shoulders, leaving me no choice but to meet his gaze.

"Don't look at me like that," he says.

"Why not? You got what you wanted." I shrug his hands off and walk away, bumping my shoulder into his.

He grabs my arm. "This isn't what I wanted."

I whirl around. "Just because your life sucks, that doesn't mean you have to make everyone else's miserable, too."

"I didn't want to make your life miserable. You or Prince Damarian's."

My blood boils when I hear that title. Has he been crowned yet? My stomach falls to my toes. Damn, I still love him.

I'm about to turn around, but he grabs my arm again. "There's a lot about my world you don't understand." Pain flashes in his eyes. "My old world."

I snort.

"It hurt me to see another child of the sea traveling freely from sea to land when I'm stuck here. You have no idea how badly I want to return home. I haven't seen my family and friends in two years."

"I do feel sorry for you, Kyle—or should I say, *Kyler*—but that didn't give you the right to threaten to expose Damarian."

He throws up his hands. "If not for me, he would have continued his little charade. How much longer did you want to stretch this out?"

I fight back the tears that are about to consume me. I can't believe the guy I thought I loved would screw me over like this.

I cross my arms. "What's the real reason you broke up with me?"

He staggers back a bit, like my question threw him off guard. "What?"

"Now that I know who you really are, why did you break up with me?"

He shifts from one foot to the other. "Are you sure you want to talk about this?"

"Were you engaged, too?"

He sighs. "I met you a little after the girl I loved broke up with me. You were my…distraction. My rebound girl." He shuts his eyes. "I loved you, but not like I loved her."

"Great," I mutter.

He moves closer. "I'm sorry, Cass."

"Whatever." I push past him and meet my kids for class.

Seriously, screw guys.

***

After finishing my class, I run into the ocean and surf until my lungs nearly collapse and my limbs turn to lead. As I wipe my forehead with my towel, something catches my attention. Golden hair, blue eyes. Not Damarian, but Doria, on the beach, a few feet away from me. I stand there, frozen in place, as she makes her way toward me, dressed in a one-piece bathing suit.

When she finally reaches me, my mouth is glued shut. I just stare at her.

"I wish to speak with you," she says in a detached tone.

My lips move, but I don't know what comes out of them.

"Pardon me?" she asks.

I clear my throat. "How…how did you get out of the ocean?"

"I shifted in the early morning, when no humans were about." She fingers the bathing suit. "I found this article of clothing. It is not comfortable."

Despite the weirdness of all of this, I laugh. Doria—who's only had cold, unfriendly eyes toward me—expression softens.

"Let's go to my house," I offer. She nods.

Kyle's standing with a group of surfers. He stares at Doria. She doesn't seem to know who he is, though.

I lead her to my house and invite her into the living room. I get some water and sardines from the kitchen. Having Doria in my house makes my skin crawl with nerves and unease. What is she doing here?

When I return with the refreshments, I find her sitting on the couch, glancing around. She looks breathtaking and exquisite, just like one would imagine a mermaid to look.

I lower the food onto the table and sit down across from her. She doesn't say anything for a bit, just continues to study the room. I open my mouth a few times to ask all the questions burning in my soul, but I keep quiet.

Finally, she turns to me. "Father threatened banishment if

Damarian dared leave the sea."

I gape at her, my heart pounding in my head, making it hard to think. "Uh…what?" is all I manage to say.

"Damarian wishes to return, but he is not certain you will have him."

The pounding in my head increases. I rub my temples to lessen the pain, but that doesn't help. Releasing a breath, I look at her. "Let me understand. Your brother wants to come to land, but your father threatened to banish him?"

Doria nods. "He wishes to return to you, but you clearly stated you do not wish to lay eyes upon him."

Tears of relief build up in my eyes. He wants to come back. He didn't forget about me. "But…what about his…the princess?"

Doria shifts in her seat. "She will find another king."

"But he said he's the rightful king. I don't understand."

She leans back. "Would you like to hear it all from the start?"

"Yes. Please."

She begins, "The children of the sea have not always lived in peace. Many moons ago, there were battles. Many of us were lost. The crown has been in my family since the beginning of time, but during the battles the Violets stole it from us." She looks down at her knees. "My father is the true king. Damarian is the true prince." She slowly raises her eyes. I don't know what my face shows, but my mind is a jumbled mess. Damarian's the prince. He will be king. All this time…

"Some clans wish the crown to return to the rightful family. The Emeralds are not fond of the Violets. Neither are the Diamonds. King Palaemon is a fair king, but he is not the true one. It is time the crown be returned to the Sapphires."

My head's reeling. This is too much to soak in.

Doria continues, "The Violets do not wish to relinquish the throne, for it was theirs for generations and they feel they are the true ruling clan. Father and King Palaemon have agreed to form an alliance and unite all the children of the sea." She lays her hands on her lap. "Damarian shall rule as king. Princess Flora shall rule as queen."

My throat gets so dry, I need a drink. But I know nothing can enter my mouth. My left foot twitches. "So Damarian wanted to have some fun before the big day?" There's no masking the pain and bitterness spewing out of me.

Doria shakes her head. "You do not understand the manner in which Damarian felt. He was promised to Princess Flora when he was a fry. All his life, he has been told how vital he is. He has spent many a time at Eteria, our capital city and the kingdom. He and his betrothed are fairly well aquatinted." She shakes her head. "But try as he might, Damarian does not love the princess."

I swallow, goose bumps forming over my skin.

"He understands his duty. He understands how imperative it is for him to take the throne. As the eldest, it is his obligation."

Every part of me cries for him. To be forced to marry someone he doesn't love, all for the sake of his people. My poor Damarian. I wish I could hug him.

"The night Damarian fled the sea during the storm," Doria says, "he and Princess Flora were to announce their mating the following morning."

Now it all makes sense. Damarian swam away in dangerous conditions because he was running away from his life.

"Father believes him to be a coward. A disappointment." She shakes her head again. "All he sees is the crown on a Sapphire head."

Again, I cry for him. I want to gather him in my arms and hold him close and comfort him.

"He fled his duty," Doria says. "A child of the sea does not act in such a manner."

I want to defend him. Why should anyone be forced to marry someone he doesn't love, even if it's for the sake of his own people? Yet at the same time, a lot of people were counting on him. I don't know what I'd do in that situation.

"He returned home," Doria says. "Father was most upset. He informed my brother that the mating shall occur that night. Damarian fled once again. He did not return."

That was when Mom came home. I thought Damarian was spending time with his family, which eased my mind. But he wasn't. He hid somewhere in the ocean, with only Fiske as his protector.

"My brother, Kiander, and I left the sea in search for my brother."

"How did you find him?" I ask.

"Children of the sea have the ability to sense when one is near, on land as well. It is how we do not injure one another in the ocean while we hunt."

I nod.

"Father was furious when Damarian returned. Damarian attempted to tell him that he did not wish to mate with Princess Flora and take the throne. I am certain you can imagine Father's reaction."

Yeah, he flipped.

"Father informed him that he was to take the crown. That is all. Damarian returned to you." She wrings her fingers. "Father understands that Damarian has found another mate."

Well, I wouldn't put it like *that*.

"When Damarian returned again, Father threatened banishment."

The day I told him I never wanted to see him again. He must have been crushed. "How can your father banish, though? I thought only kings can."

Doria nods. "Father is the true king. He has the ability to banish as well."

"Oh." I chew on my braid. "So...why are you here?"

Doria sighs. "Damarian loves you deeply. I do not understand how one can have such love for a human, but I do not question it. He remains in his quarters, refusing to see anyone."

Tears roll down my cheeks. I've hurt him so badly. I never understood why he didn't talk to me about it, but now I do. He knew I wouldn't want to be with him once I learned all of this. He didn't want to lose me.

"I persuaded my brother to speak to me," Doria says. "He informed me of the quarrel. I have never seen him so broken."

I bite my lip as more tears splash down my cheeks.

"His is prepared to risk banishment," she says, stressing her words to make sure I understand. "He is not certain Father will truly banish him. He is his son, and heir to the throne." Her voice rises a little. "He is willing to be tied to land. For you. But he is not certain you will have him. He wishes to know."

"No!" I practically yell.

Her eyes widen in shock.

I slap the tears off my cheeks. "Go back to the ocean. Tell Damarian that I love him so much. That I've never loved anyone as much as I love him, and that I won't ever love anyone like him. Tell him that it's because of my love for him that I'm letting him go. I don't want him to lose everyone he holds dear to him. I won't let him be stuck here on land. Not for me." I wipe away some more tears. "Don't let him, Doria. Don't let him risk everything for me. I love him so, so much. It'll kill me if I take his life away."

Doria studies me for a few seconds. Then she nods. "I admire you, human Cassie. I shall relay the message to my brother."

She stands up, and I do, too. "I never meant for this to happen," I tell her.

She nods. Then she hesitantly rests her hand on my arm. "You have changed my brother. He is joyful now." She twists her nose. "Before your quarrel."

I nod, forcing fresh tears away. "He has changed me, too. I will cherish my time with him forever."

She bows her head. "I shall take my leave now."

"Thanks so much for coming. I know I'm not your biggest fan."

She heads for the door, then looks back at me. "If my brother were to love a human, I am glad it is you."

That's really sweet of her to say, even though I don't think I deserve it. My feelings toward her have definitely changed. "Please don't let him ruin his life because of me. That's my only wish."

She nods and opens the door. "Very well." She stares out. "How will I return?"

I grab my bag. "Let's get a boat."

Chapter Twenty-Five

I hug my pillow to my chest and turn onto my side, shutting my eyes tight. Sleep just won't come. When I try to count sheep, I count little Damarians instead. When I count from one to a hundred, Damarian's face distracts me.

I miss him like crazy.

Squeezing my pillow even tighter, I push him out of my head. His beautiful golden hair, his dark blue eyes, the light on his face when he's happy or excited, the strong arms that made me feel loved and protected.

I groan, turning onto my back. So much for pushing him out of my head.

After some time, I must have fallen asleep, because through the fog in my mind, I hear something. The sound of the doorbell ringing.

My body tunes it out and latches onto the sleep I desperately need.

But the ringing continues. I'm slowly thrown out of Sleep Land, and my eyes open.

Ding. Ding.

I sit up. The doorbell.

Could it be…?

No, it can't be. It better not be. I don't want it to be.

Except, that's not true. Because I do want it to be. I'm dying for it to be.

I slide my feet into my slippers and make my way downstairs, opening the hallway lights. They blind me for a few seconds. The ringing continues. Whoever it is, he's not leaving until I open that door.

Once I unlock it, I pull it open. The face I've grown to know so well, the one I've etched into my memory, learned to love, stares at me.

Damarian.

He's dressed in nothing but a large, white towel wrapped around his waist. I just stand there, blinking at him. It's like the reality won't enter my head because I can't believe it.

His eyes are glued to mine, searching every feature on my face, digging into my soul.

Finally, I force myself to ask, "What are you doing here?"

He rakes his hand through his hair, uncertainty clouding his features. "May I come in?"

"Of—of course." I widen the door and step aside. He sweeps past me, his delicious scent swallowing me up. I sway for a few seconds, my eyes closed, getting absorbed in the smell that means everything to me.

I shut the door after him. We stand face to face in the narrow hallway. I feel myself starting to melt from the heat and electricity burning between us. I shake my head, knocking myself out of it, then motion toward the living room.

But instead of heading there, Damarian steps forward and gathers me in his arms. I'm not taken aback or thrown off. It's like my whole being misses him so much that I meld into him, fitting my body in all the right places. His arms tighten around me and his lips search mine. When they lock together, a symphony plays in the back of my head. Our lips come together almost violently, so passionately, as if we're drinking each other like we haven't had any water in days.

"You shouldn't have come back," I whisper when our mouths come apart. A second later, they are fastened back on each other, a desperate longing sparking between us.

Damarian slides his lips up the side of my neck. "I could not stay away from you, my love."

My head's thrown back as his lips cause explosions on my neck. I'm lost in this magical world where Damarian is not a merman and not the future king of his people and not engaged to marry the princess. In this world, nothing matters but the love between us and the feeling his warm, soft lips brings me.

With his lips still on me, he lifts me in his arms and carries me to the living room couch. He lays me down and climbs on top of me, his lips continuing their quest to kiss each and every part of my face.

Reality manages to slip inside my magical world. I push my hands against Damarian's chest, gently forcing him a few inches back. "You'll get banished."

He captures my hands in his and brings them to his mouth, kissing each one of my fingers, causing my stomach to flutter. "Father will not banish me."

"How..." A moan escapes my mouth as he sucks my pinky finger. "How can you be so sure?"

His lips graze my palm. "I am his son. He will not banish me. He only threatened me to do his bidding." He leans forward and nuzzles my nose. "Nothing can keep me away from you, my sweet Cassie. Nothing."

"What about your people? You're the true king."

Damarian sits back on his knees and lets out a breath. His eyes search mine, and I can see how pained they are. He sticks his hands under my back and draws me to his chest, burying his face in the hollow between my neck and shoulder. "I love you, Cassie. Not

Princess Flora. It would do a disservice to the children of the sea if I do not love my mate."

"Does she love you?" I ask.

He doesn't say anything.

I pull back and look at him. "Damarian. Does she love you?"

He runs his hand through his hair, his gaze on his towel. "I am not certain…"

"If she loves you—"

His gaze meets mine. "She does not love me the way you love me. I do not wish to mate with a child of the sea who does not love me. Not in the manner in which I love you."

My stomach does cartwheels. It's not fair for him to be forced to marry someone who doesn't love him. And whom he doesn't love. But…"Who will be the king, then?" I ask.

Damarian shakes his head. "I am not certain. Perhaps Princess Flora will have suitors."

"And your dad? Will he be upset with you?"

Damarian nods slightly. "Yes, but it is in Father's nature to forgive."

"And the alliance?"

"It is my hope that Princess Flora chooses a mate from another clan. The alliance will stand."

I lay my head on his chest. "What will happen to us?" I whisper.

He places his hand under my chin, lifting my head toward his. "We will be together for eternity. If you will have me."

My arms come around him and I squeeze my cheek to his. "Of course I'll have you."

"I am truly sorry for lying to you. I believed you would not want me once you were aware that I—"

I put my finger on his lips. "It's okay. I understand why you lied. I know you weren't in a good place. And I know how much you wanted to do the right thing, but how you wanted to do what made you happy. It's not an easy choice for anyone."

His lips trace my temple. "You are such a forgiving person, Cassie. So understanding. How I love you."

"I love you, too." I reach up to kiss him. "You sent Doria to me."

He shakes his head. "Doria left the sea on her own will."

I raise an eyebrow. "Why?"

"She witnessed our love for one another. She realized how I longed for you. How it pained me. All she wants is for me to be happy."

He lays me back on the couch and kisses me, his hands exploring every inch of my body. After a few minutes, he gathers me in his arms again and brings us to my room, where he lowers me onto the bed and slides in next to me.

We spend the rest of the night in each other's arms, our lips never coming apart, our hands not leaving one another.

Somehow, we fall asleep.

***

My hand automatically reaches for Damarian, and when I feel him, my heart swells. My eyes fly open and I stare at him, watching him, reveling in the way his chest rises and falls in a steady rhythm. I bend over to peck his lips. I love him so much my chest aches. I didn't know it was possible to love someone so much, with every part of me. I've heard it, read about it in romance novels and seen it in movies, and I always wondered if I'd ever love someone that way. Now I do, and it's the best feeling in the world.

His eyes flutter open and land on me. A grin appears on his face. "This must be a dream," he murmurs.

I give him a deep, heartfelt kiss that sends a flush from my head to my toes. "Would that happen in a dream?"

He smiles again. "I believe not." He wraps an arm around my waist and hauls me to his chest. "I shall wake up beside you every morning."

"What about your family? You'll want to see them."

His eyes get unfocused. "Yes, I will." He returns his gaze to me and strokes my cheek. "I shall wake up by your side when I am on land."

I laugh. "I accept."

I'll stop by the community college and get an application. Damarian and I will be discreet. No one will know our little secret. No one. Other than Leah, of course. And Kyle. Screw Kyle.

Getting to my feet, I take his hand and pull him up. "Come. Let's make breakfast."

He nods. "May I go to the pool first?"

"Sure." I hit my head. "I almost forgot."

He touches his hair with a shaky hand.

"What's wrong?" I ask.

"The banishment…"

My heart skips a beat. "You're…you're banished?"

He shakes his head. "I am not certain. I do not feel different."

I bite down on my lower lip. "Let's check."

As we make for the pool room, dread fills the pit of my stomach. If Damarian's dad banished him, I don't know what I'll do, how I'll live with the guilt. That Damarian threw away the only life he knew, all for me.

I hope he's not banished.

We enter the pool room. Damarian takes labored steps, until he reaches the edge of the pool. He looks back at me, his face anxious. I give him a reassuring nod and smile. He can't be banned. He just *can't* be.

Raising his arms, he dives into the water. I fall down on my knees and peer over the edge of the pool. The familiar bubbles are there, like the water's cooking. I feel my body sag with relief. When his tail pops out of the water, I nearly topple over with more relief.

His head breaks the surface. His smile is big and bright. "I am not banished, Cassie!" He laughs a little crazily, threading his fingers through his hair. "I am not banished."

His joy consumes me. I get to my feet and cannonball into the water—in my pajamas. His arms come around me and bring me to his chest. His lips find mine. "I'm so happy, Damarian."

He throws me onto his back and dives into the water. When he leaps, we almost touch the ceiling—that's how excited he is. Midair, I wrap my legs tightly around his torso and lift my arms. This is so amazing. The way the sun reflects off his sapphire tail, creating a rainbow on the surface of the water.

We crash inside, then leap in the air again. This time, my hands graze the ceiling. I giggle like a little kid with a big bag of candy.

Back in the water, Damarian lifts me off his back and flips me upside down so my head touches the surface of the water. He stares down at me with a mischievous grin. "Hello, Cassie."

I laugh. "The water feels so good against my scalp." I close my eyes and moan, licking my lips. His hands tighten on my waist.

"Cassie…" His voice is above a whisper.

"Yeah?"

"The feelings you invoke in me. Even as a child of the sea."

He kisses me upside down and dunks us both in the water. As we kiss, water doesn't enter my mouth, or my nose. He spins me upright with our lips still locked together. I'm not sure how long we're underwater. It could be seconds, it could be minutes. When we resurface, I jump onto him, wrapping my legs around his middle. "I can do this all day." My lips trail kisses up his neck. I feel him shudder.

"As can I," he whispers. His hands tangle in my hair as my lips make their way down his chest. "Cassie..."

"My merman," I mumble.

"My human," he mumbles back.

I laugh against his chest.

"What?"

I just continue laughing like a hyena. Maybe it's the relief, the excitement, or the realization that he and I are going to be together forever. I don't know. But I can't stop laughing. After I calm down, I say, "Calling me 'my human' sounds funny." And there I go laughing again.

His lips tickle my ear. "I am not concerned with the reason you laugh. Only that you laugh. How pretty it sounds."

Despite the cool water of the pool, I'm a pot of boiling water. "You really know exactly what to say to melt a girl's heart."

I grab the back of his head, press my lips against his, and pull him down into the water.

Chapter Twenty-Six

After we get dressed, we make breakfast—scrambled eggs. Damarian devours them like he hasn't eaten in days. "How I miss the food prepared by you," he says.

We wash the dishes together and curl in each other's arms on the couch with a movie. To say we watched the movie would be a lie. We couldn't keep our lips and hands off each other.

I called Uncle Jim and told him I wanted to cancel the surfing class this morning. Today will be Damarian and Cassie Day.

While running his lips down my throat, Damarian suddenly sits up. He clutches the sides of his head. Panic grabs hold of me. "What's wrong?"

He moans and tries to move his mouth, but more moans come out.

"Do you need to go into the salt water?" I ask. But that doesn't make sense. He was just in the water an hour ago.

That's when I realize a huge difference in his appearance. His skin is no longer translucent. It's…peachy. Like a human's.

When he opens his eyes, they are no longer that beautiful shade of ocean blue, but a dull blue.

Oh no.

"Yes," Damarian sputters. "Salt…water."

Tears enter my eyes as I see him growing more human by the second. *Banished.* His father actually did it.

"P...please," he begs.

I can't tell him. I can't.

He rolls off the couch and falls splat on the floor. I scramble to my feet and help him get up. Throwing his arm over my shoulder, I half-carry him toward the pool room. My vision blurs because I know this time his tail will no longer be there.

Banished.

This is all my fault.

We barge into the pool room. Damarian makes a run for it and dives into the pool. When I look over the edge, I don't see the water cooking. I wait—I hope—for his tail to spring up. But it doesn't. Damarian just lies on the bottom of the pool, still clutching his head.

It takes a few seconds until my mind pulls me out of my state of shock. He's no longer a merman, which means he can't breathe underwater. Without a second thought, I jump into the water.

I wrap my arms around him and drag him to the surface. As soon as his head breaks it, he coughs. He thrashes around, clearly in panic. "Stand," I tell him. "We're in shallow water."

He straightens out his legs. Then he stares down at himself, at the lower half of his body. His eyes widen in disbelief, then realization, then panic, and then pain and betrayal.

"Seawater," he says. "The pool requires more seawater."

With tears still in my eyes, I touch his arm. "Damarian—"

"Seawater," he begs. "I require seawater."

My hand rubs his arm. "There's enough sea salt. We just refilled it this morning."

Pure agony captures his face. "Please, Cassie." I see tears in the corner of his eyes.

"Okay," I tell him.

I make my way to the bucket of sea salt that I left in the corner of the pool room. It's half empty. Biting down on my lip, I drag it to the edge of the pool. Damarian doesn't look at me or at the bucket. His gaze is on the water, as though it's responsible for his lack of tail.

I tip the bucket and the salt slides inside.

Damarian splashes toward the salt and dives into the water.

Nothing happens.

That was all of the sea salt. I didn't buy more because I thought I'd never see him again. I put it aside and jump into the water. Damarian is still under. Gently, I wrap my arms around his chest and lift him. He takes in a huge gulp of air.

"Damarian." I pull him to my chest, but he pushes away.

His eyes blaze with betrayal, ache, anger. "He…he banished me."

I don't say anything, just gnaw on my bottom lip, forcing the tears to remain behind my eyes. I need to be strong, for him. "I'm so sorry, Damarian."

This time, he lets me take him in my arms. He cries into my hair, making my own tears burst out of my eyes. I pat his back. "It's okay," I tell him. "It'll be okay." Even though I know it *won't* be okay. Not at all. Damarian's no longer a merman. He's a human. Everything he's known has been ripped away from him. All because of me. Now he needs to learn to live a completely different life. It feels like my chest has been split open.

"I cannot…I cannot." He sobs on me. "Father has…" A hiccup swallows the rest of his sentence.

"I know," I whisper, wishing I knew what to say or do to make him feel better.

He wrenches himself out of my hold and slams his fists on the water. Tears run down his cheeks. "Father has banished me," he mutters. "He…he…" He grabs the sides of his head and yells a harsh, bitter yell. I've never heard anyone shout like that before. It's like every tragedy in the world has been packed into that yell.

I enclose him in my arms and press my lips to the side of his neck. "I'm here, Damarian. I'm here."

His body heaves. "Father banished me," he says, over and over again. I squeeze him tighter, continuing to press my lips to his skin. There's nothing I can do but be here for him.

He turns around and lets me comfort him. I hold him in my arms and stroke his hair. "We'll get through this. You and me, we'll be together forever. Through thick and thin. I'll be here for you. I'll always be here for you."

His tear-stained eyes stare into mine. "What shall I do, Cassie?"

Every cell in my body cries for this man that I love so much. I hug him closer, not knowing how to answer him.

***

Damarian's passed out on the couch, his face splattered with tears. His head rests on my lap. As I stare down at him, my body fills with fear and anxiety. I don't know what will happen to him. I'm scared for him.

I wipe his tears away.

My hand softly strokes his hair. I study him. He looks exactly the same as he did before he lost his tail, except for the skin, hair, and eyes. There's something missing, something magical and mesmerizing. But that doesn't change the way I feel about him.

He shifts on the couch and opens his eyes, staring into mine. He sits up, but then his eyes get unfocused. He blinks a few times and his face falls. It must have all come back to him.

"Tell me it is a terrible dream."

I bite down on my lip. "I wish I could."

His shoulders hunch over as he buries his face in his hands. "Banished."

I rub circles on his back.

"I cannot live solely on land, Cassie," he cries into his hands. "I cannot. The sea is my home."

I continue rubbing his back. "I know. Will anyone from your family come to see you?"

His shoulders heave. "One is not to associate with one who has been banished."

"Maybe Doria or Kiander—"

"No." He sobs some more. "No."

I don't say anything, just give him the chance to let it all out. After a little bit, he lays his head on my shoulder. "Thank you, Cassie," he mutters, his voice laced with despair.

I kiss his forehead. "Do you want to do something? Maybe to take your mind off things?"

He lifts his head. "May we visit the sea?"

My heart drops. "Are you sure?"

"Yes. Perhaps..." He swallows. "Perhaps..."

It's no use, but I'll do it for him. "Okay. Let's go."

The beach is busy today. Damarian and I head to an area where no one's around. He's clinging onto this hope that he might still be a merman, but I know he'll be disappointed. I lower myself onto the wet sand and hug my knees to my chest.

He takes a few tentative steps toward the shore. When the tide comes, his feet get swallowed. I hold in a breath, waiting for his legs to shift into a tail. But of course that doesn't happen. Damarian falls down to his knees and bends over, smashing his face into the wet sand. The ocean hits his face, but he remains in that position.

I get up and press my cheek to his. "Come. Let's go for smoothies.

It might make you feel better."

I need to get his mind off of this. I need to...I don't know. What can I do to help him? Nothing, absolutely nothing.

After some more coaxing, Damarian gets up and we make our way to Misty's Juice Bar.

Leah's face brightens when we walk in. But as her eyes fall on Damarian, she freezes like she's never seen a sight like him before. We sit down at the bar. She raises an eyebrow at me, but I shake my head. She nods slowly, then pastes on a smile. "What would you like to order?"

Damarian's staring at the counter, his face cloaked in anguish. I want to cry just by looking at him.

"Something to lift our spirits," I tell her.

"I got just the thing."

She goes to the machine to start working on our smoothies. I rest my hand on Damarian's thigh, trying to prompt a smile out of him. But he continues to stare at the counter with the same grief-stricken expression.

Leah watches us from the machine, her eyebrows creased. When she's finished with our orders, she holds one out to Damarian. He doesn't acknowledge her.

She places it on the counter. "Hey, Damian. You okay?"

That causes him to snap out of his daze. "Damian," he weeps, covering his face. "That is who I shall be. Damian."

A lump the size of the whole store clogs my throat. I wrap my hand around my smoothie and gulp in the liquid. I can't take seeing him so broken like this. I hate that I'm powerless to do anything.

Leah looks very confused as she watches Damarian continue to whimper into his hands. Some of the people in the shop stare. I want to tell them to quit it. If they had any idea what he's going through...

Merman's Kiss

I slip out my phone and send Leah a quick text. **He lost his tail.**

Leah's phone beeps. She plucks it out of her pants pocket and scans the screen. Her mouth falls open and her eyes widen. Her gaze springs to mine.

I nod, my lips pressed into a tight line.

She leans forward to pat Damarian's arm. "Hey, it'll all be okay. Whatever you're going through."

"It will not," he mutters into his hands. "It will never be all right."

She looks at me. I shrug helplessly. I don't know what to do, save for dressing into scuba gear and searching for his colony. I doubt they'd welcome me with open arms. Not to mention the sharks that would attack me if I get too close.

If only I could speak to Doria. Maybe she can convince her dad to lift the banishment.

I stand up. "I'll be back. Watch over him?"

She nods. "Sure thing."

I head back to the part of the beach where no one's around. Getting down on my knees, I touch the water. "Doria," I call. I look over my shoulder to make sure no one is close by. Then I turn my attention back to the ocean. "If you can hear me, please talk to your father. Your brother is miserable. I can't stand to see him so upset. He misses the ocean, misses all of you. Please."

When I close my eyes, tears drip down my cheeks. I open them, but don't see anything. Just the waves of the ocean.

I return to the juice bar and find Damarian drinking his smoothie, the same look on his face. I sit down next to him. "Hey."

He nods, his eyes so, so sad. I drink my own smoothie, hoping it'll help me blot out the pain I feel for him.

"May we return to the beach?" he mutters.

"Okay. If that's what you want."

We stand. Leah mouths "call me." I nod.

Damarian settles down near the tide, where it washes over our feet. Our shoes are tossed to the side. He takes a sip from his drink. "Never have I imagined Father betraying me so. Never have I longed so for the sea."

I lay my hand on his knee.

"I feel ill. As if I may perish."

"I understand how heartbroken you are. I wish I could do something to help you."

He wraps an arm around me, pulling me close to his chest. "You are the only light in my life. If not for you, I am not certain what shall become of me."

"What the hell?"

Kyle stares down at us. He does that merman bow thing, then gets down on his knees. "My king." He bows his head again. "What happened?" His eyes bore into Damarian's face. "You are no longer…"

"Kyle, this isn't a good time—"

"He's banished?" His eyes widen in shock. "Who—"

"Kyle, please," I ask.

"Who will be the king?"

"Kyle!"

Damarian's staring at the ocean, his jaw clenched. I brush his hair off his forehead.

"Forgive me," Kyle says, bowing his head another time. Then he disappears.

"I wish to leave," Damarian says.

Taking his hand in mine, we head home.

Chapter Twenty-Seven

He's lying under the covers in the guest room. I sit down on the edge of his bed, my hand caressing his arm. He won't accept my comfort. He won't even budge.

I've tried giving him food, but he won't eat anything. He's falling into a deep depression.

"I am sentenced to live in the same manner as Kyler of the Emerald clan," he says after a few minutes.

I continue caressing his arm. "Kyle didn't have me." I lie on top of him, feelings his warmth through the thin blanket. "You have me, Damarian."

He pulls the blanket off and looks at me, his eyes circling my face. He draws me to his chest and kisses my forehead. "Forgive me, Cassie. I am behaving like a fry. I understood the danger when I left the sea. I left so you and I could be together. You are the most vital one in my life." He threads his fingers through my hair. "I wish to be with you for all eternity." His lips skim across my cheek. "I shall learn to embrace my new life as a human, for you are part of it."

I push some hair out of his eyes. "I'm so sorry it has to be this way."

He continues to trail his lips across my skin. "It is all right. I shall learn to love this life. I shall learn to say goodbye to my family."

I hug him close and squeeze him tight. I wish he didn't have to give up everything to be with me. It's not fair.

"Fret not, Cassie. It shall be all right."

We settle down, cuddled in each other's arms. Nothing will ever be all right. I don't know how I'll live with the guilt that I tore him away from his family, from the life he loves.

I feel like such a horrible person.

***

Knocking.

I sit up, just as Damarian opens his eyes. "What is that noise?" he asks.

I rub my eyes. "The door."

Who can it be at this time?

"Stay here and go back to sleep," I tell him.

Once I get my slippers on, I make my way downstairs, stifling a yawn. I couldn't sleep at all. Thoughts and worries jammed my mind. One thing that keeps replaying over and over in my head is if I regret meeting Damarian. Had I not, he would still be in the ocean. Maybe he wouldn't enjoy his life because he would be forced to marry a girl he doesn't love, but at least he wouldn't be banned from the sea.

I don't regret falling in love with him. I didn't know I could experience something so lovely, so magical and passionate. If a genie would drop by my house and grant me only one wish, it wouldn't be to go back in time and stop myself from meeting Damarian. It would be to lift his banishment so Damarian can return to his family.

But then he'd be forced to marry Princess Flora. Did I do him a favor? I shake my head. I have no idea.

I don't realize I stopped in middle of the stairs until I hear more knocking. I push all the worry out of my head and walk to the door.

When I peek through the peephole, I stumble back. Kiander stands outside.

I just stare at the door, a million thoughts spinning in my head. Damarian's brother is here. What's he doing here? Damarian said no one's allowed to see a banished merman. Does that mean Kiander broke the law? Does that mean he'll get banished, too?

Again, this is all my fault.

The next knock makes me jump. I unlock it and slowly open the door. Immediately, I notice something different about him. He looks the same, but he also looks different. I can't pinpoint what exactly, but it looks like he's glowing.

"Kiander," I say.

He bobs his head slightly. "Cassie. I search for Damarian."

"He's—he's upstairs. What's going on?"

"May I see him?"

"Sure." I clumsily widen the door. "Of course."

I lead him up to the guestroom. Damarian lies on his back with his hands folded on his stomach. He must sense Kiander, because his eyes snap open. He sits up. "Brother."

Kiander bobs his head again. "Brother."

Damarian climbs out of bed and steps closer to Kiander. I hadn't noticed it before, but Damarian is a good few inches taller than his brother. As Damarian studies Kiander's face, his expression changes. He lifts his hands in the air and brings them together, then bows his head. "My king," he says.

I gape at them. *King?*

Kiander rests both hands on Damarian's head. "At ease, Brother."

Damarian lowers his hands and raises his head, but it's still slightly bent. Like he's his servant.

Kiander turns to me. "Where is Kyler of the Emerald clan?"

Words get caught in my throat. I open my mouth, but only manage to stutter. Finally, I say, "He's at home. What's going on?" My eyes meet Damarian's. "He's the king?"

"Brother," Damarian says. "I do not understand."

"I have taken Princess Flora as my mate."

I feel my jaw drop.

"Kiander—" Damarian starts, but his brother holds up his hand.

"It is the duty I have taken. The crown is now on a Sapphire head. The clans are united."

Damarian takes a few steps closer. "It was not your duty to take," he says softly, his voice laced with guilt.

"I have accepted the responsibility." He gestures to me. "I have no reason not to take it."

Damarian looks at me. I can see the love he has for me glimmering in his eyes. He turns back to Kiander, bowing his head. "My king. I apologize for any—"

"It is all right." Kiander holds out his hand again. "All is well. Come. Let us return to the sea." He nods to me. "Summon Kyler of the Emerald clan to rendezvous with us."

I'm still confused by what's going on, but I do as Kiander asks. I deleted Kyle's contact information from my phone months ago, but his number's engraved in my memory. I'm not sure how happy he'll be to be woken up at three AM.

"Hello?" his sleepy voice asks.

I clear my throat. "Hi, Kyle."

"Cassie?" He sounds more alive now. "Why are you calling me in the middle of the night?"

"I have Damarian's brother here. Kiander. He…he's the king now. I think. I don't know, really. But he wants you to meet us at the beach."

He's quiet. I'm not sure if he hung up. "Kyle?"

"Okay, I'll be there."

I hang up and face the brothers. "He said he'll come."

Kiander nods. "Very well."

He leaves the room. Damarian stands there, staring after him. I take his hand. "What's he doing?" I ask.

He shakes his head. "I am not certain."

His hold on my hand tightens as we head downstairs. Kiander is already outside. We follow him to the beach, where we stop a few feet away from the tide.

In the distance, I see Kyle heading our way. He's only wearing jeans. He stops before us, his eyebrows creased. When his gaze lands on Kiander, he raises his arms and bows his head, just like Damarian did. "My king."

"Stand before me," Kiander instructs Damarian and Kyle.

They do as he says.

He raises both hands and touches each one to Damarian and Kyle's chests. He closes his eyes and says, "As King Kiander of the children of the sea, I hereby grant you pardon of banishment. You may return to the sea."

As soon as he removes his hands, Damarian and Kyle bend over, clutching their necks and wailing in pain. They fall to the sand and continue to cry out like tortured whales.

They're no longer banished. They need to be in the sea.

"Help me," I tell Kiander, whose eyes are wide in shock. "They need to be put in the ocean right away."

Together, he and I heave both men and lug them into the ocean. The water starts to bubble. A few seconds later, two tails shoot out of the water, one sapphire and one emerald. My heart explodes in elation when it finally hits me that Damarian is no longer a slave to land. He's a merman. A *merman*.

Damarian and Kyle's heads pop out of the water. I run into the ocean and swim toward them. Damarian meets me halfway and lifts me in his arms. I wrap my limbs around him and laugh, kissing him. Damarian's heart is beating super fast. "You're a merman," I tell him.

"I am no longer a human," he says, surprised.

I glance at Kyle, who's floating in the water, staring at his webbed hands, fingering the gills on his neck. Touching his beautiful emerald tail.

There's a splash near us, followed by another sapphire tail sticking out of the ocean. Kiander's looks a bit shinier than Damarian's, probably because he's the king. When his face appears, Kyle swims to him, raising his arms over his head and bowing his head over and over as he mutters, "Thank you, my king."

"What happened?" I ask Damarian.

"The king has the ability to pardon banishment. My brother has granted Kyler permission to return to the sea."

Kyle's still bowing his head. "I am grateful, my king. You are most generous."

Kiander nods. "You have been absent for far too long. I am certain your family will be overjoyed to see you."

Kyle bows his head again. "As am I, my king."

Kiander nods to Damarian. "As king of the children of the sea, I give you permission to travel freely from sea to land. My only requirement is that you be discreet." He lays a hand on Damarian's shoulder. "Welcome home, Brother."

Damarian gently lowers me to the ocean and gathers Kiander in his arms. "You will be a fair king, Brother. A revered king. A great king." He pulls back and smiles to him. "I am extremely grateful for your kindness."

Kiander nods once more. "I shall return to Eteria. Will you join me, Damarian?"

He looks at me. I nod for him to go. I don't know if he'll come back, but I'm not thinking about myself now. All that matters is Damarian got his tail back and he can return to his family in the ocean.

"Shortly, Brother," Damarian tells him, taking me in his arms.

Kiander dives into the ocean.

"Cassie," Kyle says, swimming closer to us. "I'm so sorry for everything. For hurting you and threatening to tell everyone about Damarian's secret. I was so sad. All I wanted was to return to the ocean." His eyes trek to Damarian's. "I'm sorry."

"It's okay," I say. "I totally get it. I'm really happy for you."

"Thanks." He half waves before diving into the ocean.

Damarian and I are left alone. His eyes bore into mine as he raises a hand to my cheek and strokes it with the back of his fingers.

"Go home," I tell him.

His fingers continue to caress my cheek. "I must make peace with Father." He presses his forehead to mine. "I shall return to you, Cassie."

"Even if you can't return, it's okay. I want you to be happy."

"I am happy when I am with you. I shall return."

I grab the back of his head and tug his lips to mine. They stretch over mine as he kisses me with everything he has. When he pulls free, he murmurs, "I shall return to you, my love."

After giving me another kiss, he turns around and jumps into the ocean. I watch the waves as they crash into one another. When they're calm, I swim back to shore.

As I walk home, I hug myself. As hard as it'll be, I need to accept the possibility that he won't come back. Like I said, if you love someone, you need to let him go.

I'm ready to let him go.

Epilogue

Leah and I stroll around the beach. I've updated her on everything that happened. She whistles. "Forget TV. *This* is drama."

I laugh, but then I feel my lips pull into a frown.

Leah pats my arm. "He'll come back. His brother is so nice to do this for him."

I swallow. "I know. I'm just worried, I guess." I rub my forehead. "I didn't know relationships could be this stressful."

Leah grins. "For the average human relationship? Yeah, relationships are at a ten. But for a human-merman relationship? That's a hundred, easy."

I smile back. I know I can count on my best friend to make me feel better. "So what's happening with you and Jace?"

Her grin widens. "Oh, it's happening."

"Ooh."

Her gaze drops to the sand as she grins even wider. She kicks a pebble. "You were right about giving him a chance. I really like him."

"I'm so happy for you."

"Thanks."

We continue walking in silence, enjoying the beautiful scenery around us.

"What about school?" she asks.

"I sent in my application to the community college here. I'm not moving away from the ocean. I mean, assuming Damarian comes back."

"He will," Leah says.

"What about you?" I ask.

She waves her hand. "Still undecided. I think I'll spend my year working at the juice bar and figure out what I want to do with my life."

"Sounds good."

She hugs me. "We don't have to separate!"

She's right. I was so preoccupied with Damarian and my life that I didn't pay much attention to what would happen to my friendship with Leah if I were to go away for school. I'm so glad we'll be able to remain best friends.

We sit down, burying our feet in the wet sand. "Where do you go from here?" Leah asks.

"What do you mean?"

"With your relationship with Damarian. Will we tell him I know?"

I puff out some air. I hate that I've been keeping a secret from him. But if he and I will be together, I'll need to tell people. Like my mom. She's living in New York for a while, but she'll drop by often and eventually travel back home.

"I'll tell him," I say.

"And what about taking your relationship to the next level?"

I feel a blush crawl onto my face. "I guess we'll see."

She bumps her shoulder into mine. "I think you meeting Damarian is the best thing that happened to you. You were in such a dark place after Kyle broke up with you. In a way, he saved you."

I play with some sand. "We saved each other."

***

"I have a cute little apartment," Mom tells me over the phone. "You're welcome to drop by whenever you like. You'll love it."

"Thanks, Mom."

"How are you holding up?" she asks. "Everything okay with Damian? With work, college planning? Life?"

I'm sitting on Damarian's bed, inhaling his ocean scent. Even if he doesn't return, I feel at peace. It was enough just knowing him. "Everything's great," I tell Mom. "How's your job?"

"Amazing!"

I laugh.

"I'm so glad to hear that you're doing okay, honey. How are things with your dad?"

"They're going really well," I say. "I'm invited over for dinner tonight."

"I'm so happy you made the call."

I smile. "Me, too."

***

I'm standing on the rocks, watching the waves. They move in a steady beat. My heart races with anticipation and hope.

His head pops out of the ocean. I jump in my place, my lips stretched to the max. I grab the blanket and towels and race down to the shore. Damarian is already on the sand. I throw the blanket over him and jump on top. Our arms encircle each other as my lips search for his. When they come together, I'm engulfed in flames, in pixy dust, in fireworks, in everything. We roll over each other as we continue to hold onto one another like the apocalypse might come.

"There is no need to rush," Damarian whispers in my ear. "We will be together forever."

I squeeze him even closer to me. "What did your father say?"

"He understands what you mean to me. He has given his blessing."

Merman's Kiss

"Really?"

"Yes."

"I love you so much, Damarian."

His lips trail kisses down my throat. "My love for you will only blossom in the moons to come. I will always love you, Cassie. For all eternity."

Eternity. I like the sound of that.

About the Author

Dee J. Stone is the pseudonym of two sisters who write adult and young adult novels. *The Keepers of Justice series, The Merman's Kiss series, The Cruiser & Lex series, Emily's Curse,* and *Chasing Sam* are now available on Amazon. You can email them at deej.stone@yahoo.com or follow them on Facebook and Twitter.

Made in the USA
Middletown, DE
16 October 2022

12911610R00151